DEAD....If Only

Heather Haven

The Wives of Bath Press

www.thewivesofbath.com

The Wives of Bath Press
5512 Cribari Bend
San Jose, Ca 95135

http:// **www.thewivesofbath.com**

Cover Art by Heather Haven and Jeff Monaghan
Edited by Baird Nuckolls
Layout and book production by
Heather Haven and Baird Nuckolls

Print ISBN: 978-0-9892265-5-4
eBook ISBN: 978-0-9892265-4-7

The Alvarez Family Murder Mystery Series

"One of the funniest mystery authors around. You won't be able to put her books down.
A must-read 5 star series!"
National Best Selling Author, Cindy Sample

"You'll go from edge-of-your seat suspense to rolling-on-the-floor laughter. Hang on to your derriere. If you have not read Ms. Haven's books, please do so. I highly recommend."
Rochelle Webber, author

"One of the nice things about ongoing series is you get to know the characters better as they develop or perhaps it's more accurate to say, they reveal more of their quirks as time goes on. Lee, and her family are amazing...add Tugger into the mix and I LOVE this series. FIVE STARS for Ms. Haven and the ever enchanting Tugger."
Lady Bug Lin "Ladybug Lin Reviews"

~

Acknowledgements

I would like to thank Catherine Latta for her help with the dos and don'ts of sailing and boats. Charlotte (Charly) Taylor is always a treasure for her Spanish language expertise. Both these women not only make me look better, but write a more accurate book for the reader. I am grateful.

I would also like to acknowledge my writing buddies, Carter Schwonk, Myra H. Strober, and Jerry Burger who made wonderful suggestions after reading a draft of the book in its ghastly entirety. That's friendship.

I would like to acknowledge Jeff Monaghan, who is always willing to help guide me through troubled spots in my pursuit to become a better cover artist. What I lack in skill, I make up for in guts. He created the theme we use for the Alvarez Family Murder Mysteries, and every one I make for the succeeding books, are based on his vision and skill.

In particular, I would like to acknowledge Baird Nuckolls, whose expertise in all things holds me in good stead. She is a wonderful writer, editor, and friend.

Lastly, I would like to state that all the name brands within the book are of quality and worth. If they were no good, the Alvarez Family wouldn't bother with them. Life is too short.

Dedication

This book is dedicated to my mother, Mary Lee, who I miss terribly; to my husband, Norman Meister; and families everywhere. If you love and are loved, you are part of a family. Further, it is dedicated to all my readers. You help me write to the best of my ability, always trying to be truthful and entertaining. I love you all.

DEAD....*If Only*

Book Four

In

The Alvarez Family

Murder Mystery Series

Heather Haven

Chapter One
Can It Get Any Dirtier?

According to song and legend, for the past few centuries hot sulfuric mud is sucked out of caverns loitering beneath the hills of Calistoga. For the privilege of parking your backside in the stuff, big bucks are sucked out of your bank account. Only in California do you pay through the nose for something most kids can run outside and jump into after a rainy day.

I did find a twig or two earlier, but was reassured by the spa attendant, Rainbow, the trees and all their inhabitants died long ago. I tried to embrace the thought as my new phone rang out with Beethoven's Fifth.

At eight-oh-five in the morning I should have been suspicious. I should have known disaster can find you wherever you go, but I was a reluctant PI on vacation. My sixth-sense was on vacation, as well.

My name is Lee Alvarez and I'm the in-house P.I. for Discretionary Inquiries, the family owned Silicon Valley detective agency. I was tired and in need of a little R and R, having recently wrapped up a case, a big one, involving the entire Alvarez clan, God help me.

There are probably worse things than working hip-to-hip with CEO and mother, Lila Hamilton Alvarez, she who can shoot the tattoo off a fly at fifty paces in her size six stilettos, but I can't think of them. She's still your mother and there's something unnatural about it.

Throw in a techie geek of a brother, Richard Alvarez, he who fobs off the latest gewgaw on me while I'm busy taking down felons, and you have my life as of late. That's the downside of a successfully run family business, the family. The upside eluded me for the moment.

But glory hallelujah, everyone was out of my hair for an entire week, thanks to my brother's wife, Vicki. Said sister-in-law was opening a new branch of her hat shop, The Obsessive Chapeau, in New Orleans's French Quarter. Lila, Richard, and my Uncle Mateo, better known as Tío, went to help out. For one week. *Laissez le bon ton roulette*. Yup, let the good times roll.

They'd have been rolling a lot better if I'd known whether or not the mud I was laying in had been washed and hermetically sealed. I have a thing about creepy crawlies.

Regardless, when the Boston Philharmonic Orchestra plays its heart out, it's apt to get your attention. Especially when the blaring phone in question is out of reach and you're in a vat full of mud pretending to enjoy it.

The song ended but the melody lingered on, reverberating around the large white-tiled spa room. Meanwhile, I wondered who called. Not many people know my private number, just family and close friends. Still, there was the occasional carpet cleaning service drumming up business or wrong number. Was that it or was it something important? Let's face it, there's nothing more awful than an unanswered phone, even a smart one that makes you feel stupid.

"Sweetheart, I told you not to bring your phone into the mudroom." The voice of Gurn Hanson, the love of my life, wafted over the steam rising from our side-by-side tubs. He spoke in a slow, lazy voice and didn't even open his eyes; he was that relaxed. Mine were bulging out of my head.

We'd reached the point in our relationship where we could throw out the occasional 'I told you so' remark, in between proclamations of love. I hope we never neglect the proclamations.

I'd been in a disastrous early marriage, where not only were the 'I told you so's sans any declaration, but my ex-threw in the occasional punch for good measure. Thanks to a good helping of self-esteem and a black belt in Karate, I'd filed for divorce several years back.

So here I was, thirty-four years old, five foot eight inches of me, four pounds over the allotted one-hundred and thirty-five, curly dark hair in a knot atop my head, sprawled out in a revolting tub of mud, and telling myself to relax. After all, I was on a long awaited vacation, eating and drinking my way through Napa Valley, and sharing the experience with a honey of a man.

"Relax, sweetheart, relax," Gurn crooned then opened green-grey eyes and looked over at me. "Is it the phone you're worried about or leaving Tugger and Baba alone in the room?"

"No, I'm sure the cats are fine. They're noshing on kippers and catnip. I'm the one chin deep in disgusting muck. Who's sorry she's not a cat?" I muttered the last bit and wasn't sure Gurn heard me. It was just as well. I tend to complain.

The two aforementioned felines were my Tugger and Gurn's cat, Baba Ganoush, named after the eggplant dish. The fact our two cats were with us had nothing to do with the wine or mud, because I've never met a cat into that sort of thing. It was more the Alvarez clan, as previously mentioned, was off in New Orleans and I trusted no one besides Tío to take care of the little darlings. So we threw the cats into their carriers, climbed aboard Gurn's Cessna, and flew here to spend a glorious week living the high life, putting aside the current visit to a mudslide.

My phone sprang to life again. The Boston Philharmonic Orchestra and Beethoven's Fifth bounced off the walls once more. I tried not to think about it. Eventually, the phone stopped ringing, but Beethoven's 'ba ba ba bum' continued to bong around the room and in my head. I gotta change that ring one of these days.

"I think you should have left it in the room, but I probably shouldn't say that." Gurn gave me another wide grin.

I had to think for a moment of what he was talking about. Oh, yes. Phone. Mud. Yuk.

He exhaled a long, relaxed breath and closed his eyes, looking quite yummy, even covered with black gunk.

"It's your phone, sweetheart. You take it wherever you want."

"Thank you, but you're right. I am kind of indisposed and shouldn't have brought it with me." *Relax, relax, relax. Nope. Forget it.*

Too late I remembered that even as I kid, I was never the mud-cavorting type, preferring to stay clean and dry, playing with my Legos on the patio. My brother, however, sought every opportunity to be in mud. Gurn seemed to be enjoying his own foray. Maybe this was a guy thing?

I took a deep breath and choked on the sulfuric smell rising on clouds of steam. Buried under steaming dirt, I reflected on how a pig at a luau must feel. All I needed was an apple in my mouth. Then I thought about the posted warnings overhead: do not put your feet down on the bottom of the tub. I wasn't exactly sure why you couldn't, but it became my *raison d'être*. Among other things, that's French for 'What the hell did I get myself into?'

A large bubble found its way to the surface and exploded into the air. I tried not to scream. Rainbow, a flower child of the sixties, was quite firm in her introductory statement that any bubbles appearing were only trapped sulfuric gas. I chose to believe her.

Rainbow had passed what we define as 'older' decades before, and was now racing toward eighty like a thoroughbred coming down the home stretch. Dressed in a tie-dyed, free-flowing robe, slathered in patchouli oil, and weighed down by dozens of love beads, her look was finished off by two silvery-white braids hanging down to her knees.

Barely audible New Age music piped through the sound system completed our trip to the Age of Aquarius, geriatric style. The phone rang out for the third time with Ludwig's finest.

"You know, Lee, you could move over to the side, get out, shower off, find out who's calling, and then jump into the hot tub. I'll join you there in about ten minutes."

Gurn opened his eyes and looked over, his wondrous lopsided smile enchanting me down to my muddy toes. "I suspect you're not enjoying this part of spa day."

I didn't need to be told twice. With about as much grace as a beached walrus, I rolled over to the side of the tub and splashed down on the white tiles, flinging dark glop everywhere. As I stood dripping onto the once spotless floor, I realized what a bitch it must be to keep the room clean. Note to self: never use white tile on floors. Too unforgiving.

The BP Orchestra went silent.

I leaned over to see who called and a chunk of mud fell from my neck onto the phone, obscuring the ID number. I gave up and padded toward the shower area. I'd like to say I rinsed off fast and easy, but I found mud in crevices of my body I didn't even know were creviced.

The phone beeped with sounds similar to Morse code on helium.

"What the hell is that?" I shouted from behind the curtain, hoping Gurn could hear me.

"That's your messaging notification. Someone's texted you."

"What do you mean, texted me? I don't have texting."

"You must have. Otherwise, it wouldn't be beeping."

"Fer crying out loud, you need a degree in computer science to figure out these phones."

I continued to grumble and grouse, but finally turned off the water and snatched a towel. Wrapping it around me, I made a dash for the phone, which stopped beeping as I reached for it.

Gurn chortled. "Somebody's persistent. I'm glad I left mine in the room."

I chose not to answer but picked up the phone, wiped off the mud with a corner of the towel, and looked at the incoming call list. "The number's blocked. It must be Richard."

"What makes you think that?"

Gurn no longer sounded like he was being fed Prozac intravenously, but alert and back with the living.

"He's one of the few people I know who has the guts to have a blocked number and not be an insurance salesman."

"So maybe it's Met Life."

"No, it's Richard." My sixth sense returned, albeit if only on two cylinders. "And where's this texting business?"

"I'll get out and show you." He made a move for the side.

"You don't have to do that, just tell me."

"It's better if I show you."

We heard a soft knocking and without waiting for a reply, Rainbow opened the door. She wafted inside, love beads clicking in rhythm with the braids swinging from side to side. How did she keep those braids out of the mud, I wondered? Tie them in a bow around her neck?

"Love, peace, and harmony, friends," her small voice waivered. "It's only Rainbow telling you it's time for grooving in the hot tub." She saw me on my phone and got a little prickly. "Oh, no, no, no. No cell phones in the place of tranquility." She straightened up as much as possible, waggled a finger at me and came forward, assuming the attitude of an elderly drill sergeant.

Gurn tried to cut her off at the pass. "Rainbow, why don't we let Lee do her thing and we'll do ours?" Without thinking, he tossed two muddy legs over the side of the tub and with the nimbleness of an acrobat threw himself into a standing position.

Rainbow gasped and turned away. We'd been told several times rules state that men's private parts must remain beneath the mud whenever female attendants are in the room.

"Sorry, Rainbow," Gurn said, as mud sloughed off him. "You'd better leave and come back in ten."

Our octogenarian ran out of the room like a vestal virgin pursued by a legion of Roman soldiers.

"You know, that could be considered elder abuse." I raised an eyebrow at Gurn.

Gurn ignored me and went back to the phone. "What makes you think it's Rich calling? I thought everybody was in New Orleans." He pulled excess mud from his arms and hands as he spoke, flinging it down to the floor. A not so clean hand was extended in my direction, with the goal of taking the phone from me. "Here, let me see it."

I turned away from him, deep in thought. "Okay, maybe it isn't Richard. He knows I don't text. My thumbs don't work that way."

"Only one way to find out. Give me the phone, Lee. I'll see." Gurn reached out a persistent hand again. "Come on, blue eyes."

"No, you've still got mud all over yourself. This thing cost over four hundred bucks, even with the trade-in of my old phone. Go wipe your hands on one of those towels over there." I pointed to several towels neatly folded at the side of the tub. "I can find the text thingamagiggy. After all, it's my phone." I pushed buttons and managed to turn on the flashlight.

With a shake of his head and a laugh, Gurn ran a quick hand down the front of my towel and made a grab for the phone. He was playful about it. I was not. Reluctant to let go of any power I had over the phone, be it zip, we went into a mini tug of war. Hands grappling one over the other, the phone escaped our grasp in an upward motion like a slippery bar of soap. Following a neat arc, it landed with a 'kerplop' in the middle of the tub.

"Now look what you did!" I stared in horror at the phone floating belly up in mud.

"What I did? Never mind."

Gurn reached over and lifted the phone out, snatched the towel off my body, and wiped off the mud.

"Is it dead?" My voice trembled at the thought.

"No, of course not." He continued to wipe the back of the phone with care, while he inspected it. "When the mud dries completely, we'll scrape it off. It didn't get inside, because you've got the protective case on it. See? Nothing's hurt."

He handed the relatively clean phone back to me and kissed me on the nose. I rethought my position. I was being too possessive and grumpy about one of my shortcomings. Technical stuff and I do not get along. And if Gurn knows more about Smartphones, who was I not to let him help me out?

The phone in my hand started its Morse code thing again.

"Sorry I was so snarky before. You want to show me texting? At least I know where the flashlight is now. You never know when that will come in handy."

He took the phone with a grin, swiped at something, and handed it back to me. "There you go. Just touch on the messaging icon."

I followed instructions and began to read the short missive. When I finished, I sank down to the side of the tub. It took me a second or two before I could utter anything, and then it was only a single word.

"Gurn."

He turned to face me, the one word stopping him from wiping his face on his towel. He carried it with him and sat beside me.

"What's wrong?"

"It *is* from Richard." Together we read the short but disturbing message in silence.

Fly to NOLA General Hospital ASAP. Terrible danger. Think Vicki will be arrested for murder.

I looked at Gurn. His face registered all the shock, confusion, and fear I was feeling. My voice shook when I spoke.

"If this is a sample of texting, I don't like it one bit."

Chapter Two
What Life Throws at You

I pressed Richard's number on my speed dial, put the phone to my ear, and listened to it ring and ring. For somebody who'd been burning up the wires a short time before, where the hell was he?

We finished dressing in a hurry, and gathered up our things. While Gurn paid the bill, I tried Richard's number again. It rang as we dashed out of the building. I was about to hang up when I heard my brother's voice.

"Lee, thank God you got back to me. I've been calling and texting you for like an hour. Don't you answer your damned phone?" His voice was tense, accusatory, and raw; nothing like the laid back nerd of a brother I know and love.

"And what took *you* so long to answer *your* phone?" I can hold my own in the tense, accusatory, and raw department. I flung open the rental car door and jumped inside.

Richard became contrite. "Sorry about that, but the doctor had to give me an update on Vicki. They're trying to stabilize her."

"Stabilize her?" It felt like my heart thudded against my back teeth. "Is it Vicki in the hospital? You just said she might be arrested. What's happened?"

"Hang on, Lee. I'm going into the hallway, so we can talk. We're not supposed to use cell phones anywhere but in a designated place."

There were rustling noises and the sound of movement. Gurn started the car and peeled out of the parking lot, while all sorts of thoughts raced through my mind. Within our familial dynamics, Tío supplies unconditional love, Mom supplies class and grace, Richard supplies his IT genius, and I supply….the cat?

But it's Victoria Lombard Alvarez, twenty-six years old and barely five foot one, who supplies the heart. Smart enough to be the owner of a successful business at a young age, she manages to remain a warm, loving person with a forgiving nature all at the same time. And she was soon to deliver my first niece or nephew.

I tried not to panic at the thought of something being wrong with either her or the baby. And what was all this stuff about her being arrested? I nearly chewed through the phone waiting for Richard to start talking again.

"I'm back." Richard's voice sounded more normal.

"Then tell me what's going on and right now. I can't stand it. I'm putting the phone on speaker so Gurn can hear, too."

Gurn took a corner so sharply I had to hang onto the strap over the door. Richard's voice came over loud and clear throughout the car.

"You remember the man who raped and nearly beat Vicki's sister, Robin, to death?"

Whatever I thought he was going to say, that wasn't it. Throwing my mind back to Vicki's history before she became part of the Alvarez clan, I came up with a name I nearly choked on saying.

"Dennis Manning, wasn't it? What about him? Why is this coming up now? He died nine years ago."

Richard took a deep breath and expelled it noisily. "Vicki swears she saw him in the French Quarter earlier today."

"That's impossible!" My response was louder than it had to be, my protest stronger. "He blew up his own boat with him on it, for Christ's sake."

"That's what we all thought."

Richard's ragged voice went on.

"But Vicki keeps saying she recognized him, beard and all. She says he recognized her, too, because he ran when he saw her. She took off after him before I even knew what was going on. She didn't answer her phone, but I eventually tracked her down by her GPS. It was over a half an hour before I caught up with her." He gulped and stopped talking for a second before he blurted out, "By the time I did, she was lying in someone's backyard, unconscious."

"Unconscious!"

"The doctor is hoping it's a mild concussion. It's too early to tell. They're doing a CAT scan now."

"Is that safe in her condition? A CAT scan?"

"The doctor assured me there's no risk to her or the baby from radiation. And they have to see if there's any bleeding in the brain."

I gasped when the seriousness of the situation struck me, sucking in air long and noisily. Clapping a hand over my mouth, I wished I could take the reaction back. Richard didn't need anybody else reacting like this; it was a luxury the rest of us couldn't afford. He and Vicki had to come first.

Gurn gave me a look that said he agreed. Then he spoke up. "You want to tell us what happened, Rich?"

"Yes. Okay. But let me talk for a minute and don't interrupt. This is hard enough. When I found Vicki…there was a dead man lying beside her."

I swallowed hard over that one, determined not to ask the thousand questions reeling around in my head.

"From what I could see, the man's skull was crushed in. And it looked like it just happened. I freaked out; I really did. I don't know how I managed to call an ambulance and then the police."

"Who's the dead man? Manning?" Gurn's words tumbled out of him.

"No, it isn't. I don't know who it is. I don't believe Vicki does, either. She's pretty woozy, but when she's with us, she doesn't remember anything about being there. The police think she killed him; I know they do.

They haven't said as much yet, but a wrench was clutched in her hand. I know somebody put it there when she was out. It was covered with blood."

His voice broke and then he was silent, except for shallow breathing. I could tell there was more to this story.

"What else?"

"The doctors are worried about the baby. Vicki's so stressed about Manning, she can't keep her blood pressure down. And she doesn't even know about the dead man." Richard choked up again. "I'm scared, sis. I might lose her or the baby....or both."

He began to sob. I did, too, but kept it to myself. The big sister side of me kicked in.

"Stop thinking like that, Richard. The doctors will stabilize Vicki, the baby will be fine, and when we get there, we'll find out what's going on. Where are Mom and Tío?"

"They're on their way. I reached them about a half an hour ago. They were attending a fund-raising lunch over in the Garden District. You know, the one Felicity Llewellyn gives every year."

Gurn spoke up, issuing orders in an urgent tone. As Richard's former commanding officer in NROTC, it was a natural place for him to go.

"Rich, you concentrate on Vicki. And don't either of you answer any more questions by the police. Tell them you have to talk to your lawyer first. If necessary, we'll hire one when we get there. We're heading back to the hotel to check out. You're two hours later, so after I file a flight plan, we should be able to leave within an hour, probably land around seven o'clock. Meanwhile, you hang tough."

Richard's voice took on a feigned brightness. "Easier said than done, but I'll try. Just hurry up and get here. I'm out of my element on this one." The line went dead.

We stopped at one of the two red lights in town. I became quiet, trying to get my bearings. Gurn turned to me.

"How are you doing?"

"Trying to process all of this. Thinking it out."

"Don't project anything into the future, sweetheart. It never looks good when you do. Why don't you fill me in on the details of Vicki's sister? Rich has been pretty mum and I've never wanted to press it. I could tell it was a painful subject for both he and Vicki. I don't know much other than her sister had been raped then institutionalized."

"I only met her once, if you can call it that. It was very sad."

"Her name is Robin?"

"Yeah." I cleared my throat and sat up taller in the passenger's seat. I tried to be unemotional and detached, something I rarely pull off.

"I remember when I saw her at the sanatorium that one time. It was about three years ago. Robin was sitting in a chair staring out a window, looking hardly more than a child. You'd never have known she was nearly twenty-four years old. I don't think she aged a day since it happened. But that wasn't the worst part. What was terrifying was there didn't seem to be anything going on inside of her. She didn't seem to be seeing or thinking or feeling…anything. Just empty. I've never seen anything like it before or since."

"My God." Gurn swallowed hard.

The light turned green, but we sat in silence until the car behind us tooted his horn. Gurn hit the gas pedal, and the car leapt forward almost with a life of its own. He slowed down after he realized he was exceeding the speed limit and glanced over at me.

"Okay, so what exactly took place nine years ago?"

I sucked in a deep breath. "When Robin was fifteen, she was taking a summer prep course at the local junior college. Around three pm, she got off the bus from school and started walking home. It was a three-block walk. The driver of a passing delivery van confirmed he saw her and Manning together on the side of the road. An hour later, a neighborhood boy was walking his dog in the woods near his house. He saw Manning kneeling over Robin, hitting her and yelling, 'Shut up, shut up'.

Manning took off when the dog snarled and lunged at him. The boy ran home for help. Robin was barely alive when they got her to the hospital."

"What made everyone think this monster was dead?"

"When the cops did a search, Manning's boat was missing. The next morning, a fishing trawler saw it blown up off Pacifica, about a half mile from shore. There were traces of blood, but a body was never found. The Coast Guard figured it had been thrown overboard by the blast."

"Accidental explosion or planned?"

"Undetermined."

More silence.

"What else? Come on, Lee. I know you."

"The fact the Coast Guard never found a body has always nagged at me. But it happened before Vicki came into our lives, so I learned to brush the suspicions aside. Until now."

"So you're thinking it's possible Vicki could have seen Dennis Manning in the French Quarter this morning?"

"Yes."

He waited. I was silent. Finally, he prompted me.

"And? You know, whatever's going on inside your head, I'm with you one-hundred percent. Whatever you do, we're partners in this."

"Glad to hear it. Because if he's out there, if Dennis Manning is still alive after all these years, I'm going to find the son-of-a-bitch and bring him to justice."

Chapter Three
If Only It Was Like The Movies

I ran up the un-air-conditioned staircase of the New Orleans General Hospital to the fifth floor. I needed the exercise, I told myself, after sitting in a small plane for much of the day. The truth was hospital elevators are notoriously slow and I was anxious to see what was going on with Vicki. Even though the Cessna had access to phone service and I'd been calling every hour for an update, no one was answering. I was scared. Anything could have happened while we were airborne.

What I didn't need was a temperature of ninety-seven degrees with a like humidity. That's one of the minuses of living near the gorgeous Gulf Coast in the summer, the feeling of walking through a steam room whenever you move.

New Orleans General was fifteen minutes from the French Quarter and touted as one of the best in the state. Hurricane Katrina had done her damndest to engulf the hospital with her floodwaters, but only managed to damage the basement and ground-level floors before receding.

Recently done over, the lobby more resembled a luxury hotel. Comfy, dark blue couches and chairs gathered in seating areas. Well-tended plants, and watercolor paintings displayed on pale blue and green walls greeted patient and visitor alike. The only give-away it was a hospital was the steady flow of doctors, nurses, orderlies, and uniformed volunteers instead of bellboys.

Arriving at the fifth floor, I was sweaty and out of breath. I threw open the stairwell door of the head trauma wing and was hit in the face by a welcomed blast of chilled air.

At the end of a long cream-colored hallway, my mother and brother sat next to one another on similar furniture to those hanging around in the lobby. I couldn't help but notice a nearby third person, not our Tío, but a policeman. Staring into space, the officer was across the hall from the family on a hardback chair. All three were lost in their own private thoughts.

Mom's posture was that of the consummate lady, of course. Body erect, hands clasped in her lap, ankles crossed, she wore a yellow and grey patterned Bolero jacket over a sundress of the palest yellow. The look was set off by a pair of Gucci 'Ursula' ankle-strap high heels in a slightly darker yellow, matching clutch bag resting under her well-groomed hands.

Her ash blonde, shoulder-length coif was perfect, unaffected by the humidity. Just in the short time I'd been in New Orleans, my hair poofed out to three times its normal thickness, ringlets and frizz competing for space on my head.

Richard, God bless him, while he resembled Mom in the coloring department, looked like he'd been run over by a steam-roller that came back for a second round. Wearing a threadbare, wrinkled dark blue t-shirt with the Discretionary Inquiries logo across the back in white, he sat slumped over, head down, elbows resting on the thighs of a pair of faded, ripped jeans. He looked like the weight of the world sat on his thin shoulders. I guess it did.

In unison, the heads of two blondes and one cop snapped in my direction with the echoing sound of the press bar opening the door. Once they saw me, mother and brother leapt up and rushed in my direction. We went into a three-way embrace, no one saying a word for a moment. The policeman went back to his mind-numbing stare of the far wall. I turned to my brother.

"How's Vicki?"

"The doctor is with her now." My brother forced a smile to his lips.

"Liana." said Mom, embracing me again. "You've *finally* arrived. We've been *anxiously* awaiting you."

My mother tends to stress individual words within sentences when she speaks. I've often thought about contacting the CIA and suggesting they use this form of torture in their Black Ops.

She went on, "What took you so *long*? I've been *frantic*. And *where's* Gurn?"

"Gurn's driving the cats to the hotel. Seven hours cooped up in a carrier can take a toll on even a cat of Tugger's temperament. I'm sorry it took so long to get here, but I left voicemails and emails midflight for you, letting you know we had a slight delay due to bad weather. Didn't you get any of my messages?"

I looked from one face to the other. Both shook their heads.

"Sorry, sis," Richard mumbled. "They're very strict about cell phones in the head trauma unit. I have to go to another part of the hospital and I'm in texting mode only."

My kid brother's voice sounded tired, as if speaking was almost too much of an effort. I scrutinized him in more detail. Not only was his face haggard and drawn, there were smudges of dirt and dried blood on the front of his t-shirt. Were the blood smears from the dead man or Vicki? I involuntarily shuddered.

"Where's Tío?" I looked up and down the long hallway, in case I missed seeing him.

Before Richard could answer, our mother piped up. "Mateo is in with Victoria *trying* to bring her blood pressure down by using alternative measures. The doctors are being *most* cooperative."

"Ohhhh, alternative measures." I nodded my head all-knowingly. "I remember hugging a tree once, when I had the flu. I think they call it tapping into the energy of the world around us."

Mom stared at me. I went on, inserting foot in mouth up to thigh.

"Sure, like instead of the doctor pumping a sick kid full of antibiotics, his mom spreads Vicks Vaporub on his chest, bundles him up in a blanket, and makes him lay in the sun to help 'bake out a cold'."

"What kid?" Richard looked at me, puzzled. "Did I know this kid?"

"Richard, it's not a specific kid." I was filled with exasperation. "Don't you get it? I'm just using this as an example." I thought for a minute. "Of course, this works best when you live in warm climate, especially in the winter. Otherwise, frozen kid."

Mom finally found voice. "Liana, the situation is *stressful* enough without you talking *utter* nonsense to your brother and me. P*lease* do not be so trying."

"Right, Mom." I need to learn when to shut up.

She drew herself up to her full five foot four inches. She was wearing her five inch stilettos and me my flip-flops, so we met eye to eye; hers cold, mine twitching.

"Alternative medicine," she said, "is any *practice* that is put forward as having the *same* healing effects of medicine but is not based on evidence gathered using the scientific method. It has *nothing* to do with wrapping a child in a blanket. Mateo has studied the science and philosophy of different approaches to healing *extensively*, as did his mother, your paternal grandmother. You *should* know that."

"Right. I do know that. Sorry. I didn't mean to natter on. I sometimes do that. Diarrhea of the mouth."

At my last words, an expression came upon her face, as if something formerly dead for several months found consciousness and hoisted itself upon her lap. Her eyes fluttered closed. I saw my error and tried to make amends.

"Whoops. Sorry. I'll try not to try. Sorry."

Richard was silent during what is often the standard exchange of dialog between this particular mother and daughter.

Mom rallied, opened her eyes, and gave me a genuine and warm smile.

"*Nonetheless*, we're glad you're here. I *know* Victoria wants to see you, Liana; she's been asking for you *repeatedly*. After you've seen Victoria, Richard will stay with her, while you, Mateo, Gurn, and I will go out to dinner to *discuss* the situation."

Our marching orders. And she was not done. Mom looked down at what I was wearing with a raised eyebrow.

"That is, *once* you've put on appropriate attire. If Gurn is dressed in *similar* fashion, you might want to alert *him* to change, as well."

My eyes shifted down. I was still wearing the blue shorts and red and blue plaid midriff blouse I'd worn to the baths in the morning, looking like they'd been slept in for a week. She had yet to mention the rubber flip-flops on my feet, purchased two years ago when driving past a Wal-Mart parking lot two-for-one sale. Even I didn't want to be seen in them other than a Calistoga mudroom or doing my laundry.

"Right, Mom. Consider it done. But for now, I want to talk to Richard, just he and I. Why don't you sit down for a moment and try to relax? Give it a shot."

I enveloped her in a quick hug and kissed her on the cheek. Mom took a breath about to say more, thought better of it, and merely nodded. She sat down, erect of carriage, and picked up a withered magazine from a pile on a side table, one probably announcing the arrival of the Nina, the Pinta, and the Santa Maria.

I grabbed my brother and maneuvered him to the other side of the hallway. Richard glanced over at our mother before turning back to me.

"Mom's scared, that's all, Lee. I've noticed ever since Dad died she tries to control things a little more."

"Which is like saying a Great White becomes more aggressive on steroids."

He cocked his head to one side. "You're being funny, right?"

"Apparently not. Never mind. How are you? Really?"

He shrugged, but his lips were tight and grim. "Really? Just about done. The pre-natal unit is monitoring Vicki's vitals. The doctors are afraid to give her something strong to bring down her blood pressure because of the baby, but they can't seem to keep it from peaking. Tío's been in there for about twenty minutes trying to help out."

I reached out and wrapped an arm around my brother's shoulders. He's only about a half an inch taller than me, normally, but now he shrank into almost nothing, leaning his body into mine.

"I know the waiting's tough, Richard, but Vicki's young and strong. She's got everything in the world going for her. And you know Tío is crackerjack at making good things come about."

After my little pep talk, Richard's persona seemed to lighten a little. He stood taller and took a deep breath, releasing it with a hissing sound.

"True. He's crackerjack at just about everything."

"Remember how we said if he hadn't have been a chef, he would have made a great shaman?"

"*You* said that. I said nobody could sooth a growling dog the way he could. Not quite the same thing."

I need to learn when to shut up, I really do. I smiled brightly and tried again.

"Brother mine, Tío has a calming, spiritual oneness with the universe, very powerful. We've seen him use it time and time again."

Richard looked at me then chuckled.

"You'll say anything to try to make me feel better, won't you?"

"Yup. That's what big sisters are for. But it's true. Vicki is going to be fine, I can feel it."

"Who's the shaman now?"

The door to Vicki's room opened and a tall, angular, dark-skinned man emerged.

Dressed in blue hospital scrubs, he radiated the command and sympathy of a physician, along with the look of a man who'd had a long day.

"Dr. Frietas!" Richard ran to him, followed by Mom and me. The policeman looked up with momentary interest, but didn't move.

"How's my wife?" Richard planted himself in front of the doctor, vibrating from head to toe.

Dr. Frietas laid a soothing hand on Richard's shoulder, a slight Jamaican accent lilting his words. "She is better, much better. Her blood pressure has lowered by a good twenty points. If we can keep it there, she and the baby will be fine."

"What about the blow to the head?" I piped up, studying the tall man. He was around my age, but his black hair was already graced with silver. Chocolate brown eyes focused on me, questioningly. "I'm the sister."

"Ah!" He reached out a slender hand with long fingers suited equally well for a pianist as a surgeon. The doctor grasped my hand warmly and covered it with his other. "You are Lee?"

I nodded.

"She has been asking for you." He released my hand and turned back to the others. "The concussion is not as serious as we first thought, but we do want to keep her here for a day or two to make sure there are no further ramifications from the head wound and to monitor the baby."

Mom turned to her son. "This is *good news*, Richard. *Hold onto that.*" She embraced him.

"When may I see her?" I stepped closer to the doctor as I spoke, my voice eager, urgent. His remained gentle and calm. I liked this man.

"Now, if you wish. But only for a few minutes. And only if she doesn't become agitated again." He raised a slim finger for emphasis and gave me his style of my mother's eagle eye. "Mrs. Alvarez's vitals are finally stabilized, thanks in part to your uncle. I have seen a similar approach used on the islands from time to time. One was from a cousin of mine."

Dr. Frietas gave me a brilliant, white-toothed smile Colgate would have been proud to plaster on a billboard. "I am a man of medicine myself, but I cannot fault its success. I'm not saying Mrs. Alvarez is out of the woods yet, but it is very promising. Very promising. I would like to see her sleep for a couple of hours, so I have given her a mild sedative. It should take effect in about ten minutes. Why don't you go in and see her before it does?" He looked at me, adding a gentlemanly gesture to the door.

It was odd hearing Vicki referred to as Mrs. Alvarez. That was a title I thought reserved only for Mom. But when I considered it, my short, red-headed sister-in-law was next in line to become the matriarch of the family, just as Lila Hamilton Alvarez currently wore the crown. Lord knows it would never be me. Most of the time, I'm too busy chasing down bad guys who steal computer chips and playing with my cat.

Chapter Four
Reality Comes Calling

I crossed the threshold into the darkened room where monitors monitored and IV drips dripped. The room was abuzz with beeping machines and blinking colored lights. In the middle of it all lay an ashen Vicki, looking drained of life and vitality. Like her surroundings, her hospital gown and bed linens were all variations of shades of white. Even Vicki's glorious auburn hair, often set off by one of her own fun-loving chapeaus, was now constricted by a pallid gauze covering. It was pretty scary.

At her side, Tío sat on a small stool stroking her outstretched arm. The other arm had lines connecting her to various apparatuses, all giving forth their take on how she was doing.

I could hear Tío droning on with something pleasant and mesmerizing in her ear. Neither was aware of my presence. I studied the machines, trying to figure out what the displayed numbers meant. Giving up, I came to the foot of the bed and called out softly.

"Vicki, it's Lee. I'm here. *Hola*, Tío."

Tío glanced up at me and smiled, his gaze filled with so much love, I experienced the first peace of the day. Tío's gift to the world.

Vicki's eyes flew open. She blinked several times, and looked down to the foot of the bed, where I stood. Her voice cracked, sounding strained and dry.

"Lee, thank God you're here."

She let out a wretched sob and made a reaching gesture toward me with the arm wearing the IV. "He's alive. That horrible man is alive. He didn't die after all." One of the monitors began to beep faster than before.

I gave Tío a worried look, went to her side, and grasped her eager hand.

"Shhh. Easy, Victoria. Don't excite yourself. The doctor gave you a sedative to help you sleep."

Tío spoke to her, his soft Spanish accent filling the room. "You need to think the pleasant, calming thoughts, but first, the breath, *mija*. Take the slow breath, hold to the count of ten then let it out as slowly as possible. Do not think of anything else."

"Yes, yes, Tío. I will try." Vicki did as she was told, concentrating on her breathing. I squeezed her hand and did likewise, because man oh man, I needed a little calming down, myself. We both took in air, held it, then released it in unison. We did it again. I could see the tension subside within Vicki, the hot color fade somewhat from her flushed face. My own heart rate slowed down from a gallop to a trot. In less than a minute, the monitor returned to its steady, slower beep.

"Okay," I said. "Why don't we talk a little bit, Vicki, but as calmly as possible? Doctor's orders."

Even though the monitor didn't increase its beeping, a large tear gathered in the corner of Vicki's eye and slid down her upturned face. Her lips trembled as she spoke but her voice was soft and composed, almost as if she was reporting an event from someone else's life. She nodded then began to speak.

"Around nine-thirty this morning, I saw Dennis Manning coming out of Beignets on Bourbon Street. Richard and I were shopping for baby clothes across the street; it's the store right next door to mine. Richard was still browsing inside, but I had come outside and was standing on the sidewalk waiting. Then I saw him. Dennis Manning. I couldn't believe it was him. I just stared. He didn't notice me at first. He was with someone else, a short, older man."

"Do you have any idea who the older man is? Or where he might be now?" I was thinking of the dead man found beside Vicki.

She shook her head. "I never saw him before. Why would I know where he is?" Her question had an incredulous air.

"No reason, no reason."

I glanced at Tío. He was silent but listening intently, never ceasing the up and down stroking of her arm and soft chanting. I turned back to Vicki, who seemed lost in the past.

"What makes you so sure the man you saw was Dennis Manning?"

"He was thinner, older, wearing a beard, but there was something about the way he stood, leaning a little to the side. I had a crush on him when I was a teenager and I used to watch his every move. Then there was his laugh. I recognized it; I'd know it anywhere. He caught me staring at him. I saw the recognition of me on his face. I couldn't move at first. We just stared at one another. But he knew. He knew I knew who he was."

Vicki turned her head and looked at me. "I stepped off the curb to cross the street to get a better look. When I did, he walked away, nervous. It was like he didn't want to show anything was wrong, but he needed to get out of there. Then he started to run. I didn't even think to tell Richard where I was going, I just took off after him. The faster I ran, the faster Dennis Manning ran. But I could keep up because of his limp."

___

I finally spoke up. "His limp? Dennis Manning didn't have a limp that I know of."

"He has one now, Lee." She nodded slowly but emphatically. "Anyway, he stopped all of a sudden and said something to the short man, who was trailing behind. That man stopped running, too. They both turned and glared at me. That's when I realize how far we'd run and that no one else was around. In fact, I didn't even know where I was. Then the two separated. The short man took off in another direction. I almost lost him but I kept up."

"Who did you keep up with? Manning or the other man?"

"Dennis Manning." Her voice became impatient, agitated. "Always him, Dennis Manning, Dennis Manning! Why would I chase the other man?"

"Easy, Vicki, easy." I took her hand in mine and stroked her fingers, imitating Tío's methods. "Let the sedative do its stuff."

"I'm sorry. I'll try to calm down." She swallowed hard. "Can I have a drink of water? My mouth is so dry."

I looked over at Tío, my face a question mark. He nodded and pointed to a small glass on a side table filled half-way with water.

"Sure, sure." I unwrapped a nearby straw and plunged it into the liquid. I held the straw to her lips and she strained to lift her head without moving her body. Vicki took a few sips and released the straw from her mouth.

"Thanks. That's better." She gave me a weak smile and my heart went out to her.

"Go on telling me what happened. Try not to get excited, kiddo."

"As if, kiddo," she bantered, her humor returning for a moment. She squeezed my hand then looked back up at the ceiling. "I kept following him to God knows where. It seemed like forever. I didn't even think about what I'd do when I caught up with him. I didn't think about anything other than the man who'd destroyed my sister's life was still alive. I followed him into someone's backyard and woke up here." She gulped several times. "I asked what happened to him, but nobody knows what I'm talking about. He's gone. Vanished. Again."

"You don't remember anything about what happened in the backyard? Any details at all? Sights, smells, things like that?"

She shook her head.

"Maybe you remember something from before, when you were chasing the two men. Close your eyes."

She obeyed.

"Think back. You said Manning spoke to the man and the man spoke to him. Did they say anything you could hear?"

Vicki shook her head again, but was silent for a moment. I could feel her concentrating.

"Wait a minute." Her mood became eager, as if she'd made an important discovery. "The short man yelled out the name 'Sam', I think. Yes, that's right. I heard him call out, 'Sam, where are you going? Wait for me'. Then Manning said something to him I couldn't hear and the short man took off in the other direction. There was a lot of nearby traffic noise and I couldn't hear much, but the short man *did* call him Sam."

She turned her head toward me and struggled to rise, pulling her elbows under each side of her. Both Tío and I panicked.

"No, *mija*," Tío, said, standing over her and gently pressing down on her chest. "You must not move. You must rest. Think of *el bebé*. Do not make the stress."

She nodded and lay back down, anxious to please. "This is good, isn't it? I heard his name. Sam."

"This is good." I tried imitating her doctor in the toothy grin department and sound positive. I didn't want to mention how many men there must be in New Orleans with the first name of Sam, let alone in the state of Louisiana. "How was he dressed? What was he wearing?"

"Dressed?" She stuttered.

"Come on, you fashionista, you. How could you not notice what he was wearing? Even if all you design are hats." I baited her and waited. She rose to it.

"What do you mean, 'even if all I design are hats'? You're talking fiddle-faddle, Lee. A hat is the most important accessory we can add to our wardrobe. No offence, you could use one right now."

I saw the old Vicki return, if only for a moment, and it was wonderful.

She went on, seemingly as impressed as I was by her ability to recall details when tested. "Speaking of hats, he was wearing a tan Big Apple flat cap."

"What's that?"

"You know, the Great Gatsby, very thirties. And a white dress shirt, rolled up at the sleeves, khaki pants, and there were Huaraches on his feet. That's right." She gave me a proud look, like an A student would give her teacher.

"Very good. Was he carrying anything?"

"Carrying?" She screwed her eyes shut. "He *was* carrying something. A canvas bag. Yes. A canvas bag that looked kind of heavy. And a cup of coffee, which he threw away when he started running, but he kept the bag. It was slung over one shoulder and he clutched at it with his right arm."

"Nothing else?"

"That's all. You'll be able to find him now, won't you?"

"You betcha." Out of the corner of my eye I saw Tío signal me to leave with him. "Vicki, I should go and let you can catch some sleep."

She grabbed my hand and pulled me toward her with more strength than I thought her capable. I stared into her beautiful, but fearful green eyes, now bloodshot and teary.

"It's for Robin. He can't go free after what he did to Robin, can he?"

"No, he can't." I leaned over and kissed her on the forehead. "But first things first. Right now, your job is to get well and have a healthy baby. Our job is to find Dennis Manning and bring him to justice. Discretionary Inquiries at your service. " I stood, gave her a small salute, and grinned down at her. "We clear on our assignments now?"

She nodded, a brave smile on her face. I became more serious.

"You need to trust me on this. We'll find him. I promise. This is what I do best."

I saw her relax, faith in me, in what I could do, shining in her eyes. I felt a shift of the weight of the world from Richard's shoulders to mine.

"I know you will, Lee. And I am a little tired." Vicki closed her eyes and let out a long, deep sigh. "I think I'll sleep for a while."

"*Bien, mija.*" Tío said. "We will go now and you will rest."

"Thank you, Tío," she murmured. "Lee, kiss Richard for me and tell him I love him. I love you, too, Lee."

"Backatcha, kiddo."

I headed for the foot of the bed and met Tío there, who put a strong arm around me, regal bearing ever present in his six foot frame. It was only natural for me to bend into him. We left Vicki's room together.

Chapter Five
Things Are Never What They Seem

Richard was nowhere to be seen but Mom stood in deep conversation with a man of stature, tall and imposing but beginning to run to fat. Sure of his own importance, the large man looked like a policeman to me, even though he didn't wear the uniform. I labeled him as the 'brown' man, in that his hair and clothing were various shades of brown, down to skin that wore a healthy tan. He looked over at Tío and me. His piercing blue eyes were all the more vivid because of his otherwise russet appearance.

They were unsettling, those eyes. I felt like I had run a red light, ignored a speed bump, robbed a piggy bank, and knocked a little old lady around, all within the time span of stepping over the threshold. My gut told me here was a man who condemned at first sight and went out of his way to ensure his assessment was right.

Mom followed the man's stare, caught sight of us, excused herself with a small gesture of a perfectly manicured hand, and hurried over.

"How's Victoria? Did you *speak* with her, Liana?" Without waiting for an answer, she turned to Tío. "Were you able to *accomplish* what you wanted to do, Mateo?"

Her voice sounded thin, her body language more frenetic and unsure, and her face was definitely a little flushed. Whatever conversation she'd been having with the brown policeman seemed to upset her.

Tío reached out a reassuring hand, resting it on Mom's arm. "*Es major, hermana*," he said in Spanish.

Although he speaks English well, albeit with a heavy accent, he tends to revert to Spanish in times of pressure. After Dad died and Richard and I moved out, Mom was left rambling around the family's Palo Alto McMansion, the white-columned symbol of the American success story. Tío moved in some time ago, and as a retired chef, took the bottom floor with the huge kitchen. Mom took the top floor with the humungous bathroom. They lead separate lives mostly, but are there for one another in times of need, as family usually is.

"So she is *better*?" Mom visibly relaxed. "I'm *so* relieved."

"*Si.*" Tío smiled at her. "Victoria, she is resting now and will probably sleep for some hours. *Con permiso*, voy a *regressar en un momento*," he added and headed down the hall, probably in search of a men's room. I know the ladies room was whistling to me.

The need to keep up a 'strong front' temporarily subsided, tension in Mom's face drained away to be replaced by fatigue. She didn't seem so much like a drill sergeant now, just a woman trying to keep her family together in a crisis.

"Mom, where's Richard? And who's that man over there staring at us?"

"*That* is Detective Maxim Devereux. He's an old *acquaintance* of your father's and assigned to the homicide of the man found lying next to Victoria."

She looked toward him with a sniff of disapproval. He, on the other hand, glared at us like we'd committed a felony right under his nose and were about to get cuffed for it.

"As for your brother, he is in a nearby room doing research on Dennis Manning and, *hopefully*, the dead man, as well. I *arranged* to have his laptop sent over from Felicity's this afternoon. He --"

"I didn't realize Vicki and Richard were staying at Mrs. Llewellyn's with you. I thought they were booked into the Mariage Frères Chateau. That's where we're staying."

"Felicity has *plenty* of room. She --"

"Then why didn't she invite me? I thought Mrs. Llewellyn liked me, although I don't know her that well." I didn't wait for an answer, but went on with a new thought. "I don't get it, anyway. You two were never such fast friends in Palo Alto and all of a sudden when she learns Vicki is opening a new store in New Orleans, she insists the family stay with her? What's that all about?"

"If you *must* know, she is a very *big* contributor to the American Cancer Society, even chairing the Garden District's chapter, and as *I* am Chairwoman of the Palo Alto division --"

"Say no more, Mom. I know how you chairs stick together, not to make you sound like pieces of furniture."

"Initially, it was my *hope* she and I could share some marketing ideas. Contributions have been down a little, and we could use an *infusion* of new ideas. Once Felicity heard you were flying here, she said the only *reason* she didn't invite you to stay with her is her allergy to cats. Putting that aside, we should concentrate on Vicki and Richard --"

"She's allergic to Tugger? Well, where he's not welcomed, I'm not welcomed."

"Liana, where you stay or don't stay is *irrelevant* at this juncture." At my quick intake of breath to speak again, she all but stamped her foot. "Now *please* stop interrupting me while I'm--"

"Sorry, Mom. You're absolutely right. Where I stay doesn't matter. Whoops," I said, realizing I interrupted her again. But did that stop me? No. I'm not sure why I tend to babble around my mother, but I do. It's something about nerves, intimidation, and needing approval. "Don't mean to keep saying I'm sorry. Sorry about that. I mean, I'll be quiet. I promise."

"Yes, but *when*?" My mother closed her eyes and spoke through gritted teeth, often what occurs around me. "As I was *attempting* to convey to you earlier before all this nonsense about who is staying where, Richard is *forbidden* to go online in Vicki's room or out here in the hall.

He did find a hotspot in a patient conference room for his computer. You'll find him in there." She pointed in a direction.

The use of the word 'computer' for any of Richard's state-of-the-art equipment is almost an insult. It's actually a supercomputer configured into a laptop and to Richard's own specifications. A small island in the Pacific costs roughly around the same amount of money as this hunk of binary codes held inside a plastic casing. Thus, I have named it Bali Hai.

Bali Hai is a prototype, weighing in at less than a pound, fifteen inches square, pencil thin, and has the power of ten petaFLOPS. PetaFLOPS is some kind of scientific term used for computer power, speed, and performance. I can only remember the word because it's similar to the word flip flops, which I wear during the summer. Other than that, I'm clueless.

But Richard, the fount from which all things megahertz flows, is clued in like gangbusters. He even added a bunch of gewgaws on his supercomputer that do everything but fry eggs. There's a nifty monitor that swivels or can be detached and moved around within a twenty-foot radius of its mommy board. And he can make 3D images dance upon it like Nijinski. I don't know why you'd want to do that, but it's a great party trick.

Once linked to D.I.'s mainframe, Richard has the ability to find information, and run our business from anywhere in the world. And just like Mission Impossible, this baby is designed to self-destruct within five seconds if the wrong password is entered. Aloha, Bali Hai.

D.I., BTW, stands for Discretionary Inquiries. We're twenty employees strong and offer the service of bringing software, hardware, and intellectual property miscreants to justice on behalf of wounded hi-tech companies. *They Steal; We Reel* could be on our letterhead. Just a thought.

At work I am known as the ferret. I dig out who the bad guy is, even when the bad guy took a powder a long time ago.

I have a knack for solving after-the-fact crimes, which, hopefully, would enable me to sniff out Dennis Manning. Because I had no doubt he was alive and kicking, and living under a rock somewhere.

I opened the door to the conference room and whispered my brother's name, trying not to startle him. Fat chance. On hearing my voice, he leapt up from a small sofa with such ferocity he banged his shins against the table holding Bali Hai, almost tossing it to the floor.

"What…how…is everything all right?" The words came out jerky, and half-swallowed.

"Vicki's fine, just fine." I was quick to reassure him. "In fact, she's sleeping and should be for the next couple of hours. She's much better."

He fell back down on the sofa, bringing his bent arm across his face, trying to hide his emotions behind it. "Holy crap, you came in so quietly, I thought something else happened."

I sat down beside him. "I'm sorry, Richard. I guess I should have barged into the room and shouted out right away 'Vicki's okay'. I was trying to be considerate of you."

"Well, don't do that again. I'm not used to you being considerate."

I think I had just been insulted, but due to the circumstances, I let it go.

My brother lowered his arm and looked at me, fear, confusion, and love for Vicki written across his face like a newspaper ad. It made me swallow hard; the pain, the devotion. I tried to smile and be upbeat.

"She told me to give you her love. She's going to be all right, Richard. And so is the baby."

He didn't say anything but nodded. When he finally spoke, he turned his head away from me and reached down to close the lid on his laptop. "So what do you think?"

The words spoken were vague, but I knew exactly what he was talking about.

"I think a very alive Dennis Manning was in New Orleans and seen by Vicki this morning.

Even if he was only here on vacation and lives somewhere else, I'll find him. We're going to get him, Richard. You can take that to the bank."

Relief spread across my brother's face. "Thank God at least one other person besides me believes Vicki. I don't know how I could have done battle with the entire family over this, what with everything else going on." His light blue eyes so reminiscent of Mom's, were lit from behind with our father's Latino spirit.

"There's no battle to be done, Richard. At least, not between you and me."

Wordless, he reached for my hand resting in my lap, and gave it a squeeze. I squeezed right back. He looked at me with the same smile he had when we were united against the world over anything and everything, from cafeteria bullies to Dad's tough curfew hours.

"I know Dennis Manning being alive sounds crazy, Lee, but --"

"No, it doesn't, so let's not waste time going there. Vicki is way too pragmatic to have imagined this. Plus, if nothing else convinced me, a bloody wrench clenched in her hand while she lies out cold next to a dead man does. It's straight out of a bad Wes Craven movie."

He let out a laugh, the first genuine one I'd heard out of him since I arrived. "You always have the most bizarre way of looking at things." His mood instantly sobered. "But the handiness of it had crossed my mind. Vicki knocked out, the only other witness lying dead beside her, Manning gone." He paused. "Again."

"Hmmm. Vicki said the same thing. I take it you've been looking for Dennis Manning online. Or maybe the dead man's identity? Who was he?"

"Info on the dead man is nowhere to be found. I can't get a name or anything about the victim. I would say the cops are sitting on it, not putting into their system yet."

"Which begs the question, why?"

"Once it goes in there, it's fair game to anyone like me, Lee."

"That said, I'm surprised you're using the hospital's server. I would imagine it's pretty slow for our purposes."

"I'm not using that piece of crap." The affront to my words rose up from him like a geyser. "Their server can barely bring in Google." He dismissed the notion with distain and an impatient wave of his hand. Going into a field he knew well and was master at, his demeanor became more secure.

"I've captured a signal from an overhead satellite dish, and connected it to D.I.'s mainframe. It should stay in range for the next fourteen hours. Otherwise, even with my computer I would hardly be able to play a video game, much less do what I'm doing."

"And what are you doing?"

"After not finding the dead man, I dug up the Woodside Police report on Robin's assault, including the medical examiner's findings, from nine years ago. I've sent you a copy via your phone. It's encoded but be careful where you read it. I broke the law on this one."

I let out a soft whistle. "Richard, I'm shocked to hear you admit it. Usually, your philosophy is, if I can get it, it's mine. And how did you? Get a hold of it?"

Richard looked at me with raised eyebrows then a disappointed shake of his head. I was chagrined.

"Forgive me, Oh Hurdler of Firewalls. I didn't mean to doubt you. Anything interesting I should know about?"

"I didn't read it; leaving that to you, but it shouldn't have been as buried as it was. That much I know."

"Meaning what?"

He raised his shoulders in a shrug. "Since then I've been searching for Dennis Manning."

"And?"

Richard shook his head.

"Nothing?" If my voice sounded incredulous, that's exactly how I felt. "No funeral notice sans body?"

He shook his head again. I went on, emphasizing each word.

"No memorial service for the dear departed? *Nada*?"

"*Nada, nada,* and *nada*. He disappeared from existence September third, two-thousand and five and that's it."

Chapter Six
A Blast From the Past

"That's not it, Richard. It's only the beginning."

Richard grinned at me. "I knew you'd say that, so I pulled up an old photo of him from his real estate days. Then I added nine years and a beard to the image."

"Sort of Son of Photoshop meets Etch-a-sketch. Well, that's pretty good thinking."

"Not really. I made it up one night when I was nine. You should remember that."

Then he actually sniffed in a similar way Mom does when you've said something pretty lame. Blood will tell. He reopened the laptop and jabbed at it.

"Here's the image I made of Manning as he probably looks today. I'll show it to Vicki later."

A picture of a good-looking older man appeared on his monitor. Short salt and pepper hair and beard framed a face with even features. Dark brown eyes and deep-set wrinkles, the sort that come with an outdoorsy lifestyle, set off a flashy smile. I did not return the smile, but rather scowled.

"I've got a first name for you, Richard. Sam. It's not much, but Vicki remembers the other man calling out to Manning using that name. How many white males in their late forties, early fifties, go by the name of Sam in the greater New Orleans area?"

"Oh, God, there must be ten thousand." He looked stricken, so I tried to make light of it.

"Ah, but this one's got a limp. That should narrow it down to a couple of thousand. Piece of cake. Don't you have a program that can compile, search, and eliminate; maybe one of those you've done later on in life, say in your teens?" I added the last bit as a touch of sarcasm, but could have saved myself the trouble. Sarcasm is wasted on Richard.

"Given those parameters?" He thought about it. "I can probably piece something together. I helped the Palo Alto Police Department with something similar a few years ago. We don't have much to go on, but I'll do my best." He changed the subject. "The question I can't figure out is why here? Why New Orleans? Why not Switzerland or some far corner of the world, where you're less likely to be caught? This isn't that far from where he committed the crime."

"I would say two possibilities. Some people can't cope with living in a foreign country, handling a new language and culture, especially in their middle years. And second, Hurricane Katrina. He disappeared shortly after it hit, when much of the city's infrastructure was in chaos. If you had the guts and money, I'll bet you could come here and make a new life, assume the identity of somebody missing or dead. Or create a new person by doctoring up corrupted files. Make them read what you want."

"I hadn't thought of that. Maybe you're right. Have you seen the area around the Super Dome? Vicki and I took a tour of the city yesterday. Some of it still has vacant lots, nothing but debris left over from the Katrina. Might never be rebuilt."

He shook his head and turned to his computer. I reached out, stopping him with my hand.

"Actually, there's a third possibility and one that fits with what little I've already gleaned about Dennis Manning."

"What's that?" He gave me his full attention.

"He strikes me as having the kind of ego where he believes everyone else in the world is stupider than he is. That might work in our favor." I leaned in. "One more thing. Where's his wife, Richard? That's what I want to know."

"Pamela Manning? I have no idea."

"Find her. Let's see if we can track him down through her."

"You think she stayed with him after what he did?"

"They had two little kids. Besides, people are notorious for believing what they want, especially about a spouse. And find out their financial circumstances. Did she get any insurance monies when he died?"

I stood up and watched my brother typing commands into the computer with renewed energy.

"That should keep you busy for a while. Meanwhile, Mom, Tío, Gurn, and I will find some place close by for dinner and a debriefing. Can I bring you back anything?"

He muttered something unintelligible, caught up in what he was doing. I persisted.

"When was the last time you ate?"

He didn't answer, lost in his internet search. I was not deterred.

"Richard! Answer me. How about an omelet? It's hard to ruin eggs no matter where you go."

He glanced over at me with a dismissive air and gave me one of his shrugs.

"An omelet it is, Brother Mine."

He sat upright, body frozen, not even breathing. "Oh crap!"

"Okay, then. No omelet. How about a hamburger?"

Richard shot to his feet apparently not hearing me, but remembering something he didn't want to remember. Waving his hands wildly, his face became contorted with a myriad of emotions, none of them good.

"The car! I forgot to move the car from emergency when I drove to the hospital."

As if to prove he was in the final throes of panic, Richard began to talk with the rat-tat-tat of a machine gun. "Don't you see? I parked it in the emergency room section. The sign was very specific. You can only park there when the patient is in the emergency room. After that, you have to move it. Otherwise, the car is towed!

Vicki got out of emergency over six hours ago. I'll bet the car was towed. I'll bet the car was towed. Oh, my God. That's all I need."

His body jerked around like six-foot Cajun gators were nipping at his butt.

In times of crisis, you never know what the final blow is going to be that sends someone over the edge. I know from experience. A friend at Stanford lost her grandmother and father within a week of each other. She'd been remarkably self-contained until she opened the dorm refrigerator and found a carton of milk with an expired date on it.

She went ballistic, trashing the fridge, kitchen, and dining room before the paramedics arrived and sedated her. To this day, my heart starts to pound when I see an expired date on anything, even a grocery coupon.

"Richard, calm down. I'm sure it didn't get towed. And even if it did, we'll pay the fine and bail it out." I stretched out beckoning fingers. "Give me the keys. I'll go down and move it to the regular parking section of the hospital. I'll be back up in two shakes of a lamb's tail."

I, personally, have never seen a lamb shake its tail or know the speed at which a tail is shaken, but this seems to be a soothing phrase for those about to step off the deep end. If only I had used it on my college friend all those years ago, we might have saved ourselves a messy cleanup.

Releasing a trapped sigh, my brother dug around in his pockets for the keys to the rental. Once found, he pushed them in my hands. "Here. Thanks so much, Lee. It's a light blue Prius on the end of a row. I can't remember which one. If it's been towed...." He paused, building up again to his former hysteria. His right eye twitched like crazy and his fine, blonde hair stood on end. "Don't tell me. I can't take any more today."

"Right. Maybe on the way back, I can snag a couple of quarts of Valium for you, just in case."

Leaving my purse on the floor, I pocketed the keys, and hurried out of the room and through the hall, passing Mom in yet another deep conversation with the brown detective. I hit Gurn's number on my speed dial, as I galloped down the stairs two at a time. Gurn didn't answer, but I left a quick message about him bringing me a change of clothes.

I crossed through the lobby and followed the signs to emergency, quiet at the moment, then through its double doors to outside. The night was warm, the air heavy with moisture, but a slight breeze ruffled the damp curls already clinging to my forehead.

The parking area in the emergency section was well-lit but fairly empty. Of the few cars there, it was easy to make out the color and style. I went down the row and spotted Richard's rental parked by itself on the end, but in practically no light at all.

As I hurried toward it, I glanced up at the L-shaped pole overhead and saw the light bulb was dark. Chunks of glass crunched under my thin flip-flops. Wishing I had my flashlight, I looked up in the gloom to see the bulb was broken inside its fixture. Then I looked down at the glass underfoot.

Near the car, smooth river rocks sat in decorative piles on the median in between well-tended landscaping. One fist-size rock, however, lay at the base of the light pole. Surmising it had been tossed up in the air, hit its mark, and crashed back to the ground, I was offended by the vandalism of it. Then I felt an additional thrill of fear run through me and went into PI alert.

After a three-hundred and sixty degree turn scrutinizing my surroundings, I took careful steps toward Richard's rental, not the least of which was the fear a piece of glass might puncture the soles of my well-worn sandals. The driver's window was not rolled down, as it appeared at first glance, but showed jagged edges of glass around the framework.

I unlocked and opened the door. The overhead light came on to reveal glittering shards of glass covering the driver's seat. I looked over at the passenger's side.

Same thing. Glass rubble layered both chairs as if poured from a container.

This surprised me and made no sense. If someone wanted to steal from the car, they only needed to break one window to get in, not two. Besides, Vicki's expensive camera and case and Richard's new baseball cap with *If at first you don't succeed; call it version 1.0* written across the crown lay undisturbed on the backseat. What was going on?

Then I saw it. Propped up against the gearshift sat a crudely made voodoo doll, black button eyes staring out at nothing, black stitched 'x's forming a grimaced mouth. Created out of an off-white coarse burlap, it was about twelve-inches in length, and splattered with what looked like blood. Two long nails, one stuck through the head and the other piercing the heart, completed the ghastly picture.

Chapter Seven
Sometimes You're Dealing With an Idiot

I needn't have worried about the extra weight I gained in Napa Valley. Between not having any lunch and taking the stairs two at a time yet again to the fifth floor, I felt pounds lighter already. Noting Mom glaring at him from afar, I pounced on Detective Devereux as he stood shooting the breeze with the seated policeman. I should have known what his attitude was going to be when he elected to take the elevator traveling at glacial speed down to the parking lot instead of following me on the well-worn stairs, as my mother did.

Detective Devereux finally arrived, me waiting by the side of the car, Mom discreetly standing at a distance in the murky night, arms folded across her chest. I lifted an accusing finger toward the interior of the car. He merely glanced inside and grunted.

"Looks to me like a case of pure vandalism. I'm homicide. This isn't within my jurisdiction, Miss Alvarez." He said my name like he'd added a mental spit after it.

"Excuse me? You don't think this is related to Vicki or the dead man found lying beside her?" Spit all you want is my motto, just make it downwind of me. "And by the way, who was he?"

"Wouldn't you like to know?"

Up yours, I thought but merely pointed to the doll again.

Without any more words between us, he snatched it up with impatience, examined it cursorily, and chucked it back into the car like it was yesterday's newspaper.

"You can find voodoo dolls like that anywhere in New Orleans, fake blood and all. It's no big deal. And cars get broken into all the time."

"Really? That's all you get from this? You don't see anything sinister or threatening? Something happens to the car of the victim lying upstairs and you don't think it's related?" Nothing puts me more into the I-Am-A-Stanford-Graduate-So-Maybe-I'm-A-Little-Brighter-Than-You-Are mode more than the deliberate denial on someone's part just to annoy the bejesus out of me.

He knew he'd achieved his goal and snickered, the pinhead. "Tell you what I'm going to do, Miss Alvarez."

There was that mental spit again. I counted to ten.

"And what's that, Detective Devereux?" In my mind, I hock-pooed back at him as I said his name. Two can play that game.

"As a courtesy, I'll file a vandalism report for you. You should let the rental car company know. Have a pleasant evening."

He turned and walked away with a shake of his head. I watched the back of him vanish into the night.

"Man, that is one mean bastard."

"Please, Liana," Mom chastised in her best mother voice, stepping forward. "*Such* language."

I turned on her. "You don't think he's a mean bastard?"

"Of course, I do. I just wouldn't say it, that's all."

I had to laugh. "Then consider it said for both of us."

"Indeed." She was silent but we both stared at each other in a moment of truth.

"Okay, Mom. What the hell is going on? Who is this Detective Devereux and why is he so hostile? I've seen you going head to head with him and when you do, it's like you've found a pile of cow dung, sunny-side up."

She clicked her tongue in disapproval. "Where *do* you come up with these distasteful phrases, Liana?"

"Never mind my phrases. What gives?"

I could see thoughts bouncing around in her head, and then she came to a decision.

"Very well, perhaps it's time we spoke of it. Gurn has arrived and is in with Richard. He brought you a change of clothes. Let's go upstairs, call the rental car company, and then we will *converse*. Mateo already knows this but Richard and you don't. You were both teenagers at the time and your father and I didn't want to *burden* you with it."

"So my feeling Devereux has an axe to grind with the Alvarez family is true?"

She nodded, and turned toward the entrance of the hospital.

I didn't follow, but unlocked the back doors of the car with the electronic key fob. I flung a door open and retrieved Vicki's camera and Richard's cap. Hesitating, I moved forward and stared at the apparition-like bundle thrown face down among the rubble on the driver's chair.

"Can I help you carry anything?"

Mom's voice startled me out of my reverie. I hadn't known she came back and was watching me with an anxious expression, one I could see even in the gloom.

"No, it's fine, Mom."

"Are you comfortable in touching the doll? If not, I'll take it. I'd like to see it in better light."

I smiled at her with a confidence I wasn't necessarily feeling. It's an old PI trick - never let them see you shake.

"Mom, I spent much of the morning lying in a vat of hot mud from head to toe. This doll is not even close to that on my ick-odometer."

A faint smile crossed my mother's lips before she pivoted and strode toward the hospital with a determined gait. I trailed behind, bloody voodoo doll in hand. "Feel that?"

Chapter Eight
Take Your Meetings Where You Can

Tío had checked out the cafeteria when he'd left us, thinking convenience and the time factor outweighed any gourmet delicacies. Ordinarily, it would have been a tough sell to ask the mater and CEO of Discretionary Inquiries to dine in a hospital cafeteria, she who would rather eat diamond dust than processed cheese, but Tío can be very persuasive. He said he'd had a heart-to-heart with the cook, a native New Orleanian, who seemed to know his stuff and approached a cook top with honor and knowhow.

So shortly before nine p.m., Mom, Tío, Gurn and I toddled down to the cafeteria for a quick bite, sans Richard. With the promise to bring him back something, Richard continued to sift through the internet while awaiting updates on Vicki's condition.

Dressed to an acceptable level of my mother's standards in a Vera Wang orange and red sundress and red leather slingbacks, I gave silent thanks to Gurn's selections, given the choices available in my wardrobe. A man who likes cats and can coordinate a woman's accessories is a rare find, especially when he can make the temperature wherever we are climb with his kisses.

The menu comprised mostly of Cajun and Mexican dishes - how can you go wrong – with an emphasis on rice and beans. I've never met a bean I didn't like, so I shoveled in food like I hadn't eaten for days.

Tío munched on a *gordito*, a small Mexican sandwich and pronounced it *'bueno'*. Mom pecked at a garden salad, dressing on the side. She'd made the mistake of buying a glass of sweetened iced tea. An acquired taste for sure, it sat untouched and sweating by her tray before I snatched it up and gulped it down. I love sweetened tea. Gurn opted for the same platter as me, and inhaled cups of coffee as he ate. It was going to be a long night and we both needed the caffeine. Surprisingly, the food was pretty good even if it was drying out and getting on in years.

The cook, whose name was Slavio, was a rotund black man wearing a pristine white apron and cap. He hovered around the table in awe of Tío's reputation as a chef. If Tío had been Miley Cyrus singing stark naked, he couldn't have gotten more attention. Around us the rest of the cafeteria workers were closing up after a long day. Tío mentioned later he had given Slavio his secret recipe for Flan, the one that put Las Mañanitas on the Bay Area culinary map, in exchange for keeping the cafeteria open after hours. One of those win-wins.

It was a quick meal, and shortly after nine-thirty we returned to the conference room conveniently wearing a 'Do Not Disturb' sign; I'm sure Richard's undertaking. This is what happens when a geek travels with his own printer. Said geek can make signs at will.

After learning Vicki's vitals were much better and she was sleeping comfortably, we gathered around the table. Tío handed off a ham and cheese dripping with jalapeño peppers to Richard, his second favorite sandwich. His first favorite is a peanut butter sauerkraut combo, which has forced many of us to leave the room when he starts in on one. Richard held a small juice carton to his mouth, this time strawberry/grape. I watched him slurp it down. One could never call my brother a gourmand.

"Are we going to watch Richard's abysmal dining habits or should we get this meeting started?" I looked around the table.

All eyes darted over to the chair in which the sixth member of the party sat, a voodoo doll encased in a clear plastic bag obtained from one of the candy stripers.

Mom cleared her throat and took command, as usual. From this point on, we would no longer address her as anything but Lila. This was standard operating procedure, going from close-knit family to consummate professionals, something we've been doing since my early teens. Lila clasped her hands together almost in prayer and looked around at the assembled.

"Before we speak of the recent events and with Gurn's indulgence, I would like to explain the history the Alvarez family has with the New Orleans Police Department and in particular, Detective Maxim Devereux."

She flicked at her perfectly groomed blonde hair, with taut fingers. Whatever she was going to tell us, it wasn't a pleasant memory for her. We waited, while she pulled herself together.

"Nineteen years ago your father and I were in the process of making Discretionary Inquiries solvent. We had a certain amount of financial backing, the Coxe family assets to be exact. But the industry was in its infancy and Silicon Valley companies had yet to discover the need for our services. We weren't sure the business would survive. It was at that time your father received a call from an old friend, Felix Devereux, elder brother to Maxim Devereux. Felix, who originated from New Orleans, attended Stanford at the same time as your father and I. He was a lovely man and friend enough to be one of the ushers at our wedding. Roberto and I were quite fond of him."

"You keep using words in the past tense, Lila," Richard interrupted. "Does that mean he's dead?"

"Yes, sadly. But to continue, Felix was being coerced by an unknown gambling syndicate to open the doors of his string of nightclubs to them."

"And Felix Devereux called Dad?" I was surprised I hadn't known any of this. I could tell by the expression of Richard's face he was, too.

"Yes, he wanted to hire our services. Even though it was out of state and not what we saw ourselves as doing, it was for a fair amount of money. And as I mentioned, he was an old friend. Felix told us the threats were subtle at first, intimidating visits from the associates, late night phone calls, followed by harassing notes. Finally, his clubs were broken into, with great damage done. Another note was left, this time threatening his family unless he cooperated. But he never got a name or knew exactly who was doing it. The police were brought in for the break-in but, Felix shared little else with them. Maxim Devereux was a rookie cop with the department then, and Felix tried to keep him out of it, fearing he might be tainted by the connection.

"I stayed in Palo Alto while your father flew here and did some discrete investigating. Roberto found out the syndicate was out of Chicago, old and powerful. His only hope was to find information that would either coerce them into backing off or enough evidence to take to the police and have them arrested."

"Tall order," Gurn commented.

"Yes, it was," Lila agreed. "But Roberto did come up with something that linked them to an unsolved murder in nineteen seventy-seven. It was the break Felix and Roberto were looking for. Roberto's plan was to give the syndicate twenty-four hours to get out of town before the evidence was turned over to the police. Only then did they tell Maxim of the situation. What they hadn't counted on was the then Chief of Police being on the syndicate's payroll."

Lila stiffened, the expression on her face lost in the past. We were silent, waiting for her to continue.

"From what I understand, Maxim didn't know this either. Regrettably, he had, unbeknownst to Roberto and Felix, gone to the Chief of Police and confided what he'd learned. Whether he was looking for help or trying to get a promotion..."

Her voice broke off, and her fingertips stroked the wedding band on her left hand.

"....we'll never know. Of course, the Chief warned his partners, who took action immediately. Your father and Felix were sitting in the kitchen of his home. Fortunately, the children were at school, his wife was out shopping. The back door to the kitchen burst open and several men came in and started shooting. Felix was killed instantly; your father was shot in the leg. Roberto was still able to return fire, injuring one and killing the other. The third man fled."

"Oh, my God," Richard exploded. "Dad was shot?"

Chapter Nine
The Truth Comes Out

"Yes, it turned out to be a non-life threatening injury. You remember, the time we told you your father fell and hurt his hip? This is what actually happened. Your father was exonerated, especially as he had set up delivery of the evidence to the police for the following day through a well-established law firm. But it took two months for the link between the Police Chief and the syndicate to come to light. During that time, Maxim blamed Roberto for what happened. To this day, he has never forgiven the Alvarez family for our part in his brother's death."

"Holy chamoly. This is bad." I looked from one to the other. I know the shock and discomfort I felt was written all over my face.

Tío smiled at me. "*Mi sobrina,* I have known you to rise above much more. You must not let this deter you from what must be done."

The second large subject had been broached by our Tío. It was a foregone conclusion what we would be doing for the next several days. Searching for a dead man.

"Yes, time to move on to the *problem* of Dennis Manning. What do we know?" Lila Hamilton Alvarez can ask for a summary like nobody's business.

Richard jumped in without being invited. "We know that Dennis Manning, the man who attacked Vicki's sister, is not dead as previously thought. He --"

"We don't *know* that for certain, Richard," Lila interrupted. "We only *believe* that to be true."

"Mom," Richard said, instead of using her given first name. His unprecedented anger and outrage had him gyrating in his seat. "I knew you were going to say that! You don't believe her!"

Lila's eyebrows rose several centimeters. "Certainly, I do. I am merely establishing --"

"No, no. You think she's lying." Richard jumped to his feet, sending his chair skittering across the floor with a screeching sound. "He's alive. Vicki saw him. You can be so uptight in your thinking --"

"*Ricardo*," Tío said sharply. "Do not speak to your mother like that."

"All right, all right." I leaned forward and put a hand on Richard's arm in a quieting gesture.

Wordless, Gurn stood and returned the chair to its place beneath my brother, pressing him down into it. Richard seemed to deflate on the spot and running fingers through already unkempt hair, mumbled an apology.

"Lila isn't saying she doesn't believe Vicki." My aim was to return the meeting back to normal, if possible. "I think she's making it clear that at this moment we have no proof he isn't dead."

Lila shot me a grateful look, but had a grim look on her face. I wasn't sure if that's what she was saying at all, but I was going for love, peace, and harmony. A little something left over from the mud baths.

Richard deliberately didn't look at Lila. Whether he was still angry or embarrassed, he concentrated on crushing the empty juice carton then folding it again and again. This chasm between them was unusual. He was her favorite child, as I had been Dad's. It isn't that most parents don't love all their children, of course they do. But there are favorites. That's just the way life is.

Gurn jumped in. "Rich, why don't you give us a rundown on what you know about Dennis Manning?"

Richard thought for a moment then tossed the folded carton into a nearby trashcan. He picked up his laptop, keyed in a few commands, and began to read. "Dennis Manning. Born nineteen-sixty in San Mateo, California. Went to UC Santa Cruz and got a degree in Business Administration in nineteen eighty-two. Upon graduation, he sailed around the world on a thirty-two foot sailboat with two other men for eleven months. In nineteen eighty-four, he got a job as a mortgage broker at The Greater Woodside Mortgage Brokerage in Woodside. He wound up owning the business in six years. There's some question regarding that, but that's a story for another day."

As Richard continued reading, he relaxed more, tension leaving his voice and body.

"He spent nineteen years acquiring a considerable fortune as a mortgage broker and didn't marry until he was forty-two, although he was linked from time to time with a few society women. The property at forty-seven-oh-five Northgate Street in Woodside is where he lived after he married Pamela Nickels in two-thousand and two, remaining there until the time of the assault. They have two children, a boy and a girl, Simon and Ruth, named after Pamela's parents. The wife is considerably younger, twenty-one when they married. She's now thirty-two. The children are nine and eleven."

"He marries the *niña*, young enough to be his daughter?" Tío's voice registered his shock. "And her *pápa* allows this?" Sometimes my uncle's views on the world are charming, if not antiquated.

"Where is this considerable fortune now?" Lila once again cut right to the chase. "With his wife?"

"This is where it gets interesting, Lila."

Richard studied CEO Mom/Lila with cold contemplation. Apparently we weren't totally past the bad feelings yet.

"Gurn and I were talking about this earlier. So far, I can't find her or the money. And I've been looking for nearly three hours with every resource I have.

She and the children vanished about a year and a half after Manning supposedly died."

"How much is a 'considerable fortune'?" I watched Gurn as I asked the question. He was being quieter than usual, almost pensive.

"Around twenty million dollars at the time."

I raised an eyebrow. "Not bad for a mortgage broker."

"He appears to have had some underworld connections, as well, although nothing could be proven. Just a lot of sniffing around."

"An unsavory *character*, it would seem," remarked Lila. We all digested the latest developments.

"Richard," I said, formulating an idea. "Here's an angle. He was an experienced and avid sailor, as well as a money maker."

"Oh, yes," Richard nodded in agreement. "He participated in the Americas Cup when he was in his early twenties. The boat he was on came in second."

"What type of sailboat did he scuttle when he faked his death off Pacifica?"

He tapped in a few instructions on his keyboard then read, "A Westsail 32."

Gurn finally spoke up. "That's interesting. Remember the *Satori?* It was a Westsail 32. It didn't sink even when the crew abandoned it during the Perfect Storm; the real one, not the movie. It's supposed to be the unheralded workhorse of sailboats. I know a man who has one. You either love them or hate them."

"That's probably why he had to blow it up," offered Richard. "It wasn't guaranteed to sink otherwise."

"And," I said, taking back the focus of the conversation, "That could be another reason he chose New Orleans, the close proximity to open water. People don't abandon a life-long love, just like that. Even though I never was good enough to be a ballerina and these days I'm not even young enough--"

"*¿Que? ¿*You, *mi sobrina? ¡Nunca!*" Tío interrupted, protesting my statement. He's such a love-bucket.

"Tío, during my teens I was at the height of my dancing ability, which was mediocre. Add to that, a ballerina's career is in dog years and I'm thirty-four years old. By those standards, I'm an old bag. But that's not my point," I said heading off any further protestations by Tío.

"Even though I will never be a professional ballet dancer, it doesn't stop me from doing a barre every day or going to the ballet whenever I can. When something's in your blood, it's there to stay. Maybe the same is true for Dennis Manning."

Everyone's eyes lit up, latching on to my idea. The energy level rose by about five hundred percent in the room.

"*Como no, La devoción del corazón,*" murmured Tío, leaning forward.

"The devotion of the heart," echoed Lila. "You may have something."

"So brother dear," I said. "How about concentrating on someone who purchased a one-man sailboat after two-thousand five somewhere in the New Orleans area? You could start with a Westsail 32 and see what you get. There must be a listing of sales somewhere."

Gurn jumped in for the first time. "Not necessarily. These days, one person can handle almost any size boat with the right rigging. However, the boat would have to be registered in order to use marinas, docks and certain water ways, unless the owner is willing to keep it moored at sea, which I doubt. All sorts of things can happen to a boat left in open waters."

I turned to Gurn. "So you're saying tapping into the marina logs might be a better way to go?"

"What are you both are talking about?" Richard's plaintive cry was higher pitched than normal. "I've already pulled the IT team off everything else looking for Manning. Now you want to add searching through years' worth of marina logs and sales records in the greater New Orleans' area? It could take weeks if not months!"

"Hire extra help if you have to. Whatever it takes, Richard. We're here until we nail him." My voice was firm. "But maybe we can whittle this down. Maybe we --"

"How can we whittle it down? You've got me looking for everything that floats." Richard interrupted, his protest loud.

I thought for a moment. "Wait a minute. Maybe Pamela Manning was part of his crew. Was his wife a sailor, too?"

"Hardly." Richard scoffed. "A real princess. She wasn't into sports of any type. Spending money and going to day spas was more her line. Wait a minute. Maybe the local racing community knows something. Manning did compete in the America's Cup."

"Okay, that's good. You've narrowed it down. I've got another angle."

"You and your angles."

"No, seriously."

"I am serious. You've got more angles than a polygon."

"And I'm sure that's a good thing. To go on, did Manning repair his boats, himself? Some seamen like to do that. Finding those records could be another way to tracking him down, once we have his new identity."

"I'll have D.I. run checks on boat repair shops in the Bay Area for back then, Lee. I don't know how many years back businesses keep their records, especially for a supposedly dead guy. This is at least nine years ago."

"Another slant." I was on a roll and went with it. "Maybe we can drag some of our friends at Woodside and Palo Alto Police Departments in on this. There might be a report on Manning's personal life or a background check they did on him they might be willing to let us read. Maybe there's something in there that might be helpful. Richard did manage to get the police report on Robin's attack, and I'll be going over that tonight, but there could be something more."

"Appealing to some of the friends we've made in both departments crossed my mind, as well," Lila said. "In fact, an hour or so ago I contacted one of the officers at Woodside, whose run-away son, Siegfried, we located last year before he was officially declared missing and further embarrassing his family." She turned to me. "You actually found the boy, Liana, at the LA Computer Fair, remember?"

"Oh, yeah, Siggy. Hot pink Mohawk. Tattoos up the wazoo. Runs away from home periodically. The lesson here is, you name your kid Siegfried in this day and age, you're going to have to suffer the consequences. Murphy's Law."

"Yes, well, *thank you* for that insight, Liana." But it didn't sound like Lila was thanking me for the insight at all. She cleared her throat.

"To continue, *because* of our past history with his father, I felt I could ask him to place a few calls to the New Orleans Police Department on our behalf to ascertain the dead man's identity. He should call back momentarily. I'm also *overnighting* the voodoo doll to the lab we use at home, with their promise they would not only analyze the blood to see if was human, but check it for random fingerprints. Hopefully, there will be someone's other than yours, Liana, and Detective Devereux's, both of which are on file."

"You have been a busy bee, Lila." I looked at her with admiration. "And never one to let the grass grow under your Jimmy Choo's."

Lila gave me a smile then looked at her watch, taking in a quick breath.

"You need to wind this up?" I pushed the issue not only because I was tired, but wanted to see what seemed to be bothering Gurn.

"I do. I need to present the doll to UPS before they close, which is in less than a half an hour, so it will arrive in Palo Alto by ten-thirty tomorrow morning. Let's quickly go over what each of us is doing tomorrow. Richard, you will *continue* your compilation of data. Liana, you will *begin* the search for Dennis Manning. I will be at Victoria's store in the morning awaiting the workmen's arrival. They'll be finishing the sheetrock and starting placement of the shelving. Someone needs to be there to supervise until Victoria's return and I have the blueprints and work orders. I thought of cancelling, but I know Victoria would *like* to see the work continue until her return in a day or two, and it might help keep her spirits up. And as you know, we have *similar* tastes."

Okay, reality check. That was the fattest lie I've heard coming out of Lila's mouth in a long time. While my mother adores her daughter-in-law and the positive effect Vicki has on Richard, taste-wise, not so much.

Mom has long held that Vicki's skirts are too short, her footwear flamboyant, and her combination of colors, erratic and unsettling. Once, after two martinis, Mom told me she'd rather wear a San Francisco 49ers football helmet backwards to the Black and White Ball than one of Vicki's designer chapeaus to the grocery story. So much for similar tastes. However, I applauded her trying to gather the covered wagons around the campfire, so to speak. But would my brother buy it?

I need not have worried about a man getting the gist of this sort of female stuff. It goes right over their heads, the little dears. Richard turned to his mother, his look sending love beams by the bunches.

"Thank you, Mom. She wants the work to go on and it frees me to stay here with her at the hospital."

"Of *course*, my dear." She returned the mother/son love beams and whatever rift between them healed *instamunto*. Maybe Richard can teach me how to do that trick. Mom went on.

"Anything I can do to help, you know that."

It was getting a bit thick in here, and I was glad when her cell phone rang. She swiveled in her chair away from the table and answered quietly. I turned to my brother.

"Can you give me the address of where you found Vicki? I'd like to visit it myself tomorrow morning. See what I can find. Maybe you can join me?"

I directed the question to Gurn, who still remained uncharacteristically quiet and withdrawn throughout the meeting. He smiled back, but said nothing. Something was going on.

"Rather than the address," said Richard, as he pulled out his IPhone and started banging on it.

"I'm sending the GPS coordinates I got from Vicki's phone to yours. All you have to do is follow them and you will be taking her route. You might find something useful along the way."

"Good idea," I agreed, but secretly thought, *Oh, great. Now I have to find out where the hell the GPS is on my phone. I hope it's near the flashlight.*

As if reading my mind, Gurn leaned in and mouthed, "I'll show you where it is."

I mouthed back a thank you.

"I am supposed to be working at the shelter run by the Garden District Community Center tomorrow morning, cooking and serving *el desayuno*," said Tío. As a retired master chef, this was something my uncle did wherever and whenever he could. When he knew he would be visiting to New Orleans, he'd offered to spend one or two mornings cooking breakfast at a local shelter. "Maybe I will try to postpone or perhaps I ask Slavio to fill in for me --"

"Absolutely *not*, Mateo," Lila jumped in, having finished with her call. "*Please* don't disrupt your community service obligations for this. We'll all be busy with our various projects and you made these arrangements weeks ago. One hundred and fifty people are looking *forward* to a hot breakfast. And let us not forget, as coordinator of the kitchen program, Felicity is counting on you."

"She's a woman in charge of a lot of programs," I said. "I wonder how New Orleans got along without her before she moved here."

"And her good works are to be appreciated, Liana, not *criticized*." Mom did her sniffing routine again, the one that makes me want to brain her. But I smiled.

"I'm not criticizing, just observing."

"On another matter," Mom said, "the call I took a moment ago was from my source at Woodside. Unfortunately, and I quote, 'NOLA won't give me the time of day.' So much for *courtesy* between police departments."

"They're going to eventually have to tell someone. The dead man's name should show up in the papers tomorrow, won't it?" I looked around for confirmation of this.

"They could stall for weeks or even months, if they choose to." Gurn made this statement quietly. "Unless the press wants to run with this and create a stink, it might never show up."

"Hmmmm," I said. "Who do we know in the newspaper biz down here?"

Lila addressed no one in particular, but focused on a far wall. "No one. Even if we did, it seems the Alvarez Family and all our friends are *persona non grata*." She stood with a heavy sigh. "So be it. Let us see what tomorrow brings. Time to *end* this meeting and go our separate ways."

The rest of us stood and I picked up my purse. Gurn glommed to my side, wrapped one arm around my waist, and hurried me outside the door, stopping in a secluded corner of the corridor.

"Honey, listen, I need to speak to you," he whispered hoarsely in my ear.

"Okay, but first what's a polygon? I didn't want to let Richard know I didn't know."

"It's a plane figure with a lot of sides. Now listen, sweetheart --"

"You mean like a hexagram or something?"

"It can be. Now listen to me. I have something to tell you."

"Okay."

"Darling, listen to me." He looked around him furtively, paused, and gulped.

"Okay, that's a honey, a sweetheart, and a darling. What gives?"

"Listen, I need to go to D.C."

"Now?"

"Right now. Listen --"

"Stop saying 'listen'. I'm listening."

I wasn't sure if I was being condescended to or patronized, if there's a difference. In any event, I was annoyed.

"Fine," said Mr. Oblivious, "just listen. I think there's more to this situation than meets the eye. I've made a seven a.m. appointment with a friend of mine in the FBI. I think he'll tell me what's really going on."

"You're C.I.A. What --"

"Shhhh!" he interrupted, looking around him as if I'd just pulled down his pants to reveal his snow white jockey shorts.

"There's nobody within earshot, just you and me, Gurn. We both know you're in the C.I.A. no matter what you say about being a C.P.A. And by the way, there are far too many initials in your life for my liking. It's hard to keep them all straight."

"Forget the initials," he demanded, in almost a snarl.

I bristled. On seeing that, he cooed his next few words.

"Listen, sweetheart --"

"Say 'listen' or 'sweetheart' one more time and I'll belt you." I grated my teeth together in a way that would have stopped my dentist's heart.

He closed his eyes and took a deep breath. "Lee, let me start over, so we have no misunderstandings. Within the hour I'm going to fly to Washington D.C. on a commercial jet because I am dog tired and can sleep on the plane instead of having to fly it. I have arranged a seven a.m. meeting with an unnamed person or persons who might be able to shed some light on this matter. I have called in some markers and I need to go, in person, to collect them. But in case this doesn't pan out, I don't want to get your family's hopes up, so mum's the word. Okay?"

"Okay."

"Have I explained this clearly enough?"

"Yes. You're being a good guy. Dudley Do Right to the rescue."

"Dudley Do Right *maybe* to the rescue; it's a long shot. But I will return to the Big Easy with any information I can find around two, tomorrow afternoon. How's that?"

"Great, Dudley," I said with a smile.

"Does that make you Little Nell?"

"No way." I laughed and so did he. I kissed him. He kissed back. Man, did he kiss back. Laudie, laudie, laudie, he was a good kisser. I let out a sigh for the long night I'd spend without him.

"I love you. Keep that in mind as you fly over the Lincoln Memorial."

"And I love you. Keep that in mind as you drink your first Sazerac in the morning."

"I don't drink Sazeracs in the morning," I protested.

"No? Then you should. Such a lovely way to start the day."

We kissed deeply.

I broke away and looked around me. "Feel that?"

"What?" Gurn looked around him, puzzled.

I leaned in again, gazing up at him. "The temperature in the room actually starts to climb when we kiss. I think it's a scientific phenomenon."

He smiled down at me and drew me closer. "Should I alert *National Geographic* or maybe *Ripley's Believe It Or Not*?

"Just kiss me again," I whispered. And he did.

Chapter Ten
The Facts, Nothing But the Facts

After a night of cuddling with two warm cats and several pillows, I still felt lonely and anxious. Well, maybe not anxious exactly, but I woke up repeatedly wondering how Gurn was doing and exactly what kind of information he would manage to find.

I finally got up at around six a.m., which is four a.m. by my internal clock. I dressed in my practice leotard and ballet slippers, freed my mind, and did my morning ballet *barre*. Nothing gets the kinks out and centers me as much as my morning *barre*. All I need is an even floor and a wall to lean against occasionally to keep my balance. Tugger and Baba watched me from the bed beneath heavy lidded eyes. No one needed to tell them the time of their internal clocks.

Thoughts of Vicki, a young life filled with promise and her sister, Robin, a young life robbed of promise, crowded in on me as I did a series of stretches. I had to make things right. Or as much as I could make right. Some things can never be put back together. Just ask Humpty Dumpty. All the king's horses and all the king's men.

Then there was this horse pucky about Vicki possibly being arrested for killing the man in the alley. I mean, seriously? Here was a five-month pregnant woman, knocked out herself, who didn't even know the man, and she's being considered a suspect in his murder? There wasn't a self-respecting defense attorney in the world that couldn't rip that scenario to shreds. So what was really going on?

I felt my energy drain, my *arabesque* droop. That's the thing about not allowing your mind to be free. It affects the sanctity of the ballet. I forced myself to do several *pirouettes*, spotting my turns on the sleeping cats. The turns are difficult and can be dangerous if you don't concentrate, so concentrate I did. I ended with a double and almost landed pure.

That's the problem with being a not so great dancer. The heart is aching for perfection, the body gives its best shot, but they don't quite match up. Fortunately, I love the art for its own sake. Ballet will always be my first love, no matter what.

After a forty-five minute *barre* then a shower, I fed the cats, changed their litter pan, and went through my suitcase of vacation clothes. I had done some last minute shopping before we left for Napa after downing a martini. Given my mother's proclivity for them as well as mine, a well-chilled martini might be the downfall of the Alvarez women.

It's still no excuse for allowing myself to be talked into several sleazy outfits by sales ladies who should hang their heads in shame. Leave it to me to have a suitcase full of cruise wear for the tastefully challenged.

My first clue was when I donned what I thought to be a charming little number the first night Gurn and I were in Napa. Yes, cobalt blue Capri pants covered with white polka dots, topped off by a striped halter in the same colors. It's my suspicion that designers throw remnants of fabrics together, heedless of the patterns, as long as they are the same color. Then fashion school dropouts hope to convince the wearer the pieces go together when they actually don't.

And they have me to prove this form of brainwashing works very well. However, I take the fifth on the blue suede Roman gladiator style sandals with leather ties crisscrossing up mid-calf. The devil made me do it.

In any event, after parading around in front of Gurn and asking him how he liked the outfit, he said it didn't matter what I wore, I was beautiful, anyway. Then he shoved a glass of Chardonnay in my hand, and planted a big kiss on my lips.

Never trust a designer label that's seventy-five percent off. I'm just sayin'.

I didn't know what I'd be getting myself into in chasing down Dennis Manning, and as these were the only pants I had on hand, I climbed into this getup. After looking at myself in the mirror, I threw one of Gurn's denim shirts on to cover the bulk of it. I even put on the silly looking gladiator sandals, trusting I wouldn't run into Russell Crowe on the streets of New Orleans. I'm sure he'd tell me to give them back to the Coliseum. Unfortunately, these were the most comfortable shoes I've had on my feet in a long time. Life is filled with these little ironies.

Before leaving, I opened the room safe and pulled out Lady Blue, the gun I use when I carry. Something told me I should have it on me, so I grabbed my fanny pack, threw in the holstered gun, a bottle of water, my phone, other life essentials, and wrapped it around my waist.

Regarding the piece, Gurn thinks I should carry a newer, more accurate gun. I want none of it. I drive a vintage nineteen fifty-seven Chevy convertible, and carry a nineteen sixty-four Colt Detective Special, both gifts from my late father. You can say a lot of things are quirky about me, the least of which is I'm stuck in the past.

I skipped the idea of room service by our own little pool, and had some coffee with chicory in it at a corner booth of the coffee shop, rereading the police report Richard had sent the night before on my phone.

The report outlined one of those frustrating situations cops are powerless to do anything about. The year before Robin's attack, Manning had been brought in for questioning regarding him following a twelve-year old girl home from school. According to what the girl said, Manning approached her and offered her money for sex. She ran home, told her parents, and they filed charges. Several weeks later the charges were dropped and the family moved out of the area.

The report begged a lot of questions, but I suspected I knew some of the answers.

Manning certainly had the money to pay the family off and send them packing. Maybe Richard could delve into Manning's finances and see if there was a large sum of money taken out of his bank account around the time of the girl's family departure. Then again, was that necessary? At this point in time, let's just assume Manning was guilty as sin and move on to finding the bastard.

I phoned Richard for an update on Vicki while eating a *Beignet*, **a local delicacy around here**. My brother was happy, almost bubbly. Vicki and the baby were officially out of danger. Now if I could only keep her from being arrested for murder, it would be a good day.

By eight, it was already around eighty-five degrees and climbing. I was on Bourbon Street and making my way to the junction of St. Claude Avenue and Spain Street. The distance was one point four miles from Vicky's new shop on Royal and across the street from where she'd spotted Manning. The trek was certainly doable by a woman five month pregnant, even in this heat.

I was following a moving dot and verbal directions given to me by That Aspen Bitch, as I like to call her. That's the voicemail system that uses a woman's voice to boss everybody around. She started out doing telephone trees and has now worked her way up to being the voice of the GPS. She's everywhere. One cannot be free of her.

I tramped four blocks to North Rampart Street, turned right and followed her and the beeping sound. Eventually this street became McShane Place. That turned into St. Claude Avenue. All the while, the area became less affluent with pockets of definitely run-down. Whether the neighborhood was still in post-Katrina recovery or this was the way it was, I couldn't tell. One thing for sure, the birds kept singing no matter where they lived; they don't know the difference. I hung a left at Pauger Street and kept walking for a couple of more blocks.

Following the beckoning of the GPS, and at exactly one point four miles, I rounded a corner and came to the back side of a block and a row of buildings side by side on sitting on long, narrow lots. Not more than fifty to seventy-five feet wide, two and three story houses sat at the front end jammed next to one another. Each unique in style, height and character, most were kept up, but some were in serious need of a paint job.

At the rear, porches, tool sheds, and makeshift garages pretty much let nature do its thing. In between an occasional corroding refrigerator or washing machine, tropical vines with vibrant flowers in shades of orange, yellow, purple, and red twisted and crawled around, making even rusting buckets look like works of art.

A line of short dilapidated, wooden fences differed slightly in height and color, marking the boundaries of each yard. Running alongside the fences was the remnants of a sidewalk now more dirt than cement.

Across the street were mostly ex-businesses. Buildings looked ignored for decades, wearing faded and broken signs of yesteryear, with one small shoe repair inexplicably still in business. Three cars and one truck stood in the small parking lot, while a lone man wearing a leather apron leaned against the open front door smoking a cigarette. I made a mental note to visit the place to see if anyone had heard anything the day before. Otherwise, the structures looked forlorn and deserted.

I could hear the traffic from St. Claude Street, but it was almost like being in another world. Eerily so. In contrast to the distressed scene below, a canopy of majestic tropical trees dripping with either vivid flowers or exotic fruits shaded the walk. The sight made me want to burst out into Joyce Kilmer's *Trees*, if I had but known more than I Think That I Shall Never See A Poem Lovely As A Tree. I listened to the leaves rustle quietly in the welcomed breeze and marveled that if you just left nature alone for a minute, it's amazing how well it worked on its own.

The dot and blinking closed in and I knew I was nearing my destination, enough so I could turn off the vocal directives. Take that, Aspen Bitch.

In the middle of the block rose a tall fence in better shape than the rest, with an opening wide enough to accommodate a car. A thin metal chain crossed the void. It served more as a reminder of private property than a deterrent. I stepped over the sagging chain and onto the grass well-aware that I was now trespassing. The red dot and blinking aligned perfectly.

About forty feet in, and running the entire width of the lot, was a row of palm trees of at least six distinctively different varietals. They ranged in height from twelve to forty feet tall, with trunks that were fat or skinny, smooth or pocked, intricate or plain, depending on the type. Each was topped off with bright green fronds that fanned, draped or straggled against the blue of the sky. Clumped together, they shared the sun and rain as one.

As probably suspected, I love trees and of the twenty-five hundred or so species of palms growing around the world, nothing said the tropics to me more than one of them. Despite anything my mother could do or say and much to her horror, when I was a little girl I shinnied up many a palm tree, including an Indian Date Palm on a family vacation in the island of Turks and Caicos. I still remember the handful of dates I grabbed from the top of the tree as the sweetest I've eaten to this day. My regard for these swaying arbors borders on the religious. Obviously, someone else felt much the same way.

Aside from the gloriousness of them, their presence afforded a lot of privacy in this section of the lot from any prying eyes of the house. Unless you stepped back onto the sidewalk, you couldn't see the brick-colored, four-story wood-slat building looming in front of them. If I couldn't see them, then they couldn't see me. Seemed reasonable to me.

I relaxed and began to look around for where the crime had been committed. I pretty much knew where it had happened, because Richard had taken several images of the dead man, while waiting for the ambulance and police to arrive. For as freaked-out as he must have been, that was pretty smart thinking.

As in the photos, the dilapidated Adirondack chair was still sitting on three legs, the fourth missing, with two stacked cinderblocks taking its place. The chair's companion was a sad coffee table, dark wood bleached nearly white by the rain and sun. Stripped of any former glory it may have possessed inside, it was now subject to the elements of the outside world and not looking too happy about it. I sought out the yellow crime scene ribbon that should have been at the corner of the property line near the chair and table. *Nada.*

I swung around and studied the opposite corner of the property, where a child's metal swing and slide set in lively colors of red, blue, and green sat. Tufts of grass dotted the brownish clay soil beneath it, but no yellow tape was to be seen.

Two trashcans and an oil drum were lined up against the inside of the fence on the right. I opened the lid of one of the garbage cans looking for the tape and nearly gagged. Even though the garbage was contained in a black plastic bag, it still packed a mighty wallop in the heat. Before I rifled through the trash – a big downside to being a P.I. – I closed the lid in the hopes the tape might be inside the second trash can. Sure enough it was, ripped but coiled up, lying on top of several pieces of lumber and remnants of other non-smelling trash. Some days it pays to get up.

This struck me as odd, though. It wasn't quite twenty-four hours since Mr. Nameless was murdered. Where was the watchful eye of the law to make danged sure no one was trampling around or interfering with the integrity of a crime scene? Waiting for forensics to give the okay usually takes around forty-eight hours. Had they already been here and given the okay? Fast work for such a hot climate.

Puzzled, I replaced the lid, and moved back to the Adirondack chair. Several scraps of paper and a crumpled newspaper lying under the warped coffee table caught my eye. They probably meant nothing, but I dropped down to my hands and knees, and crawled under the table.

As I reached out my hand, a shrill, high-pitched sound, scaling up to 'E' above birdcall, assailed my ears. Startled, I banged my head against the underside of the table.

"Ow!" I scooted out back-ass-ward, rubbing my head. I heard a child's giggle. Sitting down on the dirt, I looked up into the face of a nine or ten-year old boy holding a clarinet. The slender boy's features were aquiline and elegant, especially for a kid, and his smile was marvelous. Possibly he had Creole in his African-American lineage. Whatever, he was a good-looking child and would probably grow up to break a lot of hearts. He put the offending instrument back in his mouth and trilled another set of notes up into the stratosphere, this time scaling back down to the note where he started.

"Hi," I said, impressed with the sounds he made come out of that glorified stick.

"Hi, yourself, ma'am. What are you doing in our backyard?"

There was something about the assuredness with which he spoke and the maturity in his eyes, that caused me to reevaluate his age. He was probably more like twelve or thirteen, just small for his age.

I began to stutter, which is my wont, when caught off-guard. "I…I…I'm looking for something."

"What?"

"I was looking for a…didn't a man…wasn't a man…uh… listen, aren't you supposed to be in school or something?"

"It's Saturday." He stared at me.

I stared back then tried to stand, clumsy and stiff. This made the kid giggle again.

For a person who lives for ballet and does a barre every day, I should really be more graceful in getting up. As residents of the Big Easy would say, what's up with that?

Regarding the kid, I decided to stop being cagy, not that I was doing such a hot job of it, but honesty is the best policy. "Look, my name is Lee Alvarez and I'm a private detective."

"Any relation to Robert E. Lee? I hear he got around."

"Not that I know of. So now that you know my name, what's yours?"

"Jasper, but everybody calls me Reed on account of I play the clarinet. You got a card?"

"Card? Ah…sure." I fumbled around in my fanny pack for one of my business cards. "Here you go."

He took it from me and scrutinized it with a jaundiced eye. He folded it in half and crammed it into his pants' pocket. Then he looked up at me inquisitively. "You're here about the guy who got offed yesterday? We still don't know what Mr. Gold was doing in our yard."

Bingo! I got a name!

"You don't happen to know Mr. Gold's first name, do you?"

"Bernie, I think. Mama didn't like him. He's from Chicago and said something to her once and she was offended. It don't do to offend Mama."

He pulled the clarinet toward his mouth, licked the tip of it, and began to do the scales again, this time with rhythm and feeling. This, too, sounded pretty good. I waited until he finished even though I was champing at the bit to learn more about Bernie Gold.

"You think your mama would be willing to talk to me about this Bernie Gold?"

He shrugged and started a song, 'String of Pearls' maybe. He was thinking. He stopped mid-stanza, took the instrument from his mouth, and looked at me. "She isn't really my mama, you know. She's my aunt, but I guess she would talk to you."

"Okay, good. What's her name then?"

He shrugged again. "The sign over the front door says Barefoot Mama Biggs, but everybody calls her Mama."

As if on cue, a woman's voice, loud and no nonsense, called out from behind the palm trees, her New Orleans Patois lilting the airwaves.

"Reed! I don't hear much playing. After what happened yesterday, I want to hear you every minute, so I know you're all right. Now if you aren't practicing, boy, you come in here and clean your room."

"Yes, ma'am. No, ma'am, I'm practicing," he called over his shoulder. Much softer, he leaned in to me. "I got to practice now or go in and make my bed. If you want to talk to Mama, go through the path and take the backstairs up to her. She's usually in the kitchen right now."

He put the clarinet back in his mouth, blew a set of notes, and gestured with an elbow to a small dirt path cutting between two Fan palm trees toward the house. I left him coaxing wonderful sounds from the wind instrument and beat my way through the glossy, green fans.

Previously untouched fronds crisscrossed one another from my chest to the top of my head, what with Reed being shorter than me. A small yellow and green bird flapped out of one frond and into the sky, as I thrashed my way through. I was sorry to have disturbed it. Once on the other side, sounds of the clarinet lessened considerably, deadened by thick fronds and trunks.

It was easy to see how someone could get murdered on the other side of the foliage and nothing heard inside the house. Unless Barefoot Mama Biggs was somehow a part of it all. A little chilling, that thought.

Chapter Eleven
The Other Side of the Garden

On this side of the line of palms, a lush and well-tended tropical garden lived. In the semi-shade of the palm fronds, blooming gardenia bushes filled the air with fragrance. Several smallish fruit trees lazed in full sun on one side of the grassy yard, burdened down by ripening fruit. Near the fence, crisp rows of herbs and vegetables grew, Farmer in the Dell style. Red, yellow, and pink Hibiscus, Birds of Paradise, climbing orange trumpet vines, and other exotic plants flowered everywhere.

An iron bench sat under the shade of another tree, maybe mango, near a terracotta birdbath filled with water. Two birds were knocking themselves out in it, obviously having a ball. All in all, I wouldn't be surprised if I saw pictures of this garden in Sunset Magazine. Oh, wait a minute. Sunset's a California mag. Well, some Louisiana magazine should snap a few pictures of this garden, if they haven't already.

I followed a narrow brick path and looked up to see a small woman, not a lot taller than Reed, watching me from the top steps of the four-story house, a house reeking with character and generations of wear.

"Good morning, ma'am," I called out at the base of the staircase, trying to be New Orleans respectful. "Reed said you would be here. If I may, I'd like to speak to you for a moment."

"Who are you and what are you doing in my backyard?"

Her tone was neutral yet commanding. She was obviously not a woman to be sweet talked, and certainly one to be respected. If she was party to a murder I had my work cut out for me.

I assessed the petite woman on the top step further before I spoke again. She had a presence having little to do with how she was dressed, impressive though it was. The colorful blue and green dashiki-like garment she wore was beautiful, as was the matching cloth wrapped around her head and tied at one side in a stylish knot. Huge, beaded hoop earrings dangled below the scarf, swinging back and forth to some secret rhythm or maybe Reed's distant playing. Slender fingers rested on the banister and glittered with a ring or two.

But it was her oval, burnished face that captivated. High cheekbones and large, deep-set eyes seemed to see anything and everything there was to see. She held herself confident and erect, meeting the world head-on. All in all, she was an arresting figure. I looked down at her feet. Sure enough, she was barefoot.

"Mrs. Biggs --"

"It's *Miss* Biggs," she interrupted. "I have never married."

"I'm sorry. Miss Biggs, my name is Lee Alvarez and my sister-in-law was the young woman who was found in your backyard alongside the dead man, Bernie Gold. The police think she killed him. I know she didn't, and I need to prove it. I'm hoping you can answer some questions that might help me find the real culprit."

She took her time looking me up and down without saying a word. Just when I thought she would banish me from the premises, she spoke.

"Then you'd better come up and have some tea."

Turning around, she stepped onto the tiny deck off the back door, and went inside her house without saying another word. I ran up the stairs as fast as I could and passed through the open door.

"Shut the screen door behind you, Missy. Flies are bad this time of year."

I reached out and closed the inside screen door, while she stood across the room with her back to me at a counter next to the stove. She poured hot water from a kettle into a large, white teapot.

"Tell me your name again."

"Lee Alvarez. I'm a private detective. My sister-in-law's name is Vicki and she's five-months pregnant. She's married to my kid brother and I love her to pieces."

After all of that came out of me, I stood breathing hard from my dash up three flights of steep stairs. I looked around the large old-fashioned kitchen painted a yellowing cream color, as wide as the house itself.

The far wall had a doorway in the corner. The rest was covered by open cabinetry revealing a mish-mashed of dishes, cutlery, and pots and pans. On the three other walls, a variety of framed cross-stitched samplers hung from midway to ceiling. The samplers were old and new, some religious, some political, but mostly proverbs. 'It's always darkest before the dawn' was my personal favorite. Because, you know, it is.

The worn but polished light oak floor gleamed under shafts of sunlight dappling in through tall, paned windows wearing soft cream-colored sheers. Pulled closed, the sheers moved languorously, keeping out the harsher rays of the sun but letting in cool air currents. One window sat directly behind a sparkling white sink. Another back window looked out over the yard where the palm trees rustled in the morning's breeze. Under that window, a small vase of colorful flowers held center court on a rectangular kitchen table decked out in a bright red and white checked tablecloth.

Completing the scene was the smell of something so delicious burbling on one of the back burners of the antiquated stove, I grew weak at the knees from hunger. I suspected any chef on the Food Network would kill for this kitchen. And they'd have to stand in line.

"Pull down two cups and saucers from the cabinet, Missy, and two teaspoons from the third drawer on the left. Milk and sugar's already on the table."

Her back still to me, she placed the lid on the teapot, picked it up, and went to the table. I chose two cups and saucers and spoons from the cornucopia before me and crossed to the table, as well, setting them down in front of two chairs.

I stood looking at a woman who could have been in her thirties, although I suspected mid-fifties was more like it. Whatever she did to keep herself looking so young, I'd have to check into. Unless it was something like eye of newt or blood of toad. Yuk.

Mama Biggs was lighter-skinned than her nephew, with a mocha honey glow, but she had the same aquiline nose as Reed. She also had a similar set of glorious, white teeth when she smiled, which she did now. There was something in the way she looked at me when she smiled, straight forward and earnest, which made me like her.

She gestured for me to sit down, so I sat. She did, too, and poured steaming tea into each cup. Fragrant, heady spices surrounded me and I inhaled deeply. I never wanted a cup of tea so much in my life.

She must have seen the appreciation on my face, because she laughed. "I make this blend myself. The secret is sun-dried Hibiscus and ginger mixed in with black China tea. Drink up."

"Thank you, Miss Biggs."

"You can call me Mama, but don't think nothing of it. Everyone does."

I nodded and her face sobered.

"I'm letting you in my house 'cause I don't like nobody getting killed in my backyard. I got a boy to raise and I don't want this hanging over our heads. If you can get to the root of it, all to the good. Now you tell me what you want and if I can, I'll answer your questions. Don't be lying to me, Missy. There's never been a lie I haven't caught up with."

I looked directly at her. "I wouldn't dream of it. I'll tell you everything I know, starting from nine years ago."

"Nine years ago," she echoed the words, her eyes suddenly far away and misty. "Bad time. Bad time. So much suffering around here, especially for the old and the little. I still pray to the good Lord for the people hurt by that time."

"I know people who were hurt around that time, too. Not here in New Orleans, but back where I live in California."

I started talking in between sips of tea and ten minutes later stopped. Mama Biggs was quiet. She seemed to be digesting this story, eyes glistening, as if unshed tears were not far behind her beautiful facade. Finally, she spoke.

"She was hurt bad, the sister. I can feel it. And it's something more than time can heal."

"The doctors say the beating probably caused irreparable brain damage."

"Probably? They don't know?"

"They claim it's hard to predict the long-term effects of such a trauma. But she's never recovered and they're relatively sure she never will."

I waited, wanting her to ask any other questions she might have. But rather than a question, Mama Biggs made an observation.

"And now your Vicki says she saw this man alive in New Orleans, although all the world says he's dead. And you believe her. That's a powerful belief."

I didn't respond right away. It's hard to put into words a gut feeling that runs deep and true.

"For all Vicki's outward flakiness and the wild hats she designs, I've found her to be a pragmatic person."

"Not one given to flights of fancy?" Mama Biggs smiled across the table at me, the first in a while.

I shook my head, but didn't reply.

"You're thinking this Dennis Manning, he sailed out to sea nine years ago, deliberately sank up his boat, made it back to shore, and come to New Orleans to start a new life?"

"Yes. Maybe he had a little help."

"Powerful maybe."

"He has a wife. If I can't find him, I'll find her."

"Law says widow."

"I say wife."

We stared at one another sipping our tea. I could feel her thinking. Mama Biggs got up and went to the counter, brought down a plate, and took the lid off a bright red cookie jar in the shape of a dancing bear. She loaded up the plate with small, square cookies and came back to the table, setting the plate between us.

"Have a cookie," she ordered.

I obeyed, chomping down on one with enthusiasm. I was starving. "Mmmmm. Delicious. You can sure tell they're homemade."

She shook her head. "Winn-Dixie's finest. Sometimes it don't pay to bake them from scratch. Have another."

The older woman sat down, studying me. While she studied me, I mulled over the phrase 'never assume, it just makes an ass out of u and me' and ate the cookie I could have sworn was home baked. Was I just as off-base about Mama Biggs being one of the good guys, as I was about the cookie? Time would tell. Her voice interrupted my thoughts.

"You want to right a great wrong, little girl. When I first looked at you at the bottom of the stairs wearing your fancy pants and sassy little shoes, I said to myself, there is a shallow, spoiled woman without the sense God gave a lemon."

"You don't like my pants? Gee, and they told me at Nordstrom's polka-dot Capri pants are the latest, especially in cobalt blue." I grinned then winked, taking another cookie from the plate.

She burst out laughing and leaned across the table. "They're telling you a falsehood, Missy. Get your derriere out of those pants as soon as you can."

She gave the French pronunciation to the word 'derriere', just like my mother does. I liked her, anyway. And she had one of the most musical laughs I'd ever heard. The sound of it made me laugh, too, lifting my spirits. But only for a moment. I sobered just as quickly.

"The rest of Vicki's family is gone and her only living relative, her sister, is in a sanitarium, probably for life. Vicki doesn't have anybody else. She's counting on us, on me."

"I know what that's like, to be leaned on. People have been leaning on me my whole life. It can be a heavy burden but it's something you learn to accept." She nodded at the truth of her words, more to herself than to me. Before speaking again, Mama Biggs smoothed a non-existent wrinkle from the tablecloth.

"Except for the sirens, I didn't hear anything yesterday, so I can't tell you about that. Mercifully, Reed was in school. I didn't even know it happened in my yard until the police knocked on my door, asked me questions, and showed me the spot. Your Vicki and that man were already gone, but the police asked me if I knew what they was doing there. I told them no and they left. When I took the garbage out this morning, everything was cleared up, though, like it never been."

"So you don't know who threw the crime scene tape in the trash?" She shook her head slowly. "Where were you yesterday?"

"Downstairs in my shop with customers. Those palm trees block out nearly every sound coming from back there. My mama asked my daddy to put those palms in fifty, sixty years ago, so she didn't have to hear him drinking and gambling back there with other men folk. But I can hear Reed if I don't play the TV. He likes it out there, same as his granddaddy."

She paused and looked around her before going on.

"My daddy was a rascal, but he built mama this top floor before he died, so he can't have been all bad. He even put this kitchen up here, so the rest of the house wouldn't get heated up. It's a fine kitchen."

There was an understatement. Her mouth took on a grim look.

"Reed promised me he would practice every minute and if anybody came into the yard he'd holler. If he does, I'll be down there with my shotgun."

"You mentioned your shop. What kind is it?"

"Voodoo."

"Excuse me?" I nearly choked on a slug of tea.

"Don't get me wrong, I'm a good Christian woman, myself, but my parents ran the shop for years and I inherited a good build up of clientele and vendors. This isn't the same trash they sell over in the French Quarter to the tourists. Besides, what I sell is mostly love potions."

"Really? Love potions. I would have never thought there was much of a market for that sort of thing."

She looked me up and down. "Then you've been blessed, Missy. Mother Teresa once said that loneliness and feeling unwanted is the most terrible poverty. So as long as I know nothing is used for evil or bad spells, I'll sell to you."

I opened my phone and searched for the picture of the bloody voodoo doll, one of several images Richard sent to me. "Do you carry something like this in your shop?"

I showed her the picture. Her musical laugh trilled again.

"Bless me, no. That looks like it was made by an Orangutan. That's the type of trash they sell in the French Quarter. Look here," she said, tapping the head of the image on the phone. "See this? It's a nail. Real Voodoo don't use nails. They use pins. Special pins. Where'd you get that thing?"

"It was a gift."

"Strange present to give someone."

She looked at me questioningly, but I didn't say anything more so she went on.

"This man they say she killed - your Vicki - he was a bad man, and he brought lots of trouble with him, too."

"That would be Bernie Gold?"

She nodded, lost in thought. I gave her time to do that.

"He came down from Chicago about eighteen months ago. In the beginning, he kept himself to the motor repair shop, about three blocks away, just like his friend. Later on, though, I seen him walking around the neighborhood, looking at people and houses.

He should have stayed at old Colbert's Place. Might not be dead now." She Frenched again on the word 'Colbert'.

"Colbert's Place is a motor repair shop?" I got excited. "You mean, like in cars, trucks, and boats?"

"Old Colbert, he repaired anything that had an engine. Lawn mowers, buzz saws, scooters, motorcycles, lots of cars, big diesel trucks, and some boats, too. They were all the same to him. Then he up and died five, six years ago. His daughter sold the place right after that to some stranger; got a high price for it, I'm told. Bad things go on there now. You can feel the ugly when you pass by, so I stopped walking that part of the street. Reed doesn't ride his bike by there, neither. At least, no more."

"Let's get back to the dead man, just to be sure." I scrolled through my pictures again until I came to the gruesome shots Richard took of the body the day before near the Adirondack chair. "Be prepared. It was taken when my brother stumbled upon his body. Is this Bernie Gold?"

She winced but pulled herself together. "That's him. Came to my door one day about six-months ago, and offered to buy my home. Offered me twice what its worth. Thought I was going to jump at it, like old Colbert's daughter done, I suppose. When I asked him why, he said it was none of my business, was I going to sell to him or not?" Her lips tightened at the memory. "I said no and then he told me, I need to reconsider. I said I never would 'cause I know what he wanted it for. You know what I mean."

She dragged the last part of the sentence out like she and I had a secret understanding. I hadn't a clue.

"Ah, no. What did he want?"

"That other man, the one who bought Colbert's Place, stopped Reed one day on his way home from school. That man stepped right in front of that boy riding his bike. He put his hands on the child's handlebars to keep him from riding away. Then he asked Reed if he wanted to make some easy money for a new bike, a better bike, if he wanted to make some new friends."

She looked at me. "You see, Reed, he looks younger than he is, more innocent, but he understands the twisted ways of some people."

"Let me get this straight. He was propositioning Reed for sex?" My voice carried the disgust I felt.

She nodded, anger bubbling up to the surface. "He shows my Reed a picture of a naked little girl and asks him if he wants to meet and play with her. Well, Reed just yanks his handlebars out of that man's grasp and rides himself home to me as quick as he can. I call the police and they go over there. Of course, he denies it, said it was a big misunderstanding, but what it did was show that man he can't fool around with me. And if he does anything like that again, I'll take my daddy's old shotgun and shoot him dead."

"I'll bet you will."

"Bernie Gold was his partner and wanted this house to do their sickness in. Set up their evil business, close enough to the City for perverts to come to. You know, this is a big enough house. I got five bedrooms, seven if you convert the two rooms I use downstairs for my business. He isn't the first one to try to buy this house from under me, but nobody ever had such evil ideas for it before."

I sat stupefied for a moment then swiped through the rest of the images Richard sent to my phone. I stopped at Dennis Manning's updated photo.

"Is he the owner of Old Colbert's Place?"

"Yes."

I was getting hits all over the place. Something in my face must have betrayed me, because Mama Biggs stared at the image for a moment, all the color draining from her face.

"Is that the man who raped and nearly killed your Vicki's sister?"

I nodded. "Do you know what his name is now?"

Mama Biggs crossed herself and sat back in her chair, as if to get as far away from his image as possible.

"Samuel Randolph. Sometimes I get his mail. He's down the street and our addresses are reversed. Sometimes the postman switches them. Look here." She rose, went over to the counter, and picked up a stack of mail.

"Here's one today from a pizza parlor. I don't know how they get all our names and addresses, but they do. If it's something like this, I just throw it out. If it looks legal, I turn it over to the postman."

"May I have that?" I reached out a hand. She shrugged and gave it to me. I finished off my tea and stood, facing the petite woman.

"I've taken up enough of your time, Mama Biggs. I should go. But before I do that, maybe you could give me a quick tour of your Voodoo shop? I've never seen one before."

She shrugged again, turned, and crossed through the doorway leading to a dark wood spiral staircase in the middle of a hall. I followed her into the hall and to the staircase that separated the kitchen from a front room that looked like a large, turn-of-the-century dining room. We went down the creaky but solid stairs for three flights, me giving each floor as much of a once-over as possible.

We arrived at the bottom into a room used mainly for storage. Behind me, a back door led out to the garden and Reed's muted riffing on the other side of the palm trees. Inside, shelving lined one wall floor to ceiling, filled with glass jars containing what looked like roots, bark, and a few things I didn't like to think about. On the opposite wall, a closed narrow door led to another room, possibly one of the bedrooms Mama Biggs had mentioned. A small sink filled with terracotta flower pots sat next to an apartment size refrigerator and stove combo. Something was brewing on a low fire on one of the burners. It had an odd smell, like sage, rubber, and walnuts.

"Sometimes these herbs smell bad, so I do my orders down here on the little stove." She threw the comment over her shoulder, as if reading my mind. "I don't like to mix my work with my home-cooking upstairs."

Mama Biggs pushed aside a curtain of multi-colored beads and gestured for me to follow her into the larger, front room serving as her shop. As I stepped through the beads, she began to give me a running lecture.

"My clientele come by appointment only. They call me, tell me what they need. I either got it or send away for it. If it's something I have to make up, like a potion or tea, I tell them when to come for it."

This room was less bright than the kitchen and had a serious air about it despite its colorful contents. I looked around at bright painted and feathered masks hanging on the walls, some beautiful, some grotesque. They were all dazzling, taking your breath away. Jewelry, statues, fabrics, books, well-filled glass jars, and more were artfully displayed on counters and tables. Dolls looking less Voodoo than folk art stood around in small clusters, as if taking a meeting.

"Wow," was all I could say. I walked over to the assortment of Voodoo dolls. None of them were as crudely made as the one I found in Richard's car. These were beautifully crafted, most dressed in gorgeous clothes similar to what Mama Biggs was wearing.

I picked one up from inside a stand, displayed next to a sterling silver necklace with a claw-like hand holding a ball. The doll had an enameled cocoa-colored head, hands, and feet, with thin hair-line cracks running through the veneer. A regal robe covered the body, once probably a brightly colored pattern, but now washed out by time to pastels. In contrast, the gold sash, trim edging the robe, and several bangle bracelets adorning tiny wrists and ankles glittered like they had been put on only that morning.

With a little practice you get to know the quality of gold. Here was at the minimum twenty-four karat gold or I am not my mother's daughter.

"Be careful with that, Missy." Mama Biggs smiled a warning. "That's nearly two-hundred years old and I'm selling it day after tomorrow for two-thousand dollars."

"Yikes." I set it back down with care. "I see there are serious bucks to be made in this business."

"Not always, but I do all right. That doll originally came from Jamaica for Marie Laveau's private collection. I have authentication. You heard of Marie Laveau?"

"She was one of the queens of Voodoo here in New Orleans."

She raised her forefinger, as if to make a point. "*The* queen. Over twenty-thousand people came to see the Voodoo priestess perform her magic at the height of her powers."

I narrowed my eyes at her. "I thought you didn't believe in this stuff."

"I believe in the power people have over one another, using their will and their minds. Use it for good is all I say."

She went to the front door and opened it. An overhead bell tinkled. The interview was over. I took out one of my cards from my fanny pack.

"Thank you, Mama Biggs, for your time and the tea. Here's my card, in case you think of something else."

I gave her my card then extended my hand. She took it and gasped.

"What is it? An electric shock? Sorry about that." I tried to pull my hand back but she held it firm, her eyes closed tight.

"You be careful, Missy. Watch the water. Stay off the water. No good can come from it."

"You mean, like a pool? That's about the only water I do."

Her eyes flickered open. "Don't you be sassy with me. You know what I mean. You watch out for the Bayou, brackish, and salt water. You be careful or you might meet your end there."

I gulped, but managed a smile. "Right. Okay then. Well, thanks, Mama Biggs. I think."

"He will kill you, if he can." She squeezed my hand so tightly, it began to hurt.

"We're talking Dennis Manning here, right?"

"You know who I'm talking about."

She dropped my hand and strode away without a backward glance, cutting her way through the curtain of colorful beads.

Chapter Twelve
The Future Looks Bleaker Than I Thought

I moved down the five steps of the wooded porch at a fair clip without looking back. I was shaken by our last exchange of words, but tried not to show it. However, at the end of the sidewalk I turned and scrutinized the four story brick-colored wood house with white trim. Over the doorframe was a small sign that read 'Barefoot Mama Biggs, Proprietress', not really noticeable unless you were looking for it, like I was.

The shimmer of a white sheer moving in one of the second floor windows caught my eye. Mama Biggs pushed the curtain aside and stood looking down at me. I waved. She didn't wave back.

So, Mama Biggs, what was that all about? You really see something or are you just trying to scare me off? Fat chance."

The sun was heating up nicely now and the few moments I stood baking in it caused beads of perspiration to sprout on my forehead and upper lip. So classy.

I walked with a slow gait toward the end of the block, but once out of any sightline from the house, broke into a run around to the backside of the block where I'd started. Anxious to get on with this, I crossed the street. The sounds of the clarinet were clearer from here and filled the morning's air with a melody to rival any songbird I've ever heard. If I hadn't seen the child play myself, I would have sworn it was a professional musician.

While walking, I called Lila. She answered on the first ring.

"Good morning, Lila. It's me."

"Liana, I was *wondering* when I would hear from you. Update me, please."

I'd used her first name instead of 'hi Mom' indicating this was D.I. business. Otherwise, she probably would have felt the need to correct my grammar. The correct phrase is 'It is I'. She knows it, I know it, but things just slip out sometimes.

"It's been a productive morning. I not only found out the name of the dead man, which is Bernie Gold out of Chicago, but I've got a lead on Dennis Manning, who supposedly calls himself Samuel Randolph these days."

"This is *indeed* progress."

Lila sounded pleased, so pleased in fact, I felt a glow of pride. I done good.

"According to Barefoot Mama Biggs – and yes, that's really her name – Dennis Manning, AKA Samuel Randolph, has owned an engine repair shop for the past five or six years a few blocks down from where Bernie Gold was found yesterday. After I pay a visit to a shoe repair store on the other side of the street to see if anyone there saw anything, I'll head for it. If need be, I'll break inside to see what's what."

"What are you wearing?"

"Excuse me? I'm thinking of doing a little B&E and my mother is worried about what I'm wearing?" We switched gears from CEO and boss back to mommy.

"What I *meant*, Liana, and there is no reason for you to be *sarcastic*, is that I hope you are more suitably dressed than when you came to the hospital last night. Something to blend in more with the scenery, more *appropriate*."

I looked down at my polka dots and gladiator shoes. "You betcha, Mom. I've got it all under control."

"Very well." I could feel her huffy mood over the airwaves.

"Apologies for whatever, Mom. I'm...I've got a lot going on and it's hotter than blazes."

Somewhat mollified, she said, "I understand. Heat *can* affect one's mood. Fortunately, Victoria's shop is equipped with an *excellent* cooling system."

"Really? I'll be right over."

Silence.

"It was a small joke," I said.

"I see. Ha ha. Well, I have some news of my *own*. Our Victoria will be able to leave the hospital tomorrow."

"Nothing about her being arrested for murder?" I stopped walking and parked myself under a shady tree.

"Not a *word*. There has also been no mention of yesterday's incident in any of the newspapers."

"So unless the Big Easy is slow in imparting the news, someone with a lot of moxie has strangled it."

I felt the huff arise again, even over the phone.

"Liana, *must* you continue to use Hollywood gangster terms? You are no longer an impressionable child and it is *so* unladylike."

My mother has been haranguing me about my affection for nineteen forties black and white crime movies since I was a kid. I saw the Maltese Falcon on TV at the tender age of nine and was set on a path for life that has caused her to repeatedly pull out her hair. When I wasn't running around the house talking out of the side of my mouth, imitating Humphrey Bogart, I was watching any old movie with a cop car in it. Then I latched on to that fab actress, Barbara Stanwyck, whose body of work I've loved since I saw her as Sugarpuss O'Shea in *Ball of Fire*. I even watched her in her later years in reruns of the television show "The Big Valley," undeterred by the fact her character was reminiscent of my own mother. I mean, lose the horsewhip and add a Dior gown and it was spot on.

"Liana, are you still there?"

"Sorry, Mom. Got lost in thought." I heard a beep indicating another call coming in. "Whoops. Got to go, it's Richard. Anything you want me to tell him?"

"Tell him to let Victoria know the workmen have completed the shelving and sixteen boxes of hats have arrived in excellent condition. Also, Mateo is on his way over to the hospital with her favorite frittata for lunch."

My protein deprived stomach grumbled. A Beignet and two cookies just didn't do it for me. But I soldiered on because I am a professional, of sorts.

"I'll tell him. Signing off for now."

"Liana." Her voice shot out over the airwaves.

"Yes, ma'am?"

"I just wanted to say, well done and be careful, my dear. Please don't take any *unnecessary* risks."

A warm rush filled me. "Will do, Mom, and thanks."

I pressed the flash button on my phone and filled Richard in with what was going on. He was elated at what I'd found, and wanted to get off the phone to initiate a new search with the updated information. It occurred to both of us that once we discovered Manning to be alive, he wasn't that hard to track down.

We hung up and I headed to the small shoe repair shop. Like every building on this block, it was narrow and long. Each of the three small stores contained within the building were barely eight feet wide.

Oscar's Shoe Repair, the only remaining open store of the three, looked forlorn and out of place, even with its relatively new sign. The doors at both ends of the shop were propped open for ventilation, but the smell of shoe polish, stale cigarettes, and cement glue was overwhelming despite the large square fan sitting on the floor pushing air around. Dozens of lathes hung on walls, along with Doctor Scholl products, such as corn pads, insoles and orthotics. The glass counter was covered mostly with men's leather wingtips and one or two sturdy-looking women's shoes.

I heard tapping coming from behind the counter and looked over to see the same man who'd been smoking outside the door earlier.

He was sitting on a bench, bent over a man's black shoe and banging the hell out of it with the small hammer. Being a cobbler seems to release a lot of aggressions.

"Excuse me."

I pretty much had to holler over the din of the fan. He still didn't hear me, so I called out again.

"Hello, back there. Excuse me. Can I talk to you for a minute?"

He looked up and squinted from behind John Lennon-like glasses, holding his small hammer midair. "What do you want?"

"Information, if you've got it."

"If you don't have a pair of shoes that need work, go away. I'm busy."

I reached behind me and pulled a fifty-dollar bill out of my fanny pack. I never go anywhere without the correct change. I stretched it out in both hands.

"I've got a Ulysses S. Grant here in need of repair."

He wrinkled his nose and pushed the glasses closer to his eyes with his free hand. "What the hell are you talking about?"

"I'll give you fifty dollars if you talk to me for five minutes."

"Well, why didn't you say so?" He put down his hammer, swung one leg over the vise encased shoe, and came to his side of the counter. "I don't know who the hell is on a fifty-dollar bill. Who the hell does?"

Well, I the hell do, I wanted to say, but let it pass.

"Mind if I turn off the fan for a minute? It's a little noisy." I reached over for the switch.

"Yeah, I do. Leave it on. What do you want to know?"

Even over the buzz saw noise of the fan, his accent was about as far from the south as you can get. I'm guessing Brooklyn, maybe the Bronx. Black curly hair, slack jaw line, and five o'clock stubble etched a face worn and tired.

He sounded like a lot of the cops in the nineteen-forties movies I often watch, the dumb ones, without a lot of lines to say but a lot of attitude. I suspected he didn't care who I was or what my goals were for being there, as long as he got his dough. I launched into what I wanted without any preamble.

"You heard about the murder yesterday across the street?"

"Hell, yes. There were cop cars everywhere for hours. Sirens blaring, lights flashing. Cops running around asking a lot of questions. Even this morning a cop car showed up, but no sirens. Just the flashing lights. He stayed for about fifteen minutes."

"This morning? Around what time?"

"Early. Maybe six-thirty, seven o'clock. My apartment's upstairs. Otherwise, I couldn't afford to stay in business. That and making break-away shoes for funeral parlors."

I stared at him. "I don't even want to think about what that is."

"Funny, that's what my wife says."

"Did you recognize the policeman from yesterday?"

"Sure. A big, surly guy."

"Running to fat? Wears a lot of brown?"

"That's the one. Acts like he owns the world. To hell with that."

"Amen, brother. You hear anything suspicious yesterday morning? Or see anything? Maybe when you stepped outside for a smoke?"

He looked at me and scoffed. "You're kidding, right? Like I told the cops, honey, I seen nothing." Then he leaned in, sincere for a moment. "And even if I did, I know enough to keep my mouth shut. Soon as I can, I'm taking me and my business out of here." He held out his hand. "Now give."

I gave him the fifty and turned to leave. An idea struck me. I turned back.

"You own this building?"

"Naw. Wish I did. I could have sold it for plenty."

"You mean to Bernie Gold, right?"

I could see the expression on his face change, as if I'd thrown cold water on it.

"You got your money's worth, honey. Now get the hell out of here." He turned and went back to his bench behind the counter.

"Sure thing, honey. Getting the hell out."

* * * *

I stepped outside, glanced at the time on my phone, and wondered what was going on with Gurn, temporarily MIA. It was pushing eleven-thirty a.m. Looking up at the blazing sky, I thought of the old saying, *Only mad dogs and Englishmen go out in the noon day sun.* I felt the urge to bark.

Just then the phone rang and I looked at the caller info. My heart literally skipped a beat - love does that - and answered the call.

"Hi, darling man! I was just wondering about you."

"Hi, sweetheart. Sorry I didn't call earlier, but I've been busy."

"What's wrong?"

His voice sounded sad and concerned. I had a feeling he didn't have good news for me on the Manning front. Unless he'd met a gorgeous flight attendant on United Airlines and they were running away to Argentina together. Hmmm. Sometimes I need to sit on my imagination, I really do.

Unaware of my weird thought processes, Gurn went on.

"I've called in every favor I can think of and finally found somebody willing to talk. Wherever you are, I hope you can sit down for this."

I followed his advise and plopped myself under a shade tree.

"I'm sitting."

"The FBI knows all about Dennis Manning. They found him three years ago. He's in the Witness Protection Program. He uses the name --"

"Samuel Randolph." I finished for him without thinking.

"Yes. How did you know?" His astonishment radiated over the phone.

"I got a lead on him this morning. How could the FBI be protecting him after what he did? Did they always know he'd faked his death?"

"Not until they came across him dealing with some other people they've been following. Once they found Manning, they decided to use him to get to the bigger fish. He's about to give evidence to the Grand Jury on a nationwide child pornography ring. The man who got killed was one of the lesser partners in the syndicate, sent down to keep an eye on Manning."

"You mean Bernie Gold?"

"So that's his name. I couldn't get any information about him. But the main boss, Rodrigo Santiago, is the one they want to hang and they're willing to give Manning a get-out-of-jail-free card to do it. The scuttlebutt is Manning took the opportunity to get rid of Gold and pin it on Vicki, maybe with the idea of taking off on both parties. The Feds are watching Manning like a hawk. Here's the tough part and you're not going to like it. Manning gives evidence in less than three days. After that they ship him and his wife off to parts unknown to start a new life. Even my pals don't know where that is."

"So if I don't nail him soon, we could lose him forever?"

Gurn let out a long sigh. "There's nothing to nail. Once he testifies, he starts a new life. As far as the law is concerned, Dennis Manning is as dead as if he had died on that boat nine years ago."

"Wait a minute! Does that means Vicki goes to jail for killing Bernie Gold? If that's what they're thinking, I'm not letting that scumbag get away with this."

"I've been thinking that over. Maybe we can negotiate something."

"You negotiate all you want. I'm going to *do* something."

"That's my girl."

I could feel his grin on the other side of the line.

"But Lee, be careful. These are dangerous people. Why don't you wait until I get back to NOLA, which should be in a few hours. How about that?"

"How about if I promise to keep you updated as I go along? Like right now, I'm on my way to Colbert's Motor Repair, which is owned by said scumbag. I'm going to look around, maybe do a little B&E. I'm wearing your denim shirt. Hope you don't mind."

"Not in the least. What do you have with you?"

"If you mean a weapon, I've got Lady Blue and a box of cartridges. I don't plan of having a shootout with anybody but thanks for taking me to the shooting range last week, just in case. I should go, Gurn. All of a sudden the sky is clouding up. It looks like it might rain. I may have my gun with me, but I don't have an umbrella."

"Could be nature's way of telling you to wait until I get there."

"Could be nature's way of telling me to get on with it."

He laughed. "Be careful, sweetheart. I love you."

"Backatcha."

Chapter Thirteen
When life Hands You Lemons, Make Limoncello

Several blocks later I came to a corrugated, half-moon shaped Quonset Hut type building, looking straight out of World War Two. It sat on another narrow strip of land, like everything else around here, surrounded by dull grey gravel instead of grass or weeds. Dense, tall bushes ran around the outer three sides of the perimeter.

A white sign with 'Colbert Motors' written in peeling red paint hung above the center of two wide corrugated doors. The doors were closed and locked, a heavy duty hasp binding them together. A battered black pickup truck with balding tires sat in one of the three spaces allotted for cars. The truck door opened willingly to me, so I searched the cab for anything interesting, keeping an eye out for passersby. Not one scrap of paper, not even in the glove box.

I banged the door of the truck shut, and walked the graveled perimeter of the forty-foot building, aware of only the sound of birds, the occasional toot of a car horn in the distance, and the crunching sound of my feet on the small rocks.

Along the side of the building were oil drums, tools, and other mysterious paraphernalia I suspected were used to repair engines. Even I could see, a person who knows nothing about tools, most of what lying around outside cost money. Left where they were they would either start rusting or 'taking a walk' soon, indications to me this place had been recently and hurriedly deserted.

That thought made me charge around to the back of the building. Was I already too late?

An old boat trailer sat on two flat tires, the long hitch resting on a bed of coiled, rusty chains. Back here everything looked like it had been in place for years, if not decades.

There was a back entrance to the shop, a door crudely welded into the siding by blowtorch. I yanked on the door, but it was locked. There isn't a lock I can't get into given enough time, but I planned on trying one of the three sliding windows on either side of the building first. Just then I heard two vehicles pull up in the front and turn their motors off. A man with an authoritative voice started barking orders.

"Get all those files out of the office, take them around to the back, and burn them in one of the oil drums back there. I don't want a single thing left for anybody to find."

A car door slammed shut and someone crunched up the gravel at the front of the building. His gait was irregular. The screeching sound of the corrugated front doors being forced open drowned out anything else he might have said.

Meanwhile, I was in a panic. I danced around in circles looking for a way out of this one. Sure, I had my gun and could shoot my way out if I had to – we'd already covered that - but I really, really didn't want to. So loud and messy.

Suddenly, I heard a set of uneven, but fast striding feet on the gravel heading toward me. Was it Manning with his limp? More importantly, if I stayed where I was, my only recourse was to hop into an oil drum, and hope it wasn't the drum they'd start a fire in.

The densely packed bushes lining the property called to me. I hightailed it over. Pushing and beating at stiff, prickly brushwood, I tried to wedge my body inside. Limbs, twigs, and branches grabbed at me from the top of my hair to the ties on my leather shoes. Scratches burned my face, neck, hands, and feet and still I plunged deeper into it. Man oh man, what I do for a living.

I managed to get in about two feet, and came nose to nose with a garter snake hanging out on one of the limbs.

I started to scream and maybe the snake did, too, but the back door flew open, banging against the tin siding with such force, we both froze. I could only pray I was inside the bushes deep enough so my cobalt blue Capri pants didn't show.

Through a tiny break in the branches, I could barely see a bald, older white man and a younger black man exit the building carrying boxes filled with file folders. The limping man had come around the outside of the building and stood with his back to me holding a one-gallon red can. On his head was a **tan cap.**

I couldn't see enough of him to make sure it was Dennis Manning, but it added up. I mean, if it looks like a rabbit, hops like a rabbit, and wears a **tan Great Gatsby cap**, it's Manning, right? Well, maybe. Okay, I needed to see his face. The tan capped man continued to stand in silence, apparently watching the two men. I thought this out.

The young black man dumped the contents of his box into a drum then the older white man did the same. They threw the empty cardboard boxes away, maybe under the awning of the building. Then they moved out of my pathetic line of vision, but it was clear the man with the tan **cap** gave the orders.

"Get out of the way, old man," he said. "You'll get splashed with gasoline." I heard the sound of a liquid being poured.

"You're using too much, boss," the young black man said. "Let me do it."

More sounds of pouring liquid. I was getting nervous. Unless you were burning down the Empire State Building, it was a lot of gasoline.

"Stand back," tan cap ordered.

I didn't hear the strike of a match, but a second later, there was more of an explosion than the roar of a bonfire. I think the snake fainted. I know the thought crossed my mind.

Thick black smoke curled and twisted in the ever-darkening sky. I could feel the heat even from where I was.

"Go get the rest of the files," the tan capped man shouted. The underlings went back into the building. Something else was yelled to the men inside, but the words were masked by the sounds of the blaze.

Was this Dennis Manning, now known as Samuel Randolph? I needed to be certain. *Think, think*, I demanded of myself, trying to ignore the feeling of being in the middle of a cactus patch. *The camera on your smart phone! And it can zoom in!*

But if I wanted to take pictures with my phone, plus see what was going on, I'd have to move. And if I made any form of movement, I might attract attention. Just when I felt frustrated beyond belief, a wind kicked up, sort of a precursor to it's-gonna-rain-big-time. Unburned papers broke free from their boxes. A few partially burned ones from the drum were pulled into the swirling updrafts and across the small yard. The three men scrambled after them.

I used this opportunity to squat, breaking small branches and limbs on my way down. Then I scrunched down on my hands and knees, sticking my butt up in the air. I maneuvered myself below the branch line and in between two narrow trunks. Lowering my face to the ground, I got a clear view.

I reached up behind me, pulled the fanny pack around to my front, and unzipped it. I was pricked at every point by the sharp, needle-like undergrowth. I withdrew my phone then Lady Blue, setting the gun on the ground in front of me. You never know.

The men retrieved all the flyaway documents and tossed them into the oil drum with the rest of the burning material. I opened the phone, put the camera on zoom, and started taking pictures madly. The zoom allowed me to see the two underlings up close and personal, tattoos, twitching noses and all. Writing showed up on many of the file covers. I couldn't make out what was written, but maybe Richard could enlarge the names, numbers, whatever, later on. It was worth a shot. So shoot I did, taking nearly fifty pictures.

The tan capped man finally turned and faced my direction, pausing for a moment. As I took his picture, I knew then for sure it was Dennis Manning. Richard had done a bang up job of projecting what he looked like nine years after the fact.

Then Manning did something that surprised me, right out of a James Bond movie. He lifted the hitch of the boat trailer, dragged it to one side, and dropped it to the ground. Then he returned to the coiled chains on the ground and reached down. Instead of heavy chains, they seemed to be one glued together piece, weighing next to nothing. Another version of the pseudo rocks people use to hide their house keys. How do people come up with these ideas? It's all I can do to run my espresso machine.

Manning set the chain facade on top of the trailer hitch and went back to the spot where they had been. With the heel of his shoe, he scraped a portion of the gravel away. Once cleared, he bent down and pulled up on a metal ring.

A large trap door opened, and Manning descended a set of steps into a cellar. He came back up moments later carrying an armful of files. Man oh man, I sure wanted to have those files but I didn't feel like shooting three men to get them, so I stayed put. He threw the files on the fire and descended the stairs again. It began to sprinkle.

As he returned from the cellar with the second batch of files, the cell phone clipped to his belt rang. He threw the files on the ground and answered his phone with a curt "Yes."

After that he only listened, but I could see whatever was said on the other end of the line upset him. He snapped the phone closed and turned to the men.

"Something's happened. I have to leave immediately. Burn the last of these files along with the rest of the ones on the fire. Then put the boat trailer over the storage room again." He looked up at the sky. "And hurry up before the downpour. When you're done, dispose of the truck in the front. It's clean but take it somewhere where it will never be found. You got that?"

The older man nodded but kept his head down, as if afraid to look Manning in the eye. The black one grinned and said, "You know I do you a good job, boss. You know that."

I kept taking pictures, even though the phone was signaling yellow, a low battery charge.

"Just do this right and I'll see you're taken care of." With that vague promise, Manning ran to the front of the building. I heard a car door open, slam shut, and the start of an engine. The back wheels of a white Jaguar spewed gravel everywhere, as he reversed next to the right side of the building. Something in my life was going right, because the back end of the car was directly in my line of vision. I managed to snap a partial license plate number before the phone blinked red twice then died. Manning careened away, the screech of tires and smell of burning rubber filling the air.

The men looked after the departing car. Then with zero gusto, picked up a stack of files and tossed them into the consuming inferno. The heavens opened up at that moment, and the onslaught doused the flames to not much more than a flicker. The men didn't seem to notice. They drew into themselves, drenched, and uncomfortable by the deluge. Sissies.

I of course, was fairly dry at this point, protected by the thick canopy of branches and leaves. After several more seconds, however, icy rainwater poured off branches and leaves, ran down slender trunks, and got me. The ground, soaked with water, turned to mud. There's no escaping the stuff.

Protecting my smart phone, I shook it and hoped to fool it into thinking it had a little life left in it. It didn't. Meanwhile, the men threw the last of the files onto the former bonfire. The black man turned to the other, and said something lost to me in the noise of pounding rain. Then he ran to the front of the building. I heard the truck's motor start and it, too, careened away.

Meanwhile, the older man hurriedly shut the trapdoor, threw the chains to the ground, and lifted the hitch of the trailer, dumping it onto the chains. Then he took off like his butt was on fire, which it couldn't have been, because he was too wet.

I waited only a split second then stood. The rain beat down on the world; water ran off the top of my head and down my back. Returning my phone and gun to the fanny pack, I fought my way out of the brush as fast as I could. I had one purpose in mind, save whatever files hadn't burned yet. My muddy Capri pants caught on a particularly nasty branch and I heard a long ripping sound. I didn't even look down; these pants weren't working for me, anyway.

I ran over to the smoldering oil drum and reached out. Despite the cooling rain, the sides were still too hot to touch. I kicked the drum over on its side with my foot. A pile of smoking rubble tumbled out. I looked around then picked up two soggy cardboard boxes and using them as potholders, grabbed the bottom of the drum, turned it upside down, and shook it. The rest of the contents plummeted out. I tossed the drum aside and it rolled several feet away.

The smoldering pile on the ground was just as I'd hoped. Papers in the middle of the drum hadn't had a chance to burn. The blessed rain had seen to that. With glee, I watched the deluge put out any remaining fire. The winds kicked up again but the papers were saturated with water and almost welded together as one. I sneezed, drenched to the skin.

I looked around for something to throw the precious unburned papers into and found a cardboard box at the bottom of the stack under the overhang, not quite wet through. Careful not to disturb the unburned pile any more than I had to, I lifted it up and placed it into the box.

My hands, arms, and feet previously spotted with mud, now was covered in soot. That didn't bother me as much as the papers I worked so valiantly to recover were being smashed down by heavy drops of rain, possibly destroying even more evidence.

I removed Gurn's denim shirt and covered the top of the box, shivering as I did so. I sneezed again and wiped away the water running down my face with my free hand. Too late I realized I'd smeared my scratched up face with all kinds of black stuff. Great.

I set the box under the overhand then turned back to the empty boat trailer with a big sigh. Duty called. I had to go down into the cellar and check for more evidence.

I lifted the ice-cold hitch off the chains with a big grunt, it being heavier than I had thought it would be. After I humped the sucker over to the side, I was rewarded with a twinge in my lower back. Tomorrow Bengay for strained muscles, Neosporin for scratches. What a life.

After throwing open the hatch, I descended the stairs into a six by six cellar made of cement. The rain hammered down on the stairs, but I saw the floor, ceiling, and walls were musty-smelling but relatively dry. Barely six feet in height, a single bulb dangled from overhead. I gave the string a yank. The low-watt bulb offered little in the way of illumination. I'm guessing the cellar was rarely used other than for storage.

Eight metal filing cabinets were crammed against two opposite walls of the cellar, four on each side facing one another. All the drawers were opened, and there was barely enough room to walk in between. Other than the eight filing cabinets, the cellar was empty, with not even room for a chair.

I examined the drawers one by one, even removing them from the cabinets for a good look behind. I was rewarded with a crumpled sheet of paper containing email addresses, and a small frog. I popped the crumpled paper into my pants pocket, snatched up the frog – because I'm not the sort of person who believes the old wives' tale about getting warts if you touch a frog – and climbed the stairs again.

I thought about dropping the frog into the brush near my pal, the garter snake, with a hurried introduction. But I wasn't sure about the culinary tastes of either one of them and there had been enough carnage for one day. Better off to release 'Kermit' farther away. So I did.

After he hopped off, I put the cellar's disguise back in place and took stock of my situation. Or rather, my predicament.

There I was, no phone to call for a cab or help, drenched, cold, wearing torn clothes, wet hair filled with leaves and branches, and slathered in mud and soot. And I was ravenous. Not for the first time, I wondered if it was too late to become a nurse. This P.I. stuff was highly overrated.

Chapter Fourteen
Just Shoot Me

Carrying my precious box, I crunched around to the front of the building, looking for a drier spot. *Nada.* The hard rain stopped as quickly as it had begun, becoming a light sprinkle again. I needed to recharge my phone and me, before I could even deal with anything else. I remembered a small corner bar about a block away and sloshed toward it.

Rivulets of water ran over, around, and through my toes. I looked down to see my feet and calves being dyed a lovely shade of blue from squishy, ruined sandals. Suede really is too volatile a material for a P.I. to wear, so I need to get over myself. This isn't the first time I've had it bleed all over me when I was caught in the elements. It's enough to break a girl's heart.

I arrived at the neighborhood bar, which was a pretty seedy-looking place. The top half of the front door featured cracked, dirty, and missing stained glass. The bottom half held warped and rotting wood. I'm guessing the last time it saw a paintbrush was maybe around the Civil War. Given how I looked, it was the ideal place for me.

I pushed open the door and waited for my eyes to adjust to the lack of light. The empty room had a dozen or so tiny round tables and an odd assortment of chairs, all in varying shades of faded black, mange brown, and mottled grey.

There was no sign of life, other than a barkeep and an overhead television, showing two teams of men having a fine time kicking a big ball around.

The barkeep was picture perfect for his surroundings and seemed about the same age, plus or minus a few hundred years. He glanced up, as the door swung shut with a drawn-out creak, not unlike the sound in a horror film. Then he stopped wiping down the bar with the filthiest cloth I'd seen in years, and stared. I forced a bright smile to my face and tried to keep a positive attitude, even though he looked at me as if I'd just crawled out of a grave.

"Hi," I said, in a voice so high-pitched and loud the glasses behind him vibrated. "Listen, I know how this looks but it's not really what it seems. Well, maybe it is, but I…"

I stopped speaking. He continued to stare at me open-mouthed. I stared back, nixing the positive attitude.

"Oh, never mind. Just give me a Sazerac cocktail."

I dropped the box on the nearest table, thankful that with the décor of choice, the soot wouldn't show. The thud of the box on the tabletop caused the barkeep to back up, as if he'd been struck.

"Sazerac cocktail?" He stuttered. "I don't even know what goes into that."

"Okay. What do you have?"

"I got whiskey, I got beer."

"A Boiler Maker it is. Where's your ladies room?"

"My ladies room?" He stuttered again. "We don't have a ladies room. We got a bathroom, but men and women use it." He pointed a shaky hand toward the back of the bar.

"Well, not at the same time, I hope."

I gave him an idiot grin. He blinked.

"Oh, criminy," I muttered. "Why do I bother?"

I headed for the back, and pushed open a door with the letters W.C. on it.

No matter how much you tell yourself you're prepared for it, you never are. I mean, once I got a gander of my reflection in the cracked mirror over the stained and dirty sink, I blinked just like the barkeep. I had several long but superficial scratches on my face and nose and a few smaller ones on my neck.

The rest of me was covered with soot, as black as boot polish. In my hair, a twig stood upright like an antenna, a small leaf dangling from the end. Another twig was entangled in damp curls over my left ear and several others acted as bangs on my forehead. I looked at my scratched and sooty hands and arms. Then down at my mud-dappled Capri pants, a large rip running halfway across the thigh. By God, I did look like I'd crawled out from a grave. Give the barkeep a prize.

Not one to wallow in my patheticness, I scrubbed as much of the soot off me as I could, and smeared Neosporin on the scratches from the tube I always carry, me being in the business I'm in. Then I unraveled some of the larger twigs out of my hair. The rest would have to be cut out later. I couldn't do anything about the tear in my pants and didn't have the energy to try. I returned to the bar lusting for my Boiler Maker.

A shot of whisky and a large glass of beer sat on the edge of the bar. The barkeep kept as much distance between me and him as possible. I said nothing, but pulled a twenty out of my fanny pack, and dropped it on the bar. He didn't come over to retrieve the twenty until after I picked up the two glasses, and crossed back to the table. He also didn't offer change.

I pulled out my solar charger, grateful the fanny pack was waterproof, and set it on the table. I made sure Lady Blue was hidden from sight, because that just might be the thing to send the barkeep over the edge. I plunked the phone down on top of the charger, heard the 'bleep-bleep' and knew it was charging. While I juiced the sucker up, I dropped the shot of whisky in the glass of beer with a kerplop, watched it foam over, and drank down half of it in one greedy gulp.

After a satisfying burp, I turned to the barkeep, still studying me with a look of horror. I no longer cared.

"Do you have anything to eat?'

"Eat?"

"Food? Do you have any?"

"No, no. I only have beer nuts and potato chips, bar-b-q flavored."

"Okay, give me one of each. Please," I added when he didn't move.

He nodded, turned around, and pulled two bags down from a stand behind him. He tossed them on the bar then stepped back.

I got up, went over, and snatched up the bags. "You let me know when I use up that twenty. There's plenty more where that came from." I winked, tearing open the bag of nuts. His jaw dropped open.

This was kind of fun, I decided. After a minute or two, my phone did that beep-be-de-beep-beep thing it does when there's text coming in. Obviously it had been juiced up enough to receive messages.

I sauntered over and looked down at my beeping phone. The beauty of texting hit me then. The barkeep was watching me like I was a rattlesnake that had returned to its hole but could pop back up at any minute. He concentrated on my every move with his total being. He may have even had a shotgun hidden behind the bar for all I knew. I smiled and almost flicked my tongue at him. Maybe it was forked by now.

I sat down and pulled the phone and charger to me, and went into messaging. It was Richard.

L- Where are you? Found 3 Samuel Randolph's. Still looking. Anymore info?

I hit reply. A space to type in showed up on the screen. So far, so good.

I started banging away with my thumbs and found the phone offered certain words it thought you wanted before you even finished typing. I can see why it's called 'smart'. A little wunderkind. I finally managed to do one sentence consisting of six words in about ten minute's time. As I said before, I'm pretty stupid with these things.

R – Partial plate # attached. See photo.

Then I got an idea. I was in no condition to hike back to the hotel, especially carrying a heavy, wet box. Probably no self-respecting cabbie would stop and take me there, either. I resumed typing.

Come get me. Desperate. Bring towels. Am at...

I looked over at the man still watching me.

"What's the address here?"

The barkeep told me with a stutter and I typed it in. The address, not the stutter. I attached the photo of the Jag's backend and sent the message off. This wasn't so tough. I crammed more nuts into my mouth and decided to text Gurn, if for no other reason than practice.

G - Hurry back. Luv ya, L

Twenty minutes later, I finished the bag of nuts, the Boiler Maker, and was working my way through the chips when the door burst open. Richard stepped inside, Tío directly behind him. They stood gawking at me, frozen in the doorway.

"Good God," Richard said.

"*Dios mio*," Tío said.

"Yeah, yeah, it's me, not Al Jolson," I said.

Tío raced to the table and hugged me. He smelled of something lemony; I smelled of burned rubbish. Soot, twigs, wringing wet, and off-putting smells never stopped this man from showing his love. Then he wrapped two towels around me, one over my shoulders and the other around my unruly mop, all the while cooing in Spanish. Everybody should have a Tío in their lives. I mean, really.

Richard came to the table gingerly.

"I'd ask what happened, but maybe I don't want to know."

"Let's go." I stood, feeling warm and a little woozy from the booze. "I need some real food."

"I bring with me left-over frittata I make at the shelter. It's in the car," Tío said. "It's not hot but --"

"It sounds delicious, Tío. I'll love it."

I turned to the man behind the bar, who was watching us with an even increased level of alarm. Now it was three against one. I gave him a charming smile or tried to.

"Do you have a large plastic bag?"

He gaped.

"Bag. Plastic. Large. Do you have one? Make that two. I want to put this box into one and I'd better sit on the other or my brother will never get his deposit back from the car rental. They're already pretty miffed at him."

Mr. Barkeep bent over and disappeared behind the bar. Seconds later he came up with two black plastic bags. How he found them in the dark, I'll never know.

I walked to the bar, the keep backed away, and I picked up the plastic bags. Feeling sorry for the man, I tossed another twenty on the bar then turned my attention to my guys.

"You'd better let me do this, gentlemen. There's no need for either you to get dirty. As you can see, I am beyond repair."

"What's in the box besides incinerated trash?" Richard whispered, coming up from behind. I turned to him and whispered in kind.

"Evidence of a child pornography ring, courtesy of Dennis Manning. And enough, I'm hoping, to take a lot of people down. But I'm turning this over to you. I've done my bit."

We went back to the table, and I handed one plastic bag off to Richard who opened it wide. I shoved the soot-covered box inside. Holding it as far from him as possible, Richard carried it outside without saying another word. With Tío's arm around me, I walked to the door, but paused before I left, addressing the man behind the bar.

"Thank you, my good man, for an excellent repast."

I looked at Tío. "Yes, I'm being sarcastic." We exited.

Chapter Fifteen
Priorities Will Tell

Tío opened the back door of the car for me, spread the plastic bag on the seat next to the other bulging black plastic bag, and handed me a paper plate. The plate was piled high with his world-famous frittata, filled with chorizo, potatoes and seasonings.

Richard stood next to the driver's side of the car talking on his phone with a local lab about drying out and separating the papers he'd taken. While looking me up and down, he mentioned words like 'rush' 'urgent' and 'vital' then threw in the phrase 'life and death' in case they hadn't gotten the message. I guess having a pregnant wife accused of murder does something to a man, even my nerdy baby brother. I was impressed.

Meanwhile, I climbed into the back of the car, frittata in one hand, charging phone in the other. Tío sat in the passenger's seat and handed me a plastic fork and napkin. Setting the charging phone on the seat, I took a huge bite of food and nearly passed out from pleasure. Some people say chocolate can be better than sex. Well, Tío's frittatas are better than any chocolate I've had. But I didn't realize I was making guttural sounds.

"Shhh, Lee!" Richard leaned in the car window and looked at me, annoyance written all over his face. "I can't hear what they're saying."

"Sorry."

I slowed down a little or at least, kept quiet as I ate.

After a few minutes, Richard hung up, got in the car, and looked at me in the rearview mirror. "The plan is to drop the box off to them before I take you to your hotel. This way they can get started right away. Did you know your feet were blue?"

"Yes, I know. Blue is the In color this year."

"You can be so weird, Lee."

He clucked and shook his head just the way Mom does. I stuck my tongue out at him and he cleared his throat.

"Never mind. You can last for a few more minutes, right?" He studied me in the rearview mirror, as he pulled out into the street. "Are you okay?"

"Sure. As long as I've got my frittata, I'm good. How's Vicki doing, Richard?" I chomped into a chorizo. Nirvana.

"Much better. I don't know what you said to her, but thanks, Lee. Even the doctors are surprised at her rapid recovery. She and the baby are out of danger, but that cop, Devereux, is still hanging around. As soon as I get done with this, I'm going to take her back to Mrs. Llewellyn's. That is, if Vicki doesn't get arrested."

"She still doesn't know about the dead man?"

"She knows, *Sobrina*," Tío answered. "But she does not know she might be blamed for his death."

"Maybe we should tell her," I offered. "Just sort of as a heads up."

"Your brother thinks it is unwise," said Tío. The expression on Tío's face showed he didn't share the opinion.

"There's no point in worrying her," said Richard.

Honestly, sometimes men like to protect us women right into prison.

"Moving on," my brother said, not wanting to have a discussion about his decision regarding his wife. "The report came back on the voodoo doll. Covered in chicken blood. Sells on the internet for about fifteen dollars."

"The chicken blood?" I made a face.

"No, the doll, you ninny. Why would anybody buy chicken blood off the internet?"

"I don't know," I countered. "Maybe because that's the way you phrased it. And don't call me a ninny because you can't explain yourself."

"Says she with the blue feet."

"*Niños, basta*. We are all the adults here." Tío's commanding tone made the both of us stop our sibling silliness.

"You're right. Sorry, Tío." Richard said. "Sorry, Lee."

"Yeah, yeah, me, too. Go ahead, Richard. Update me, please."

"Before I called the lab, I texted Andy to take the first flight here and help me go through this stuff. He arrives in a few hours. You think there's enough there to convict Manning and all those involved? It has to be, right? Or else he wouldn't be burning it."

"It's not last week's laundry list, for sure. But whatever's there, let's keep it to ourselves. Might be a handy-dandy bargaining chip with the Feds. You know, in case Vicki gets arrested. You'll have to tell her then, Richard." I shoved another forkful in my already full mouth.

"*Sobrina*," Tío chided me with a smile. "There is no need to be the *comilona*. No one steals the food from you."

Before I could reply, my phone made a completely different set of sounds. I looked over at it in horror.

"What does it want now? It's not ringing, it's not doing the Morse code thing. What the hell is this?" Richard took a corner so fast, it almost threw me, the phone, and the plastic covered box off the seat. "And take it easy. I'd like to take a shower before I get killed in an automobile accident."

"Your phone is signaling you have voicemail messages. Don't you know anything?" He didn't acknowledge my comment on his driving.

I picked up the phone, charged enough for jazz, and pressed voice mail.

There was one message from Gurn and two from the hotel where we were staying, with only the curt words to 'call them immediately' in both messages. I did so, as we careened down the streets of New Orleans for I know not where. I'd call Gurn later.

"Hello?" I said when the hotel answered. "This is Lee Alvarez, suite one-oh-one. You wanted to speak to me?"

A suave male voice answered on the other line, with just enough courtesy and authority to be effective. "Yes, Miss Alvarez, this is Mr. Lemans, the hotel manager. We wanted to let you know that while we allow pets to stay with our patrons in their rooms, the animals are not permitted to wander the premises unaccompanied.

"Excuse me?"

"Yes," he went on smoothly. "Both cats were sitting on the table under the umbrella near your pool. They were out of the rain, watching the passing people. However, even though it is a private pool --"

"Tugger and Baba were outside the room by the pool?" My voice raised in pitch and was so filled with alarm, both Richard and Tío looked back at me in concern. "Oh my God! How did they get out? Where are they now?"

"Please, Miss Alvarez, calm yourself. Everything is fine." The manager made soothing clucking sounds. "My staff and I gathered up your pets. It was quite easy. They are very sweet docile cats, and we returned them to your room. They weren't even wet."

"How did they get out?" I asked again, my voice riddled with fear. "And you're sure they're okay?"

"They are, Miss Alvarez. I have a cat, myself. As to how they escaped, Miriam, she's your housekeeper, shut a window next to the patio-pool area when she went in to clean. You should check all the windows before you vacate, Miss Alvarez, to prevent this in the future. Miriam also collected the clothing from the floor, folded it, and put it in the drawers. Miss Alvarez, are you still there?"

He'd asked the last question because I had been momentarily rendered speechless.

"I'll be right there." I hung up and smacked Richard on the back of the head. "Richard! Turn around immediately and drive with the same breakneck speed to my hotel. Somebody broke into the room."

* * * *

We arrived at the hotel about ten minutes later. I jumped out of Richard's car, streaked through the lobby like a madwoman, followed by Tío. I'm supposing Richard drove on to the lab with the plastic bag full of documents I saved from the fire. Frankly, I never gave it a second thought.

I opened the door to the room with a shaky hand, only to observe a tranquil scene, the first one of the day. Tugger and Baba were curled up in a yin and yang position on the made-up bed, both sound asleep. I rushed to them, calling out. Tugger opened one eye but didn't move. Baba opened both eyes, stretched languorously, and smelled my outstretched hand only to resume her previous position once more. I guess the Tugger-and-Baba-Great-Outdoor-Adventure wore them out. I picked one sleeping cat up then the other, examining them but holding them away from me to keep them from getting dirty or wet.

"You see, *mi sobrina*, they are fine." Tío came to my side, stroking them after I set them down again on the bed.

"I guess they are, Tío, but who let them out? And is anything missing?"

I pilfered through my clothes, now neatly folded and put back in place by the housekeeper. Yup, the same silly stuff I'd bought for Napa still lived inside. Too bad they weren't gone. I opened Gurn's drawers. All his clothes were there, as well. Strangely, my silver and onyx earrings, worth a couple of hundred bucks, were still on the tray near the ice bucket, where I'd thrown them the night before.

I went over in my mind any papers I might have left around that would be of interest to someone. Outside of the receipt for the rental car, there would be nothing. Then I went to the safe in the closet. It looked secured. There were no scratches, chips, no tale-tell sign of forced entry, *nada*. It's fairly easy to get into a room but harder to break into one of these safes. I punched in the combination to make sure everything was still inside.

Gurn's revolver and two boxes of cartridges lay undisturbed. My Bulgari earrings, turquoise, coral, and pearls set in platinum, sparkled back at me. I didn't want to think about what they were worth; it gave me the willies. If I'd lost them, Mom would have had my head. She's always for leaving expensive jewelry in the home safe, but I say, what's the point of having it if you never wear it? I closed the safe, let out a sigh of relief then sneezed.

"Liana, you must take first the shower then lie down and rest. Or you will get sick. I can tell."

Tío is the only person in the world who can call me Liana and not have it bother me. I smiled at him, nodded, and grabbed one of the spa robes from the closet. Truth be told, I was going on fumes at this point and did feel peculiar.

"You bring with you the vitamin C? If not, there is a *farmacia* on the corner. I will go there."

"No need to go to the pharmacy, Tío. I have plenty of vitamin C. It's on the nightstand. I'll be out in a minute."

I closed the door, stripped, and found the crumpled paper of email addresses in the pocket of my pants. I tossed it on the bathroom counter and threw my clothes in the trash along with the soggy sandals.

It took nearly a bottle of crème rinse to get the twigs out of my hair, but by gawd, I did it. Then I had to scrub blue stain off my toes and the soles of my feet. All told, I stayed in the shower for forty-five minutes, a record for me. I'm from the in-and-out school of thought, especially with the frequent droughts we have in California.

Squeaky clean, wrapped in the robe, wet hair in towel, I joined Tío. In my absence, he'd folded down the bed linens, and lined up five one-thousand unit capsules of vitamin C in a row, next to a glass of water on the nightstand. On another table sat a tray with a tea setup, steam rising from the lip of the teapot.

"You called room service. Thank you so much, Tío." I stood next to the bed and watched him pour me a cup of tea.

"*Sí, sí.* Now you go to bed and sleep. A small *siesta.* The world will not end if you rest. I will go back to the hospital." He placed the cup and saucer on the nightstand.

"Do you want to take our rental car, Tío? It's down in the parking lot. I can pick it up at the hospital later, when Gurn and I go there. We'll take a cab." Tío is over seventy years old now, a fact I often push out of my mind. But he is. Salt and pepper hair and eyebrows are a constant reminder.

"No, I have the taxi coming."

I got in bed and Tío rearranged the covers around me before kissing me on the forehead.

"Drink the tea and take the vitamin C every hour on the hour for five hours. Then twice a day. You do as I say, *mi sobrina*, and maybe we nip the cold back." He shook his finger in my face.

I laughed. "It's nip it in the bud, Tío. And don't worry, I'll behave. A nap right now sounds wonderful."

I reached up to him. He bent over and we went into a big bear hug. Everyone should have a Tío in their life. Wait a minute, I already said that. But it's well worth repeating.

Tío left and I lay there for several minutes, trying not to freak out over the fact someone broke into the room, searched through everything I owned, and deliberately opened the window to let the cats out. I was lucky whoever broke in hadn't hurt Tugger and Baba. It made me feel vulnerable, violated, and angry.

I got up and took Lady Blue from my fanny pack and shoved it under my pillow. Mama Biggs' warning reverberated in my ears over and over.

Maybe I could coerce Tío into returning to the Bay Area with the cats, just to relieve my mind. This was going to get ugly. The people I loved and my pets were a way to get to me. Anybody who knew me knew that.

Chapter Sixteen
On The Move, PI Style

The sound of someone coming through the door into the darkened room awakened me. I was reaching under the pillow for Lady Blue when I heard Gurn's voice, doing a not too bad imitation of Ricky Ricardo in I Love Lucy, complete with the heavy Cuban accent.

"Lucy, I'm home."

He turned on the hall light and stood there, all six foot one of him, smiling his lopsided smile. I pulled my hand out from under the pillow and switched on the nightstand light. He threw a plastic garment bag thick with clothes onto the foot of the bed. I looked up at him, rubbing the sleep from my eyes.

"Hi there. Welcome back. What time is it?"

"Four-thirty, Saturday afternoon. How's my girl?"

I almost answered but realized he was talking to Baba. He picked her up, cuddled her for a moment, and dropped her back on the bed. Then he roughed up Tugger's neck fur in a very manly way. They both seemed to enjoy it. Another guy thing.

He finally paid attention to me, third in line as it were, as I propped myself up on pillows. He bent over and we went into a kiss. Gurn straightened up and studied me. "You don't look too bad, considering the day you've had."

"You know about that? Who told you?"

"Spoke to Rich. He gave me a blow by blow. He's going through the papers now --"

"They're dry already?"

"Hey, modern technology. Chemicals and ultra violet light. And word has it you've been passed out for about three hours."

I looked at the bedside clock. "Wow! Three hours and fifteen minutes."

"And a lot can happen in that time. Especially in the Alvarez Family."

He let out a hoot of laugher and so did I. More serious, he sat down on the edge of the bed and took my hand. "Sweetheart, I think we should move from this hotel. Somebody knows we're staying here and I don't like that."

"That's what I was thinking."

"I've got a line on a safe house. One of my FBI buddies offered it to me when I was in D.C. It's nearby, a few doors down from Preservation Hall."

"In the French Quarter? You're kidding me."

"Nope. Safest place to be, among hundreds of frolicking, happy-go-lucky people."

"Did you just say 'frolicking, happy-go-luck people'? First Desi Arnez and then P.G. Wodehouse. You're sounding more like me every day."

"Well, maybe there's a pill for it. So get up, let's pack, and get going. Your mother's at the hospital with Vicki, who's being released in about an hour. We can unload the cats at our new digs and meet the family at the hospital. What do you say?"

"I say get off the bed, so I can stand up." He did and I did. "What's in the garment bag? A new suit?"

"I don't know. It's from your mother. It was waiting downstairs at the concierge. She told them not to wake you with it."

I dashed to the foot of the bed, opened the card pinned to the neck of the hanger, and read it aloud.

Liana - I know you didn't have time to bring clothes suitable for either New Orleans or the tasks at hand. These are from a shop near Victoria's. A beginning designer but one with promise.

I think you will like the selections I made. Consider it an early birthday present. Love, Mom

"Awwww. This is so sweet. I'm touched." I looked over at Gurn with glistening eyes. "Richard or Tío must have blabbed on me."

"What do you mean?"

"I think it was the gladiator shoes that tipped the scales. Anyway, she knows my size, but I can only hope she didn't pick something out in her favorite shades of tan, beige and grey. I hate those colors."

"Only one way to find out."

I unzipped the bag and pulled out a to-die-for turquoise pantsuit in shantung silk, jacket and slacks, with a paisley-patterned lime green and turquoise spaghetti strap blouse. It was gorgeous and my Bulgari earrings would set it off perfectly. Behind the suit hung a cotton knit dress, the color somewhere between teal and turquoise. Scoop necked, cap sleeves, and triangular insets of fabric started mid-thigh, giving it a lot of flounce at the hemline. In short, adorable and very me. Behind that hung a pair of navy-blue pull-on pants with matching sweater, and three sleeveless knit blouses, hot pink, powder blue, and lavender, all in summery cotton fabrics. At the bottom of the bag was a pair of ballerina flats in navy patent leather and a fuchsia folding umbrella. She done good.

"What the weather like outside? Has it cleared up or should I carry this umbrella?" I looked over Gurn wearing a lightweight all-weather jacket.

"I'd bring it along, if I was you. There's a high pressure area in a holding pattern off the Gulf. It might rain on and off for a couple of days; it might not. It could also go away or get worse."

"Well, you certainly covered your arse with that weather report. The only thing left out was snow."

"Slight chance of snow."

I laughed and threw on the hot pink blouse, navy pants and shoes then crammed the little umbrella into my bag.

You gotta love these folding umbrellas; so convenient.

After we packed up, we decided not to officially check out. Staying registered at the hotel was a great smoke screen. Gurn brought the car around the back. Laden down with the bags and cats, we had everything out of the room within twenty minutes.

Driving in the heart of the French Quarter, especially during rush-hour traffic, is a slow process. Add to that the locals prepping for another Saints football game, and you had near chaos. As we neared Bourbon Street, we decided to find a parking place on a side street. Our destination of St. Peter Street was close by, maybe a six minute walk across Bourbon Street. With Gurn humping the cat carriers and me pulling the luggage on wheels, we made our way through ecstatic revelers celebrating the local team. This was my first time seeing this spectacle and I didn't know where to look first.

Shouts of joy came from every direction. The New Orleans official song "We Ready," or fight songs from by-gone years happily competed with one another. Handmade banners and signs were bobbing up and down everywhere. The French fleur-de-lys and "Who dat?" signs were dominant, gold paint on a black background.

Many of the carousing held hurricane lantern-shaped plastic containers, filled with one of NOLA's favorite cocktails, The Hurricane. I hadn't had one yet, but they are reported to be tall, tasty, and lethal.

Hundreds of Mardi Gras beads were being tossed from either balconies above or at street level. I understand it's a year round tradition, this tossing of beads, symbols of a fun time. Green, purple, and gold plastic beads dangled from not just people, but car antennas, lampposts, tree limbs, street signs, or littered the sidewalks and pavement.

A few strands were flung at me by a couple of high-spirited men whooping it up on a second-floor balcony. The intricately designed black wrought iron railing they leaned on stood out against the brightly painted stucco exterior of the building.

Draped in colorful, cascading flowers, it looked like so many in the French Quarter, reminiscent of the Caribbean, graceful, old world, and elegant.

As tense as we were, I couldn't help but pick up some of the spirit of the partygoers. I wrapped several strands of beads around my neck, laughing, and looked at Gurn. He was laughing, too, as he trudged along. I suspected neither Tugger nor Baba were laughing, but rather caterwauling, but I couldn't hear either of them over the din.

Minutes later we arrived at a quieter street just off Bourbon. The safe house was over a ground-level pizza shop with the two floors above looking like private residences. The third floor had one of those darling wrought iron balconies, but behind the balcony, floor to ceiling hurricane shutters were shut tight. Gurn set the carriers down on the sidewalk in front of a narrow door at the side of the building. He tapped in a sequence of numbers and opened the door that led to a hallway and a set of stairs going up.

"It's on the top floor, Lee." He picked up the cats. "Real convenient. We can order pizza any time."

"Works for me." I pulled the suitcase up the stairs, the echoing thud of the wheels filling the empty hallway.

We arrived at the only apartment on the third floor, and the first thing I noticed was the door. Painted a dark brown, the shade almost hid the fact it wasn't made of wood, but steel. The door had three locks, each one looking more serious than the next. Gurn inserted the first key. It slid open on well-tended tumblers. The second lock grumbled but seemed to work when Gurn jiggled the key a little. As the last key turned, the grating sound of metal against metal moved on the other side of the door. Gurn pushed it halfway open, where the door stuck.

We slipped inside sideways to find a thick, iron rod set almost at a forty-five degree angle propped up against the inside of the door. The bottom of the rod fit into a small steel pocket recessed in the middle of the floor of the narrow hallway.

The top end dropped into the lock and moved sideways when you unlocked or locked the door. When unlocked, you can remove the rod completely, which Gurn did. He leaned it against the wall and opened the door completely.

"From inside, you put the rod in the lock and move it to the right. Whenever you exit, return the bottom end of it to its position in the floor, and place the top end back into the lock against the door." Gurn did a fast demonstration. "Keying the bolt from the other side slides the rod into place. You'd have to knock down the wall before getting in with the iron door and iron rod locked in place."

"Wow! That's clever. I'm mightily impressed with the FBI."

"Don't look so awestruck, sweetheart. They borrowed the idea from Hell's Kitchen in New York City. These were used there over a hundred years ago, and throughout the early part of the twentieth century. Probably in a lot of other high crime areas, too. Very effective."

We entered the small hallway, painted off-white. I left the suitcase there, my hand cramped from the pulling of it. A doorway off one end of the hall led to two bedrooms separated by a Jack and Jill bathroom. The other end of the hall brought you into the living room/dining room. Straight ahead was the kitchen. The small apartment was stripped of most things to make it homey, but the bones were charming. White birch floors, crown molding, and built-in cabinetry showed old-fashioned care and attention.

"Let's take care of the cats first." Carriers in hand, Gurn led us into one of the small bedrooms. Other than two made-up single beds and a dresser drawer, the room was empty.

I went to the lone window, popped up the shade, and looked out over rooftops. Below was a small courtyard from which a massive tree rose. A canopy of graceful, dark green feathery branches, still wet from recent rains and covered with hundreds of red-orange blossoms, glittered in random puffs of wind. Above streaks of gold ran through silver grey clouds quickly changing to the lavender hues of twilight.

It was easy to understand why so many artists came to New Orleans. And I could see why Satchmo loved the city like no other. No matter where you looked, NOLA was filled with larger than life color and vibrancy. If you could capture it in any form, what a coup.

Gurn set the carriers on the bed and I unlatched the doors. The cats came out almost as one, slow and suspicious. Gurn turned to leave and I followed on his heels.

"While the three of you look around, I'll go get their litter pans and whatever else is left in the car. Check out the kitchen. It even has a cappuccino maker."

"Sounds like you've been here before."

"Only once, several years ago. Tied in with the oil slick. Washington wanted a few answers."

"Did you have them? The answers, I mean, not the oil slick." We stood at the door and I watched him replace the rod in the recess of the floor and back of the door like an expert.

"Eventually." He grinned at me. "Even though I'm only going to be gone a few minutes, you may as well practice locking the door. Oh, and don't open the hurricane shutters on the balcony. They have to stay closed."

I saluted smartly and he left, the sound of his feet clomping down the stairs. I waited a moment then slid the pole into place behind the door. Easy enough to do. I experimented a little and tried to yank open the door to see if there was any play in it. There wasn't.

I went back into the bedroom. The cats were getting acquainted with their new surroundings, Tugger sniffing a floorboard and Baba giving the army blanket what for. I crossed through the Jack and Jill bathroom and into the second bedroom. It was nearly a duplicate of the first, down to the army green wool blankets, except against one wall was an aluminum set of bunk beds. This room slept a snug four people. I left the shade down in this room.

The eat-in kitchen, almost the same size as the living room, turned out to be well-stocked with staples and glory hallelujah, a stacked washer/dryer.

I returned to the hallway, rolled the suitcase into the kitchen, found detergent under the sink, and started a laundry. Hopefully, to get rid of the fact a burglar pawed through our underwear.

The apartment was very clean, no dust or dirt anywhere. Somebody in the FBI was a good housekeeper. Deep in thought, I turned on the ceiling fan in the living room for air movement and did a little thinking. I sorted through the few things that on the surface of it that didn't make sense to me. Things like who would want to toss our clothes around but take nothing, including a pair of silver onyx earrings easily pawn-able? And who would want to open a window and release the cats from the room?

The thought of the cats made me return to the bedroom, where I checked on them. Baba was now watching Tugger, who was still on the floor studying the plank of wood. I wondered what odor emanated from the wood that attracted Tugger for so long a time. Obviously, Baba wondered, too, because she hopped down to join him.

Two sniffing cats got me curious, so I crossed over to examine the plank with them. Kneeling down and much to their displeasure, I pushed them away and yanked at the floorboard.

It came up surprisingly easily and revealed a small safe secured in place between the flooring and the ceiling of the apartment below. The safe was locked, but that didn't deter me. While my singing skills are sub-par and moose-like, my safe cracking is right up there with Plácido Domingo. This one promised to be pretty easy to open. I leaned down, my right ear where the tumblers lurked, duff in the air, and started twirling. In less than five minutes, I heard the click.

I opened the safe door and saw a smallish Smith and Wesson handgun, mucho dirty and in need of cleaning. Before grabbing it, I hesitated, and reached up for some Kleenex on the bureau. I picked the gun up by the butt with the tissue, just as the front door opened.

"Hello," Gurn called out from the hallway. "Where are you?"

"I'm here in the bedroom with a surprise."

"A black negligee?" He chortled as he came down the hall toward the room. "Whatcha got there?" Gurn stood in the doorway, studying me and the hovering cats.

"It's a gun." My voice was puzzled, but I held it out to him. "There's also a box of shells."

Gurn dropped his jacket on the bed and came over. Not moving from the floor, I handed off the gun and he examined it.

"It's a Smith and Wesson MP357."

"So I noticed. It's written on the side."

"The serial number's been filed off, though, and it's filthy." He pulled the magazine out. "Jesus Christ! It's loaded." Gurn's shock reverberated throughout the room.

He crossed over to the desk, emptied the bullets from the magazine into his hand, laying them out on the hard wooden surface one by one. Each rolled with a smooth metallic sound until it found a resting place. He then began to dissemble the handgun with a proficiency I'd only seen in the movies.

"You're taking it apart?" I asked, rising from my crouching position. Tugger, now bored, leapt up on the window sill and looked out, probably searching for birds or bugs. Baba joined him.

"You bet I am. A dirty, loaded gun is just an accident waiting to happen. How did you find this thing, anyway?"

"I didn't, Tugger did. He kept sniffing at the floorboard, so I took a look."

"Anything else in there?"

"Just the box of cartridges, like I said."

Hands on hips, Gurn looked down at the parts lying on the desk. "It's been fired several times. Then put away, but never cleaned."

"Maybe they were in a hurry."

"Two cartridges are missing from the magazine. I don't understand how someone can pay the kind of money these things cost, take on the responsibility of owning a handgun, and then not treat them with the respect they deserve."

"You make it sound like owning a pet."

"In some ways, it's the same. Only potentially a lot more dangerous."

"What are you going to do with it?"

"Clean it. Check it over. Reassemble it."

"Then what? And who's is it?"

"That's the fifty-thousand dollar question, Lee. I can't imagine any of the men I know doing such a thing. It's unconscionable."Gurn's face took on a grim look I'd rarely seen.

"The safe looks to me like it was put under the floorboards in a hurry, so maybe it wasn't any of the good guys. I'm sure glad it was Tugger that found it, and not some nefarious thug."

"Well, if it works, the gun is yours now."

"Mine? Wait a minute. Doesn't it belong to somebody?"

"Probably not anyone who wants to claim it. It's a good weapon. More accurate than the Detective Special you insist on carrying. Later on, I'll take it out to a range and see how it does."

"Don't do it on my account. I love Lady Blue and I don't intend on giving her up."

"You can't hit the broadside of a barn with that thing."

"Excuse me! I have hit many a barn in my day." I rose and glared at him.

"I make an exaggeration, Lee, but given how fire arms have evolved since the sixties, the Colt Detective Special is obsolete."

"It is not obsolete! You take that back. I get some pretty good scores on the firing range with Lady Blue."

"That's because you're an exceptional shot, especially when you have the right equipment. And you're ambidextrous. Remember how you got fifty-out-of-fifty last month using either hand? Sharpshooters can't always do that. But you were using my Beretta M9. It's a better gun."

"I'm not giving up Lady Blue." I folded my arms across my chest and stomped in the direction of the bathroom.

Gurn made a grab for me as I passed him and twirled me into his arms.

"I'm sorry, sweetheart. Maybe I shouldn't have said those things." He nuzzled my neck. "It's just I worry about you. You're in a dangerous business. You should have a better gun."

I relaxed into his arms. "I love Lady Blue, Gurn," I whispered into a shoulder warm and all man. "It's easy to hide. It's lightweight. And…and it's the first gun my Dad gave me when I became a detective." I looked at him appealingly. "I don't think I can --"

"Enough said, Lee." He interrupted me with his lopsided smile and kissed my forehead. "The part about your father giving it to you makes me agree to table the discussion. Let's be friends."

"Friends." I looked up at him. "You know, this is our first fight. And it's over guns. I would have thought it would be over my mother."

Gurn shook his head with a laugh. "Not Lila. Never Lila. I wouldn't touch that one with a ten-foot pole."

"Hmmm. Men have been telling me that for years."

Chapter Seventeen
Freedom Comes At Last

Followed by Gurn, I entered the hospital room to find Mom and Vicki almost packed up. Richard was still at the lab going through papers with his assistant, Andy. Tío waited for us at Mrs. Llewellyn's.

Vicki looked up as the door opened, a little less energy than her usual dazzling, bubbly self. Over the bandage, she wore one of the ubiquitous hats she is rarely without. This one was a wide-brimmed straw job with a large bow on one side. If it hadn't been done in a vivid purple edged with bright green, it might have worked for me. Several gold fleur de lys baubles danced within the center of the green bow, catching the eye. We were pandering to the Mardi Gras crowd and if I knew Miss Vicki, this lid would set the panderee back several hundred bucks.

A large grin crossed her face as she rushed over to greet me, but her eyes had the same sunken, worried look I'd seen the day before. Vicki's small body enveloped me in a giant hug.

"Lee! How are you? Hi, Gurn." She gave my man a friendly, acknowledging nod. "I understand your room was broken into. Is everything all right?"

"It's been dealt with. We've moved somewhere safer," Gurn said.

"Details later," I added, and hugged her back.

Vicki nodded. "Any news on the other front? Richard told me you found Dennis Manning. You lost him right after that, but if you found him once, you'll find him again, won't you!" She changed the subject with hardly taking a breath.

"Did you know they were going to arrest me for some man's murder? He was lying dead right beside me, with me passed out!" She let out a shudder at the thought, but didn't wait for any of us to answer. "I'll bet you Manning killed him. That's why the charges against me were dropped."

After she stopped talking, it took me a moment to process what she'd said.

"Dropped? The charges against you have been dropped? Is that why the cop isn't outside the door?"

I gave a fast look over my shoulder at Gurn then back at Mom. Her blonde hair was up in French twist, smart and sleek. The up do revealed the ever present pearl button clip-on earrings, my father's last gift to her before his death. Dressed in the pale lavender two-piece knit suit trimmed in suede she'd had since before I can remember, Lila Hamilton Alvarez was every inch the sophisticated, chic matron. As Coco Chanel once said, "fashion changes but style endures." Mom's suit was a living monument to that statement.

On her feet and flawlessly dyed to match, were a pair of Italian suede five-inch stilettos by a big buck designer whose name escapes me, but his prices never do. My mother is a shoe fiend as well as a clothes horse, and to her way of thinking, a closet full of shoes is a glorious thing.

I mean, how silly is that? As for me, I only have thirty, forty pairs. Well, maybe a little more. I haven't done a count lately, but I'm absolutely nothing like my –

Hmmmm. Uh-oh.

"We were so relieved." Mom flashed us a smile, but never stopped arranging Vicki's belongings in a small overnight case.

Relieved about what? I did a fast rewind, my mind wandering again on life's accessories, as it is wont to do.

Oh yes, Vicki being released from the hospital with no charges of murder against her.

She went on, neatening the already neat clothing in the bag. "Welcome back, Gurn, and thank you for all you did in Washington. I see the wardrobe I chose for you, Liana, works perfectly."

"Yes, thanks so much, Mom; I'm very grateful. I love everything. So that means the jackass dropped the charges? Finally."

"A lady never calls a man a jackass, even when he is." Mom actually sniffed. "*Detective Devereux* was here only a few moments ago to tell us Victoria is free to go, in his own heavy-handed way, of course."

"So he's a heavy-handed jackass?" I grinned at her. She broke down and grinned back. I love my mother.

"Possibly more accurate. But the charges have been dismissed. That's all that matters. Victoria, hand me your toiletries over on the sink." Vicki left my side with an apologetic glance.

"Maybe Devereux's still around. If I can find him, I need to talk to him." I turned for the door.

"I'll go with you, Lee." There was a serious glint in Gurn's eyes.

"Not this time, please. I have something private I need to say to him. Okay, hun?" I blushed at excluding Gurn, especially as he had traveled most of the night helping the family out.

He reached out and touched my arm with a gentle hand and nodded. "This is your bailiwick, Lee. I'm just along for a little support."

"You give a lot of support, buster." I gave him a grateful look and he rewarded me with a loving smile.

"All part of the service. Why don't I start bringing things down to the car? Rich is going to meet us at Mrs. Llewellyn's house after he and Andy finish up. Then you and I will head off to Arnaud's for dinner. I believe that's the scenario."

"Everybody's being so wonderful to me," Vicki said, in a small voice. "Working so hard to help me. I just don't know what to say --" She stopped talking, her face scrunching up with emotion.

"There's no need to say anything, my dear." Mom's no-nonsense tone of voice filled the room, as she shut the lid on the small piece of luggage. "Naturally, we're helping. We're family. Now you stop this. You need to marshal your energy for the baby. Try not to be needlessly sentimental, Victoria."

Gurn and I snuck a waggle of eyebrows at one another before he took the case from Mom's extended hand. He crossed back and picked up the large suitcase near the door. "Have you gotten the discharge papers yet, Lila?"

"They're waiting at Admissions. We'll go there first then meet you outside the front of the hospital. The nurses insist Victoria exit in a wheelchair. So dramatic, but they have their reasons, I suppose." She glanced over at Vicki, her eyes growing misty. "It will be good to have you out of here, my dear, dear Victoria." Her voice caught in her throat.

"Try not to be needlessly sentimental, Lila," Gurn quipped. Everyone laughed, Mom the longest.

"I'll be down as soon as I can," I said. "This won't take but a minute."

I left with purpose and found Devereux in the hallway talking to the officer who had guarded Vicki's room. Everybody's favorite jackass saw me out of the corner of his eye, but kept his steady conversation with the other man going. I waited patiently on the sidelines deliberately looking unperturbed no matter what. Just when I thought I was going to have to throw my Prada bag at him – the one with the heavy chains - the detective dismissed the man and turned to me.

"You wanted to see me, Miss Alvarez?" He stressed the word 'miss' and gave me a smirk just to be annoying. I didn't rise to the bait.

"A word, Detective Devereux."

I turned and went into the waiting room, having seen it empty through the plate glass window. Devereux followed and shut the door behind him. I wheeled around and extended a clenched hand, as if about to offer him something from my unopened palm.

"You dropped this button when you searched my room."

Without hesitating he reached out, looking down at the complete set of buttons on his suit, and then up at me. I opened my palm to show it was empty then let my hand fall to my side.

A 'you got me' look crossed his face. He brazened it through, though; the caught look exchanged for one of defiance. "I don't know what you're talking about. And you'll have a tough time proving --"

"Cut the crap, Devereux. I know it was you. And if need be, I'll get a team of fingerprint experts in there to prove it. *You'll* have a tough time explaining why your prints are all over that room." We both stared at one another. "You know, I don't care you if hate us the way you do, but it takes a real low life to try to get to me through innocent animals."

His face now wore a mask of astonishment. "What are you talking about? What animals?"

"You opened a window hoping my two cats would leave the room, which they did. They could have been hit by a car, attacked by another animal, lost or --"

"What cats? I never saw any cats." He licked dry lips, and seemed to search inside his mind. "I was in there for less than two minutes. I tossed everything out of the drawers and opened the window so you would think someone entered the room that way. Maybe you'd think somebody was stalking you and leave town. I got the idea from the voodoo doll the night before."

"The cats weren't lying on the bed when you went in?" He shook his head. "Didn't you see their litter pans in the bathroom?"

"I didn't go into the bathroom. Good Lord, my kids have a cat."

As if just comprehending the thread of the conversation, he turned to me. "Wait a minute. You're more pissed off about me letting the cats out than breaking into your room?"

"You're damn straight."

He shook his head and chuckled. "Man, you are one for the books. For the record, I did not deliberately let your cats out. Are they all right?"

"Yeah, they're all right, no thanks to you. And I'm glad to hear you didn't do the voodoo doll. I was hoping your mind wasn't quite that warped."

He shook his head and studied me. I let him have his silence. I could see he was thinking.

"Okay. I'm sorry about your cats. But if you tell anybody I was in the room, I'll deny it."

He sat down heavily on the small couch and hunched over. Leaning his elbows on his knees, he stared down at his highly polished brown shoes.

"I don't ordinarily do that sort of thing. I got…there was some disturbing news earlier and --" He broke off and looked up at me, anger rising from him again. "Who do you think you are, coming into my town and taking over like this? Think you own the world."

I sat down across from him and leaned forward. "What are you talking about? Be more specific."

He looked up, his eyes meeting mine. "You want more specific? How about this? You went to the mayor. Or the commissioner or someone 'up' there, and got them to drop the murder charges against one of your own. Gold's death is now being classified as accidental death, by person or persons unknown. The man gets the back of his skull crushed in and it's called an accident? Give me a break."

"Whoa. Back up. We're not the ones who pushed to have the charges dropped. And as for changing it from homicide to accidental death, nuh-huh." I shook my head emphatically. "If you think Discretionary Inquiries wields that kind of power, you are sadly mistaken."

"Now *you* cut the crap. I know somebody did something. If not you, who?"

I let out a trapped breath and looked away.

"You know something, don't you? Mind telling me what going on in my own town?" Anger burbled out of him again. "You come here and think you can take over. Do anything you want. Get people killed. Have --"

"It wasn't us," I interrupted. "We're just in the way, same as you. This revolves around Dennis Manning, the man Vicki was chasing."

He stared at me in disbelief. "Manning is dead. I checked it out. He died nine years ago."

"No, he didn't and the FBI knows that. They're the ones behind this."

"Come on. The FBI? Come on," he repeated.

I mused for a moment, talking out loud. "I think they would have been perfectly content to have Vicki go down for killing Gold, but we were putting up too much resistance, digging to find who really did it. They dropped the charges so we would go away, which we're not. We want Manning. And we've got two days left to get him before the FBI sends him off into a new life."

Devereux gave me a shocked expression then burst out laughing. "Good Lord, you are one delusional, paranoid woman. I'll bet you don't even have cats."

"Hey! I may be many things, but delusional is not one of them." I hesitated for a moment, not sure if telling him the whole story was the way to go. "Oh, the hell with it. It started with Vicki's sister nine years ago."

I gave him chapter and verse, leading up to but not including my trip to Colbert's Motors. I'd hold on to that one for a while. If he didn't believe me after I finished, tough noogies.

It took a full five minutes. I ignored the buzzing phone in my bag and finished with, "And I do have two cats, Tugger and Baba. Well, technically, Baba is my boyfriend's cat, not mine, but – never mind. Too much information."

He leaned back, face to the ceiling, as if studying a crack running above him. Silence filled the room, and once more, I could feel the intensity of his thinking. My phone vibrated again. This time I took it out, read the missive, and texted back to Gurn that I would be right down.

"This might explain a few things." Devereux finally said, sitting up. He glared at me, the same malevolent look taking over his face. "Every time you Alvarez people show up in town, somebody dies."

"I'm going to repeat, we're not the ones. Not now nor nineteen years ago." I stood, ready to leave and get on with things. "Look Devereux, you want to hate me and my family? You go right ahead. But you're a grown man now, not a twenty-year old kid. If you can put those feelings aside, you'd realize the person responsible for your brother's death was the hired gun who came through the kitchen door shooting, not my father."

I headed for the door but turned back to him. He hadn't moved but sat leaning back on the small sofa, his body looking completely relaxed, except for the burning hatred in his eyes. I was getting used to that look and it didn't stop me from adding one final comment.

"I understand if you don't want be become involved in something as politically charged as this. I'm sure there's a lot of pressure on your department to wrap this up, but we're not going anywhere until we get Manning. And that's for the record."

Chapter Eighteen
Fancy Schmancy Digs

Mrs. Llewellyn's housekeeper, Delphine Robochaux, answered the door of the impressive three-story Greek revival mansion, complete with brass plaque touting its historical place in the community. A tall, aristocratic woman of a 'certain age', Delphine Robochaux's heritage was possibly a blend of French and African-American. Her thick, black hair was worn in a braid atop her head, and nothing softened the stark black dress she wore, other than small, gold coin earrings in her lobes.

"Good evening, Mrs. Alvarez." Delphine's voice was low and cultured. Many a jazz station would have killed for a D.J. with those dulcet tones. "Welcome back, Mrs. Alvarez. I'm so pleased you are well enough to leave the hospital."

The second Mrs. Alvarez greeting was addressed to Vicki. I was getting used to this double Mrs. Alvarez stuff, although it must be hard on the two ladies in question.

Mom introduced Gurn and me to Delphine, who welcomed us with professional but sincere warmth. She took our umbrellas, and moved aside to let us enter.

I stepped into at least a twenty-foot high foyer, airy and bright, despite the outside showers and early evening gloom. The floor was a checkerboard of large black and white marble squares. Pale yellow walls held floor to ceiling windows on the entry side of the room, each framed in layers of diaphanous, white fabric.

Several paintings hung on a wall to my left, vivid scenes depicting seventeenth- and eighteenth-century life in New Orleans. Directly opposite, a grand, circular staircase led to the second story of the home. At either end of the wall before me, two sets of double doors led to other rooms, probably even more imposing.

Overhead, a swaged, multi-tiered crystal chandelier sparkled with small inset lights. Directly below, an arrangement of bud-bearing branches and perky flowers in white, yellow, and lavender was worn like a summer bonnet by a cream-color round table. Dark green vegetation dallied around on tables, in windows, and corners of the room, luxuriating in their mosaic tile or ceramic pots. A little opulent for my tastes, but I certainly saw that a Grecian style could be punched up with tropical touches, especially when money-is-no-object guided you.

"Mrs. Llewellyn asked me to apologize for her absence," said Delphine, bringing me back to the land of mere mortals. "As she is one of the board members for the Governor's Ball, she is obligated to participate in many of the meetings regarding it, and will not return until late this evening. Mrs. Llewellyn asked me to ready the library for your use, as you mentioned to her earlier you may want to have a family business discussion. I have taken the liberty of laying out tea and light refreshments."

"Thank you, Delphine." Mom bowed her head in acknowledgment of superior service. "That's very kind of you."

"Chef Mateo is in the kitchen preparing dinner. He wanted me to tell you it will be ready around eight o'clock. I believe in honor of the occasion, he is making Crawfish Étouffée, a New Orleans specialty."

"We thank you for graciously allowing him into your kitchen," my mother said in her best lady of the manor voice.

"It's actually Cook's kitchen, Mrs. Alvarez," Delphine said with a smile. "And she is quite content to hand the job over to someone of his expertise."

"You ain't just whistling Dixie," I said, before I could stop myself. Mom shot me a dirty look, but in a very dignified manner. Breeding will tell. Gurn turned his head away, laughing.

"In particular, he wanted to extend the invitation to Miss Alvarez and her companion, Mr. Hanson." Delphine looked at us with a smile.

I turned to Gurn. "I guess dinner at Arnaud's will have to postponed."

"For Tío's Crawfish Étouffée? I can live with that." He smacked his lips and let out another laugh. Gurn is one of the most easy-going guys I know. I'm keeping him.

"I hope you don't mind, but I'd like to go upstairs and lie down," Vicki said interrupting us with a shaky voice.

"Are you all right, my dear?" Mom's tone returned to normal, but was filled with concern.

"Oh, yes. Please don't worry about me. It's just a slight headache. The doctor told me to expect these for the next few days and to lie down when I felt one coming on."

Before Mom could say more, Delphine spoke up. "Allow me to escort you upstairs, Mrs. Alvarez." She crossed to Vicki's side and took her by the elbow before my mother could make a counteroffer. "I have laid out your night wear and prepared a hot water bottle for your feet, to ward off a chill." She led Vicki to the staircase and both began to ascend the stairs, thus ending our impromptu visit to Downton Abby.

I looked around. "Okay, so where's the library? And are we going to meet Coronel Mustard with the candlestick in there?"

"Liana, sometimes your *irreverence* for the appropriate can be quite trying." Mom exhaled sharply.

"But quite funny," Gurn said with a grin.

Giving no response, Mom led us to double doors on the right. She opened one and stepped aside to allow us to enter the dark oak room. Inside was a true library. It, too, had a twenty-plus foot high ceiling.

Filled from top to bottom with hundreds of books, it rivaled many small town libraries across America. Now if Mrs. Llewellyn only had a book loaning program, Ben Franklin would have been proud.

Mom reached for a switch on the wall. Recessed lights in the ceiling sprang into action, illuminating clusters of wine-colored, leather wingback chairs and matching sofas gathered around low tables in intimate groupings. Beneath their legs, Persian rugs, sumptuous in shades of cream, black and red, covered rich wood floors.

In front of a line of draped windows along the outside wall, an ornately carved conference table sat surrounded by ten matching chairs. A huge, gilded dictionary rested at one end of the table on a gold-hinged bookstand, awaiting perusal. At the other end a multi-colored, stained glass Tiffany lamp shaped like a large mushroom cast soft hues on the surrounding area.

French doors led outside to a small garden surrounded by walkways and lush foliage. Centered within the garden was a lit marble fountain featuring nymphs cavorting with dogs, all having a grand time in the cascading waters.

My attention came back to inside the room, and mainly a buffet table holding an ornate silver tea service on a gleaming tray. White porcelain cups and saucers sat close by as did a tri-tiered silver salver brimming over with cucumber sandwiches, petit fours, cakes, and other goodies.

"Okay," I said. "So if this is how the other half lives, I can do this." I picked up a scone and poured myself a cup of hot tea.

"Or to be more accurate, the top one percent," Gurn added, crossing over to a nearby book stack, and picking out a couple of books at random. "My father is a bibliophile and if I'm not mistaken, many of these are rare first editions. Look at the ones locked in this curio. Particularly valuable. There's *The Waves* by Virginia Woolf and Charles Dickens' *American Notes for General Circulation*. One of those went for over sixty-thousand dollars last year, Dad said."

He opened the books in his hand with care, returned each to the shelving, and stepped back giving the room a once over. "My father would love to have this collection. It has to be worth a fortune."

"Did you have any idea Mrs. Llewellyn was rolling in dough like this, Mom? Anybody want some tea?" I took a bite of the buttery scone. Heaven.

"In truth, I did not. A cup of tea would be very nice, Liana; thank you."

"Me, too," said Gurn.

"When Felicity lived in Palo Alto, her home was not as *impressive*," Mom said. "But I don't think it's proper etiquette to *gossip* about one's hostess."

I poured another cup of tea and was handing it to my mother, as the door to the library burst open. Richard rushed in carrying a stack of papers, laptop case slung over one shoulder. His usual fly-away hair was wet and plastered to his head

"Cripes, is it pouring outside; I could have used an umbrella. Sorry if I've kept you waiting, but thanks to the partial license plate, I found the scuzzbag. And you're never going to believe this --"

"Richard! Please control yourself. When you sit down I'll call this meeting to order," Lila interrupted, always one for Robert's Rules of Order. Moving the dictionary aside, she sat at the head of the conference table. I poured Gurn a cup of tea, set it on the table in front of him, and sat down.

"Man I am wasted," said Richard, ignoring Mom and running a hand over his face. "I haven't had more than three hours sleep in the past two days."

My brother paused to drop the bound papers on the table and take off his carrying case. He unzipped the case and pulled out his computer. "But never mind about that. How's Vicki and where is she?" He looked around as if she might materialize from one of the stacks.

"She's upstairs resting, Richard," Lila said. "Delphine is with her."

"She all right?" His voice was anxious.

"She's fine, Richard, just fine." My reply was firm and no-nonsense, in a fair imitation of Lila's tone. "Now tell us where the man is, fer crying out loud. You made a helluva entrance. Now give."

"Dennis Manning's home is less than three blocks away."

"You're saying Dennis Manning lives here? In the Garden District?" Gurn's voice carried an incredulous tone, similar to what I was feeling. Richard was unmoved by the tone.

"Where'd you get that scone, Lee?"

"Behind you. There's tea, too." I pointed to the tea service.

He went to it, poured a cup of tea, and piled a small plate high with every variety of food available. "Not only does Manning live down the street from Anne Rice, I drove by it on my way here. It's the green house with the high, wrought iron fence around it. A dog is in the front yard, too; mean-looking thing. A Rottweiler. God, is it wet outside." Richard flung droplets of water from his briefcase onto the floor.

"Dennis Manning lives here in the Garden District?" Lila was still grappling with the facts.

"Dennis Manning leaves his dog out in the pouring rain?" I asked.

"There's a dog house, Miss Animal Protection League," My brother said, cramming half a scone in his mouth. Crumbs spilled on the table and carpet. Oblivious, he sat down chewing.

"Don't talk with your mouth full and be careful of the crumbs," Lila reprimanded.

Richard went on as if Lila hadn't spoken. "I wanted to go right over to that scuzbag's house --"

"But you knew that would have been an unprofessional move. Correct, Richard?" Lila said, giving him her severe monarch stare-down.

Richard ignored her. He's good at ignoring anyone and everyone, especially if he is in the midst of imparting information or eating.

Now that he was doing both, there would be no dealing with him. We'd have to let him run his course, knowing he would grace us with his knowledge in his own good time.

Gurn, Mom and I watched in silence as Richard shoved a half a cucumber sandwich in his already full mouth, and continued to masticate. This is the drawback to having a computer genius for a brother. They're pretty deficit in the social skills department.

Richard gulped his tea to help wash things down. He swallowed and continued chewing, as if we were not even there. Finally, he spoke.

"The bastard is living in the Garden District under the name of Samuel Randolph. The first record of him is a visit to a local doctor about a leg wound, about two weeks after the incident on the boat in Pacifica. My guess is he was wounded in the blast and when he established his new identity in New Orleans, he went to a doctor. According to the doctor's report, he had a knee replacement, but not much more could be done for the damage to the muscles in his thigh. His wife lives with him under the name of Laura Randolph. Get this; their kids live with her mother in Wisconsin. The records show them as orphans. Says she died in a car crash four years ago."

"After her husband faked his death, she faked her own, and left the *children* with her mother?" Lila's voice was filled with shock and condemnation. She took a long sip of tea, probably to calm her nerves.

"And you should see her now. Talk about a changed woman." Richard banged a few keys on his computer with the hand not holding a teacup, and turned it around for us to see the screen. "Look."

Several candid images of an emaciated woman, bearing tattoos on her neck, wrists, and hands came into view one after another in slideshow form. Instead of a youthful and curvaceous long-legged blonde, this middle-aged, boney, and dry-looking woman had light brown hair worn in a brush cut.

"Look at her arms," Gurn said. "No matter what outfit she's in, she's wearing long sleeves. I think she's using, and the sleeves cover her tracks."

"From Miss Palo Alto to heroin addict," I muttered.

"Here's something else that's bizarre," Richard said, "I found an ad of Manning's or rather, Randolph's on Craig's List. Seems he's looking for a private, resident chef, although, I don't understand why. Isn't he scheduled to testify for the Grand Jury on Tuesday and then depart for places unknown, along with his wife? Why advertise for a chef?"

"Great way of keeping up appearances," I said.

"Makes it look to his pals like he's here to stay. If they knew what he was up to, they'd probably kill him," Gurn added.

"We need to be careful with this." Lila's voice was quiet and thoughtful. "We're very close to being in over our heads. We don't have the manpower or expertise to handle a mob syndicate and the FBI. We need to be prepared to end this investigation, if necessary."

"Never," I said.

"I won't endanger anyone at this table," Lila said in a stern voice.

"I'm with Lee on this, Lila." Richard matched Lila, stern for stern. "We need to stick with it. This is for Vicki."

"Not to the point of making her a widow, Rich," Gurn said. "And I don't particularly feel like taking care of Tugger and Baba on my own, either." He focused in on me.

"Exactly," Lila said. "We have other options. We can turn over what we have to the police or --"

"No! At this point, we can't trust them or the FBI." I was adamant. "We started this. We need to finish it."

"Lee." Gurn turned to me. "Manning needs to go down; we all agree. But does it matter who takes him down? It could be too big for us, just as Lila says."

"I want to know if there's enough in what I salvaged from the fire to do a deal with the FBI."

My voice was strong and took center stage.

"Speaking of that, Richard, here's an email list I found in the bunker. I haven't looked through it yet, but it seems to be in a very small font. There must be easily two-hundred names on this one page."

He took the paper from me and shoved it in his pocket. "Okay, thanks. I'll look at it later. So what deal are you talking about?" Richard looked perplexed.

"An exchange for Manning," Gurn said quietly.

"If what we've got is enough to break this child porno ring wide open," I said, "they don't need his testimony and they'll no longer protect him. We can take him back to Palo Alto and he can stand trial for what he did to Robin."

"Well, Vicki would love that, seeing the man pay for what he did to her sister. I haven't told her yet about the FBI's plans to set him free." Richard looked down at the stack of papers, and riffled through them nervously. He was probably remembering me giving him flack about him not telling Vicki about the murder charges.

"I believe that's wise, Richard." Lila's voice was soft, the authoritative quality all but gone. "There's no point in worrying her about what hasn't happened yet. She needs to get well."

Lila reached out and covered his hand with hers. An intimate moment was shared between mother and son, the likes of which I'd never seen in one of our business meetings before.

"I'm with Mom," I said, taking my cue from Lila. I glanced over at Gurn, who leaned back letting the 'family' take over for a time. After a moment I said, "I've got an idea. Even though the Feds are probably watching the place, let's hire our own people for the next couple of days. It's expensive, but maybe we'll learn something outside the box."

"Agreed," everyone said in unison.

Gurn leaned forward. "I know a couple of men who freelance out of Atlanta. They're good. I'll give them a call, see if they can show up first thing tomorrow morning," he said, directing his last comment to Lila, who nodded.

After clearing his throat, my brother said, "What Lee managed to save was about fifty manila folders and around four hundred individual papers, many singed with areas currently unreadable. Right now Andy is scanning everything into a database. What I hope to do is link the database with a program that's far more sensitive than the naked eye in word discovery, comparison, and recognition. Once it captures everything possible on the papers, we can have it eliminate particular non-noun repeat words, such as 'the' 'that', 'this', 'those', etc. Then we can collate names, dates, and so forth. We can probably whip through what's left of the data once the program does its stuff, in a matter of hours instead of weeks."

"Sounds good," I said.

"This program is sweet." Richard clucked in appreciation. "Sweet. Fortunately, a lot of the tabs on the file folders were not burned, probably due to their thickness, with names of dozens of people, businesses, and email addresses. Exactly how they link up, we don't know yet. Good job, Lee." His face wore a momentary hero worshiper's expression.

"Yes, but is it enough to indict?" I rubbed my eyes, hot and tired.

"I can't say for sure. Even with the names easily read, there's missing data and it takes time to connect the dots. There could be some good guys in there, as well as bad."

"You mean like law-enforcement agents they were keeping tabs on," said Gurn to Richard.

"Right. So far, we have several 'for-sure' names, people there is no doubt are mixed up in this in a bad way. And I've learned some of them are criminals known to police and the FBI, but others are up-standing citizens across the country, even a few celebrities."

"The latter possibly being clientele, but just as guilty." Gurn's voice was ripe with emotion. Child pornography can affect one like that. "I have some lawyer friends at a D.C. firm who have paralegals and research assistants. Maybe their team can take a look at what we've got so far and see if any of it translates into admissible evidence."

"You've just got friends everywhere, Mr. Popular," I piped up, beaming in his direction.

"What can I say?" He winked at me then became serious again. "I mention them because they specialize in child molestation cases. If we send them the papers, I'll bet they'd know in a few hours time if there's enough evidence to bring a case before a judge. And it would be attorney-client privilege, so no leakage problem."

"It sounds like a good idea but it's up to Lila." Richard looked over at D.I.'s CEO.

Lila wore a grim look on her face, but I could see the wheels turning. "I wouldn't want to send it by any hack-able method," Lila finally said.

"That nixes email, the internet, and faxing," I said. "Courier's the only way."

"And carried by someone we trust implicitly," Lila muttered.

"Looks like I've got a return trip to D.C. coming up tonight or tomorrow." Gurn looked at each of us.

"Tomorrow's Sunday," I said. "Do they work on Sundays?"

"Attorneys?" Gurn gave out a chuckle. "It's easy to see you've never been involved with one."

"Well, not intimately."

Gurn smiled at me. "Anyway, they work pretty much twenty-four seven, if they want to get ahead."

"Gurn, thank you for the offer, but I think you are of more value here." Lila smiled in his direction then turned to Richard. "Why don't we send Andy with the package?"

"Sure," said Richard. "He's almost finished scanning the smaller pieces and laminating them for safe keeping. Meanwhile, I'll continue to feed the information into the database and have the program analyze them. We should be done with the bulk of it by late tonight, probably before three am. Who needs sleep, anyway?"

"Agreed," said Lila.

"Gurn, you set everything up in Washington with your contacts and Andy will take a plane to their offices first thing in the morning. Be sure to tell them to bill Discretionary Inquiries."

Gurn nodded. "And any conversations with them over the phone needn't reveal much. They're pretty savvy guys and we've worked together before."

"Is that as CIA or as a CPA who did their taxes?" I let out a chortle.

"Neither. NROTC, smarty pants, just like I came to know Rich."

Richard joined the Navy Reserves in college, where Gurn was his commanding officer. They maintained a friendship afterward, and I met Gurn when Richard persuaded him to tail me on a previous case, and unnecessarily so, I might add. But it turned out well, both the case and the romance.

"Are you two going to keep that up, the ceaseless banter?" Richard rolled his eyes in our direction. "Because I'd like to go upstairs and see my wife before I head back to the lab, if we're finished with important matters."

"On the police report you gave me, Richard," I said. "Other than it mentioning that Manning was brought in for questioning for following a young girl home from school the year before, there wasn't anything pertaining to Robin or her case in there."

"He assaulted another girl?" Lila turned to me. "Were any charges filed against him?"

I shook my head. "It wasn't the same scenario as Robin. He scared the girl, but she managed to run home. The charges were dropped, but the girl's family moved out of the Bay Area shortly after that. Were they leaving, anyway, or did they get paid to go away? Manning certainly had the money."

"We'll never know unless we do an investigation," Lila said.

"If need be," said Gurn, "we could track them down and try to find out."

"Let's hope it doesn't come to that; we've got enough on our plate." I leaned back in my chair, suddenly very tired. "So let's leave that waiting in the wings."

"Then we're finished, as far as I know," Lila said.

"Good," said Gurn, rising. "I'd better call my pals in D.C. and give them the heads up. Then I'll call Atlanta."

"There is one more thing," I said. Gurn sat down again. "I have something else to tell you now that we've got the Manning business out of the way. Detective Devereux is the one who broke into our room this morning. He admitted it."

After several ohs and ahs from everyone at the table, I repeated the conversation verbatim between the police detective and myself. I have a near photographic memory for verbiage, but not numbers. Whatever that condition is, I've got it.

"Devereux says the voodoo doll episode wasn't his and I believe him. Although, I still don't trust him. He's got a hidden agenda, I can smell it. I didn't tell him about my visit to Colbert's Motors or the papers, but I did let him know we're not leaving town without Manning."

"Was that wise, I wonder?" asked Lila, musing. "Well, what's done is done."

"And you know we moved, Lila, to a safe house over on St. Peters," Gurn said. "If you call the hotel, we're still registered, but we're not there. Call our phones."

Richard stood. "I'm going up to see Vicki now. Someone let me know when food is ready. I understand Tío is making dinner and I'm starved."

"You just ate a plateful of anything you could get your grubby little hands on," I said. "You must have a hollow leg, I swear."

"Never pass up Tío's cooking, that's my motto." Richard's tone was reverent. "And he's making Crawfish Étouffée."

"Hmmm," I said, thinking out loud. "Too bad we can't send him into Manning's house under the guise of being the new chef."

"Liana, you behave yourself." Mom shot me a warning glance.

"Kidding, only kidding," I said.

But was I? Dennis Manning only three blocks away and in need of a private chef. What were the odds?

Chapter Nineteen
It's All in How You Present Yourself

"Are you ready, Tío?"

I adjusted the white Dodin cap on my head, which looked like one of those upside-down paper cups you put inside a cupcake baking pan, only bigger. That and my pristine, white jacket were perfect. My outfit had been obtained courtesy of Tío's pal, Slavio, from the hospital's kitchen after a fast call. I also wore my reading glasses as a bit of a disguise, even though they made me squint.

"Now just follow my lead."

I looked over at my uncle. Tall and elegant, he was also dressed in one of his own spiffy white chef uniforms, minus the toque. That would have been overkill. He did, however, bring along his chef knives. No chef worth his or her salt travels without them. They were encased in his black canvas eighteen-piece knife case, complete with a full accessory compartment.

Experience has taught me that in the game of pretend, wearing the right costume goes a long way to making whomever believe whatever it is you want them to believe. Standing before the double-doors of the Samuel Randolph mansion was a master chef and his sous-chef applying for the recently advertised position.

It had taken everything I had or could think of to talk the family into doing this. By seven-thirty we were set. The Étouffée had been set on a back burner for consumption when we returned later.

The rain still fell, but it was completely dark, save any light coming from the porch and landscaping. I didn't hear a dog, but figured it was off duty and in its doghouse, trying to stay dry. I lowered the mammoth umbrella I held over us and dropped it into the outdoor umbrella stand when one of the doors swung open. A gaunt-looking man in his early thirties and dressed completely in black, stared at us in outright disbelief as we stood there in all our sparkling white beauty.

"What the…" His jaw dropped open and he froze in place, the door half opened.

"Good evening." I all but chirped. "My name is Margaret Lee. Please allow me to introduce to you Chef Manuel Rodriguez."

I thrust a lengthy résumé into one of his hands, printed out by Richard from online, very impressive in its looks and content. My uncle stood silently beside me with a noble but grim look on his face. I prattled on with a big smile.

"We are here for the eight p.m. interview with Mr. Randolph for the position of private chef to the household. I'm Chef Manuel's interpreter, as well as his *sous-chef*. While he is the chef extraordinaire, as I'm sure you know from having read articles about him, he --"

"Well, no, no. I hadn't. I haven't read…" The man stuttered, but continued to gape. "What?"

"Chef Manuel's English skills are not on the same level as his cooking, so he relies upon me totally." I went on.

"*Si*," Tío put in, pointing to himself. "*Solamente Español.*"

"What?" Completely thrown, the man looked down at the resume then around him, as if hoping to conjure up someone who knew what was going on.

I continued to beam. Tío continued to look regal and important.

"Wait a minute." The man's eyes narrowed. "I don't know anything about this. I need to check. I don't even think Mr. Randolph is here."

His eyes kept flitting from place to place, as if Samuel Randolph might materialize at any moment and straighten this out or take over. "I don't…you need to…I'll go see…"

"You do that." I used my most soothing voice. "And meanwhile, Chef Manuel and I will check out the kitchen to see if it's up to his standards. The kitchen would be where?"

I pushed my way inside followed by Tío, and looked around at the massive living room, done in shades of industrial grey and white marble. I've seen warmer-looking mausoleums.

With a shaky hand the man in black pointed in the direction of a chrome dining room. While he tottered off looking for someone in the know, Tío and I scurried through the glossy but boring dining room and into the kitchen.

Dressed more like a maid in training than kitchen staff, a young woman, still probably in her teens, was attempting to make coffee from an espresso machine. After some unsuccessful attempts, she didn't seem to know which buttons to push and had already made a mess. She wore the look of someone who wanted to be anywhere but here. Tío took over.

"*¡Con permiso!*" His voice was gracious, but authoritative. He relieved her of the duty with a smile. With expert hands he wiped up the spilled milk and coffee grounds and filled the carafe with water from the sink, proceeding to set the espresso machine up for use.

"Thank you, sir." Her voice was filled with relief and gratitude. "I really am supposed to be doing laundry now."

"Then you go right ahead," I said.

She seemed to notice me for the first time. I smiled brightly and she opened a door going into a long hallway, disappearing as she closed the door behind her.

Tío and I were alone and we both looked around. The stainless steel kitchen had all the modern conveniences and while it resembled a morgue in every way except for the dead bodies, it could serve the purpose of getting out a decent meal.

"Tío, you stay here and do what you can to look busy, while I check the place out. If I can find either of the Mannings or what they're up to, so much the better."

"And you will do what when you find them?" The challenge in Tío's voice surprised me, because we had already been through this. "You will do *nunca*. Remember, you promise not to make the unwise gesture. You are on their *tierra, mi sobrina. Cuidado.*"

"I'll be careful, Tío, but Manning took off earlier today in such a rush, I have to know why. Something tells me it's important. Also, I'd like to know if he's still here. There's been talk about him doing a bunk."

"Bunk? Bunk? What is this bunk?"

"Leave. Flee. Run away. He might be gone already. But I'm not here to make any trouble, just to have a look-see. We'll be in and out, just like the burger."

I opened the door to the hallway the maid had vanished through. While I had noticed a marble staircase leading up to the second floor off the living room, I knew there had to be a back staircase used by staff. My search for it didn't take too long. I heard a washing machine spinning and peeked inside the laundry room next to the narrow staircase. With her back to me, the young maid was taking clothes out of the dryer and folding them with a concentration on the task I could only think of as commendable. It's all I can do to keep from falling into a deep sleep during something like that. The washing machine was going with another load and the noise covered my actions. On little cat feet, I checked out a small bedroom, probably hers, a door leading to the backyard and one leading to the garage. Other than the girl, there was no one else around.

I took the carpeted stairs up to the second floor landing as quietly as possible, opened the door to the second floor hall, and looked both ways. No one was around, but I heard muffled voices coming from one of the rooms near the front staircase.

I tiptoed down the hall and saw a sleek, modern office with a long desk holding a computer, printer and fax machine. Behind were black wall-to-wall bookshelves holding more sculpture and artwork than books. Done mostly in dark grey furnishings, a corner of the room held a mottled grey sofa and wing back chair facing a humongous TV hanging on a wall. The TV was on, a racecar derby or some such thing running in the background.

Two men were in earnest conversation, one of them being my guy in black. The other guy wore a grey suit, so like the sofa he blended into it with the exception of his skin color. I couldn't understand what they were saying due to the droning sounds of the racing cars. But I surmised by both men's expressions I had limited time.

I wheeled around and began to open doors on the floor, quickly but quietly. Two empty bedrooms, with only a bed and dresser in each room, were sparsely decorated in more muted shades of grey. A small off-white rug on a dark grey granite floor provided the only warmth in each room. Apparently the Mannings were minimalists and super-duper boring in their tastes. Compared to them, the décor in a dentist's office was exciting.

Then I hit the third bedroom. It was anything but boring. Once I opened the door, I stood frozen for a moment just outside the doorframe. Then I crossed the threshold and closed the door behind me with a soft click. But I didn't move inside the room, but rather, leaned against the inside of the door panting heavily, trying not to gag.

Laying the king-sized bed, white satin covers askew, was a woman I recognized as Pamela Manning, the now very dead Pamela Manning.

Even against the white background of the linens, her skin seemed shockingly pale as she lay at an angle across the messy bedding. Rake thin and dressed in a red silk belted robe, one arm was extended over her head. A dark blue rubber tourniquet was tied tightly around the other outstretched arm just above the elbow.

A syringe, still a quarter filled with a clear liquid, protruded from a needle halfway inside the crook of her arm. She didn't have a peaceful look on her face, like I would expect from someone doing high-volume drugs. She actually looked a little scared, with half opened eyes, and a touch of shock about her mouth.

Her cell phone lay at her side. Was she the person who called Manning this afternoon? I had to know. Besides, if it was her phone, I might be able to find Manning with it. With hesitant steps, I crossed over to the bed and picked up the phone, careful not to touch or disturb anything else. I shoved it into my pocket and backed up. Still staring at the body, I groped behind me for the door handle. Using the hem of my uniform, I wiped the handle clean of any fingerprints, unable to tear my eyes away from the horrible sight, a woman dead before her time. That's always been my take on drug casualties, the needless waste.

I stepped into the hallway just as the two men came tearing out of the study. I moved back inside the dead woman's room again. The men raced down the main staircase. I knew where they were going. I took the time to wipe the outside doorknob, and flew down the staff stairs taking them two at a time. I was back in the kitchen a split second before they opened the door from the dining room.

They came inside like two parents about to tell a twenty-three year old Hell's Angel to get out of their house and leave their thirteen-year old daughter alone. Did they know about Pamela Manning's death? I touched the phone inside my white smock. I pushed forward from the hall-door, as if I had been in the kitchen the entire time.

"Hey!" The man in the grey suit took charge, his demeanor intimidating and angry. He shook the résumé in my uncle's face. "Just who are you and what's going on here? There's no interviews scheduled --"

"Ah," interrupted Tío, completely at ease, "*Aqui, tiene.*"

He handed a small, white cup of espresso, complete with two small brown sugar cubes and a lemon slice decorating the saucer, to the angry man. Then Tío, bless him, rattled off a lot of nonsense in Spanish about how he'd added a touch of chocolate to the beans and so forth, playing the part to the hilt. But, of course, he didn't know about the dead body upstairs.

"The interview will not take place." I snatched the résumé from the man's hand, using my haughtiest Lila Hamilton Alvarez tone of voice.

"This kitchen is unsuitable, *completely* unsuitable for the standards of Chef Manuel Rodriguez. Why there's not even a six-burner stove or a Sub Zero refrigerator. In a nutshell, it is subpar. We're leaving. Right now." I looked at the two men and waggled my finger in their stunned faces. "Do not even try to convince us to stay. It is useless."

I grabbed Tío by his sleeve and tugged him toward the dining room door. Tío managed to snatch up his chef knives with his free hand, as I dragged him to the door. We were followed out by two stuttering men.

"But who sent you here? I don't remember Mr. Randolph - -"

I ignored them and marched with Tío through the dining and living rooms and toward the front door. Tío followed without looking at me or betraying his own surprise at our hasty exit. I pulled the front door open then shoved my uncle outside. Tío gathered up our umbrella, while I turned back to the no longer angry but confused grey-suited man. I gave the word snooty new meaning as I squinted at him through my reading glasses.

"There is absolutely no way Chef Manuel would even consider taking this job, sir. Entreat us how you will. I shall try not to look upon this as a personal insult to a man of his fame and stature. I will merely say he does not work under these conditions. Possibly in the future, Mr. Randolph will leave the staffing of his kitchen to the more experienced in the field. There is nothing worse than an amateur meddling in these affairs."

Tío was half-way down the walk and I ran to catch up with him.

"Hurry, hurry, hurry, Tío," I whispered.

I glanced back at the two men standing in the doorway, befuddled and unsure of what had happened or what to do. Before they came to their senses, I wanted to be long gone. Also, if they did know about Pamela Manning's death, they were very cool customers. I don't like cool customers. I shoved Tío into the car, started it up, and went from zero to sixty to get out of there.

Chapter Twenty
One Step In Front of the Other

I slept little that night and awoke with a start shortly after eight a.m. It wasn't just the shock of finding Pamela Manning's body the night before, although that was bad enough. It was the fear of being caught, and by Devereux. We had no friends in the NOLA Police Department, an oddity for us. We were used to being liked. Not so here in Louisiana.

I'd relayed what I'd found to Gurn and the Alvarez clan as soon as we arrived back at Mrs. Llewellyn's home the night before. Even though Tío knew something was up, he had no idea it was as serious as it was. He was not happy. Nobody was.

After much discussion of the pros and cons, it was decided not to report the death to the police. If Devereux found out Tío and I were there, he'd probably arrest us for something, anything. I didn't have the time to spend in jail if I was to catch Manning. Fortunately, I hadn't used our real names and did manage to get the résumé back, but still this was very dicey.

Within many companies, Manning's Rottweiler would have had nothing on me about lodgings. I would have been in a major doghouse, held entirely responsible for what happened. But such is not the case at D.I.

Even though I'd done a lot of convincing to get everyone on board with the idea, once they agreed, we shared mutual responsibility for the deed. It was one of the upsides of our family business.

My credibility was still intact, even though in the privacy of my own room, I'd done a little barking at myself. Woof. Woof.

I redeemed myself somewhat in my mind with Pamela Manning's cell phone. Hers was an older one, not a smart phone, but at least we had something. Richard started ripping it apart the minute he got his geeky little hands on it.

Her last call had been around the same time I saw Manning answer the phone and leave Colbert's Motors. Not exact proof, but we believed we now had Dennis Manning's phone number. As to tracking his movements via his cell phone, that was proving more difficult. Richard couldn't trace a GPS on him, no matter what. Maybe it was a throwaway phone. Go to Target or Wal-Mart, and you'll find plenty of them. And all untraceable.

Remembering all this caused me to shudder violently. Both cats were curled up at my feet, but jarred awake by my sudden movements. I reached out for Gurn in the next bed, but saw it was empty. A note on his pillow explained he had gone out to a nearby firing range with the Smith and Wesson, with plans to return around eight-thirty. Reluctant to start a day I knew would be long and hellacious, I returned to my small, narrow bed reminiscent of my summer camp days, and lay back down. The more I came to, the more I could feel the tension rising in my gut. Less than forty-eight hours to find Manning or he would be gone forever.

Truth be told, I was tired and feeling stuffed. Tío outdid himself the night before, even with the delay of serving dinner until after nine o'clock. Mine is a hardy stomach, and finding a dead body did nothing to deter my appetite. In one single sitting, I probably Étoufféed back the four pounds I'd just lost.

I could feel the sticky morning air even with the overhead fan going. Sitting up, I glanced out the window. The sun was fighting to burn off low, grey clouds and there wasn't a wind stirring. The gorgeous tree with the red-orange flowers was as still as a painting in the Louvre.

It had to be over ninety degrees and ninety percent humidity. The air felt weighty and oppressive, and not a breeze to stir it.

The sliding metal of the front door and the return of the lock snapped my head in that direction. I waited, hand under my pillow resting on Lady Blue. Gurn tiptoed in, saw I was awake and beamed at me. He came over to the bed and leaned down, maybe for a morning's kiss. I grabbed him and pulled him down on top of me, where we rolled around for few seconds. This was a man worth waking up to.

"So tell me, Mr. Hanson, how's life treating you?"

"Better, now that I've got you in my arms." He looked down at me and waggled his eyebrows.

I let out a disappointed sigh before I spoke again. "But we have to get going. We have a meeting with Lila at nine at Mrs. Llewellyn's place, remember?"

He sat up, in an attempt to cool things down. "That's right. Your hot body threw me off my game." He got up and pulled the spiffy, clean Smith and Wesson from his knapsack and held the barrel to the ceiling. "I was at the firing range around six-thirty this morning. This is a first-rate gun."

"I'm so glad."

"The front and rear sites are about as accurate as you can get."

"I'm so glad."

"It wouldn't be a bad idea for you to carry this gun."

"Not happening."

"In addition to, not *instead* of the Detective Special. Please, Lee."

"Carry two guns? Who do you think I am, Rambo?"

"Think about it. Given what's going on and who we're dealing with, it couldn't hurt. I've got more than one, myself."

He turned away and pulled the magazine out of the gun, checking the chamber to make sure a bullet wasn't in it. I sat up and studied the man who was fastidious in so many ways, yet easy going in the important ones. He liked my family. He liked my cat.

He even had one of his own, with whom I was often in sort of a competition for his affections, if I may call a female feline a 'whom'. That stated, he seriously liked me. No, correction. He loved me. I have come to believe that.

Gurn has two jobs that transect in the weirdest way possible, a certified public accountant and a commander in the Navy Reserves. What's up with that? I mean, how come a CPA has a direct line to Washington D.C. and is summoned there periodically, sometimes in the middle of the night? Okay, so he's got a cute little plane, but still. One of these days, I may get the whole story. Or not.

That stated, I loved him.

I waffled. *Maybe I should consider upgrading my handgun. Mine was from the sixties. Time marches on, as my crow's feet remind me every day.*

"Okay, put the sucker in my bag and I'll give it serious thought, okay?"

"That's all I ask. Think about it seriously. I'll even include some ammo, free of charge."

Gurn gave me a glorious smile and once again, I remembered that compromise is the key to a successful relationship. Not a sellout but a compromise.

"I have a suggestion, Gurn. After our meeting, let's walk by Manning's new digs; see if anything has been discovered."

"I'm kind of curious myself. You're sure she was dead?"

"They don't get any deader. Trust me. Oh! And Andy should be on the plane, right?"

"Supposedly, he took a six a.m. flight with copies of the papers. I figure I'll give the legal eagles 'til three o'clock before I started calling for an update. Last night they said they'd drop everything and get right on it. I made coffee. Take your shower. I'll run over to Beignet's for some to go, and bring the car around. Downstairs in fifteen minutes?"

"Fifteen minutes."

I fed the cats, emptied the litter pan, showered, put on my new teal dress and navy flats, and threw my shoulder bag around my neck, all in less than ten. And they say women can't get ready in time.

Chapter Twenty-one
Another Set of Surprises

Due to traffic, we pulled into Mrs. Llewellyn's driveway five minutes late despite me being ready ahead of time. Delphine greeted us at the door.

"Good morning, Miss Alvarez, Mr. Hanson. The other members of your family are in the breakfast nook, where a hot breakfast is awaiting you."

"Thank you, Delphine," both Gurn and I said in unison and then looked at one another. This to the manor born stuff was a little hard to get used to.

"And Mrs. Llewellyn asked me to apologize for her absence again this morning. Her meeting ran longer than expected last night and she decided to stay at her *pied-à-terre* downtown. She should return mid-morning and hopes to see you both then to welcome you to New Orleans. She asked me to convey an invitation for a late lunch, if you are free."

Gurn and I started to say thank you in unison again, but hesitated, trying not to laugh. He nodded to me and I took the lead.

"Please thank Mrs. Llewellyn for us, Delphine, but we have some urgent business we need to take care of today. Possibly we can meet for drinks or something this evening?"

Delphine nodded with a smile, "Of course. I will relay the message to Mrs. Llewellyn when she returns later this morning. May I show you to the breakfast nook?"

She gestured with her hand in the direction of one of the doors off the foyer.

"That's quite all right," Gurn said. "We can find it on our own."

"We'll just follow the sounds of chomping," I added.

"In that case, if you will excuse me, I have some brief errands to attend to, and will bid you a good morning."

"Absolutely." I suppressed the urge to curtsy. "You just carry on. And good morning to you."

We watched her take her handbag from behind a vase on a table, open the door, and with a smiling glance in our direction she left, closing the door silently behind her.

"She seems to make you nervous." Gurn took me by the arm and pulled me toward the door Delphine had pointed out earlier.

"I know and I'm not sure why. I mean, I grew up with Guadalupe working at our house, but she never treated me like the queen mother. I was just one of her kids. Still am. I even get her Mother's Day cards."

"Well, Delphine has a different style, more like Anthony Hopkins in 'Remains of the Day'.

"Was that a great movie or what? Although I'm surprised you know it."

"What are you talking about? You made me watch it twice."

"Oh, that's right."

"I have to admit, it's pretty good."

And that inane conversation brought us into what was laughingly called the breakfast nook, a room nearly as big as my entire garage apartment back in Palo Alto. It was a circular room, decorated in a way that gave the illusion of being inside an amusement park's old-fashioned merry-go-round. Spaced along the sides of the curved walls and galloping in still-life, were four white, life-size wooden horses, looking very authentic and old. Their original condition only added to their beauty and wonder.

Time worn, with flecks of paint missing here and there, the horses' colorful plumes, jewels, and harnesses stirred the childhood memories of giving yourself over to a ride on a carousel. Candy-striped poles, worn in places where decades of small hands gripped tightly, spiraled up toward the ceiling and finished off with multi-colored felt banners representing real or imagined royal houses. Everything about the horses seemed to invite you to jump on and take a ride, even at my age.

I ripped my eyes from them and looked at the walls. They were decorated in elaborate panels of muted red, blue and yellow wallpaper. Overhead, similarly striped fabric came from the top of the walls and gather at the center of the ceiling in a twisted knot, finishing off in gold braids and tassels. A huge mirror-ball hung down from that and rotated slowly, casting blings of light everywhere. Beneath it sat a white round table and six chairs at which Mom, Tío, and Richard were already seated and eating.

After our usual greetings, and us not saying a word about my discovery the night before, I turned to the side table holding steamers of scrambled eggs, grits, bacon, hash browns, toast and a carafe of coffee. Being the good doobies we were, we offered the beignets, as well, but it was a little like bringing poker chips to Vegas.

I turned to my brother. "So is Vicki still in her room resting?"

"No," Richard said. "I accidentally woke her up when I came in around five am and crashed. She's been up ever since, ate earlier, and is out in the garden, reading."

"Sounds like she's better," I said.

"The dress suits you, Liana," Mom said, as I perused the table for some goodies.

"Thank you, Mom. You've got wonderful taste and I love everything you gave me." I turned to Mom after picking up a plate and loading it down. Suddenly I was starved.

"So our hostess is on yet another board doing yet more good works? She gets around."

"Yes, she left a message with Delphine last night. She should be back sometime soon."

"Well, for an absentee hostess, she sure can lay out a table." I sat down and took a huge bite of eggs and buttered grits. Yum.

"That would actually be Delphine," Mom corrected. "And should she ever decide to move to the Bay Area, I would be hard pressed not to invite her to work for us."

"We could not afford her, *mi hermana*," Tío said. Mom being his deceased younger brother's wife, he often called her his little sister. "Last night, Cook, she tells me on the slice how much the housekeeper makes. And it is considerable."

"That's 'on the sly', Tío," I said, biting down on a piece of crunchy bacon. "But I like 'on the slice'."

"You like anything that reminds you of food," Gurn said with a laugh, pouring himself coffee.

"Ah! On the sly. But that makes more sense," Tío said. "To continue, even Cook, who does not appear to have a name, makes almost as much as I did when I run the kitchen at *Las Mañanitas*."

I put down the fork, but before I could reply Mom's phone rang. She excused herself and took the call in one corner near a particularly lovely horse with a red plume, green saddle, and blue eyes. I watched her listen intently, close her phone, think for a moment, and come back to the table. Her brows were furrowed, very unlike her. She's from the Botox school of thought.

"That was one of the gentlemen we hired last night to keep the Manning home under surveillance. I think we should all take a walk there. We know what has been discovered."

"About time." I said, tossing my napkin on the table and rising. The three men rose to their feet, as well. "When do you think we know what got discovered?"

She shook her head and opened the door to the hallway. "We'll discuss it later."

* * * *

It was three short blocks to Manning's place, which I would have been drawn to, in any event, due to the commotion outside the house. Two cop cars with flashing lights were at the curb. Policemen stood in a small grouping on the sidewalk talking to each other. The gates to the garage were open, although the garage door was shut, and in the driveway paramedics loaded a gurney bearing a sheet-covered body into the back of an ambulance. Nearby, Detective Devereux was writing in a small notepad, deep in conversation with another paramedic.

Everyone else in our party hung back on the sidewalk at the property line, reluctant to call attention to themselves, especially Tío. Tilting one of Richard's caps over his face, he turned away from the house, in case the two goons from last night were anywhere around and might recognize him.

I decided to take a chance. Pulling the brim of my sunhat down over my eyes, I went to the wrought iron fence, grabbed onto it with both hands, and shouted out.

"Hey, Devereux, a moment of your time!"

I figured with catching Devereux's B&E in our room yesterday and not making any trouble for him, he owed me. Of course, if he caught me in what I did here last night, it was all over for me.

At the sound of my voice, which has its shrill moments, every head within twenty feet snapped around and looked at me. Devereux glared for a split second, but sauntered over taking it slow and easy. Apparently, keeping me waiting was one of his greatest pleasures.

Two young men, one tall, and one short, stood at the other end of the fence near a shady Magnolia tree. They noticed us or, rather, Gurn and moved toward him at a pretty fast clip. The shorter one reached out a hand toward Gurn with a smile.

"Commander," he said. "Good to see you again, sir. And thanks for the recommend."

"Call me Gurn, Steve. No commander stuff now." Gurn grasped the man's hand in a quick but friendly shake. He looked to the taller man coming up behind the other and extended his hand once more. "Lance, good to see you."

"Thank you, sir." The younger man was easily over six foot six inches high and probably weighed less than me. He had a shy way about him, but a ready smile.

Gurn looked over at the snail-like approach of the detective in my direction and stepped in the middle of the two men. "Gentlemen, let's take a walk." He led the way across the street, and they followed. Once standing on the far sidewalk, all three men began to converse.

"Well, look who's showed up," Devereux said, when he finally arrived at the other side of the fencing.

He glanced over at Mom, Tío, and Richard deep in their own conversation and half hidden behind another Magnolia tree. There was a lot of grouping going on. I think it's sort of a tribal thing. When time demands certain tasks be done by someone else before anything can be done by you, people tend to cluster around an invisible water cooler. As for me, I wanted a tribal chit-chat with the detective.

Devereux's face wore a slight sneer, but now it seemed to come more from habit than intent. His eyes actually held amusement instead of rancor. I think he knew I'd dropped the idea of breaking and entering charges against him, if I'd ever intended to file them, and he had a modicum of gratitude. I think. With this guy, one never knew. He seemed awfully eager to rip away the crime scene tape yesterday morning. Basically, was he a good guy or a bad guy? *Quien sabe?*

He went on, "Another death in the Big Easy and can the Alvarez Clan be far behind?"

"Yeah, yeah," I said, with a dismissive air. "But what's going on, Devereux? You know whose place this is?"

"I know whose place you say it is, but according to our records, Dennis Manning is long dead. This is the home of Mr. and Mrs. Samuel Randolph."

He stared at me. I stared back. Good gawd, next to him molasses broke speed limits.

"And?" I finally asked.

"All right." He gave out a small laugh. "I'll tell you and then I want you and the rest of the Alvarez's to take a hike. You're contaminating the place."

"Crudely said, but it's a deal."

"We got a call early this morning. Mrs. Randolph was found in her bed by the maid, dead from an apparent drug overdose."

And what was your big clue? The needle sticking out of her arm? "No! Drug overdose, you say?"

"Yes, but don't ask me of what exactly. I don't know."

I do. Heroin. "How long has she been dead?"

"We don't know yet. We're on the lookout for two people claiming to be chefs looking for work that showed up here around eight o'clock last night."

Uh-oh. "No kidding. Where's Mr. Randolph? Inside?"

"We don't know where he is. He's not here. Nobody is. Now blast off. And I mean it, before I arrest you for loitering."

I backed up holding my hands in a surrender gesture then I waved goodbye. This time unamused, he turned away from the fence and went back to the paramedic.

I raced back to Lila, Richard and Tío hovering on the sidelines. Tío was the first to speak.

"So this Manning, where is he? Inside the house?"

My uncle looked behind us at the large three-story house. We all followed his gaze. With the exception of the constabulary business of carting the body off to the morgue, it was as if the house was totally empty.

"According to Devereux, Manning's not around," I said. "Or else he was deliberately leading me astray. When I asked him about the man's whereabouts, his exact words were 'we don't know where he is'. I don't believe Manning was here last night, either. He would have shown himself."

"I don't like this," Lila commented.

Richard opened his phone.

"What are you doing?" I asked, as he pounded on rather than touched his screen.

"I'm finding my notes. Okay, the research I did on the inhabitants of the house showed Manning, his wife, two servants and two bodyguards. Unfortunately, her cell phone gave me little, other than the last number she called, which we think was his."

"Not sure?"

"Unclear. I can't track it and I've tried everything."

I thought for a moment. "He might have dumped the phone. So where is everybody? Even the dog is missing."

Tío looked at me. "Do I not hear barking coming from inside the garage?"

I glanced in the direction of Gurn and the two men talking. "It sounds like a neighbor's dog, Tío." I looked in Gurn's direction. "I sure hope Gurn's got more information."

As if hearing my words, Gurn broke free from his huddle, crossed the street on a diagonal, and headed for us. The two men disappeared into a car and drove away.

"Get this," he said as he strode within hearing range. "Seems Lance has a way with the gentler sex."

"Who? The beanpole?" I looked behind him at the two men getting into newish Range Rover.

"Liana, there is no *need* to be unkind." Lila jumped in with a raised eyebrow in my direction.

I turned on her. "What? He's over six foot six and weighs about three pounds. And he isn't within hearing range."

"*Nonetheless*," Mom continued in her vein of reprimand.

"Honestly, Mom, I --"

"Ladies, ladies." Gurn raised his voice in protest. "Don't you want to know what I learned?"

"You will find that when *la familia* is under the pressure," Tío said, with a smile. "They have much to say to one another having nothing to do with the business at hand."

"Do we do that, Tío?" I was shocked.

"Lee, please!" Gurn's voice was sharp. "Let me tell you what went down."

"Sorry."

"'Beanpole,'" he said, with a nod toward me, "got friendly with the maid, a girl no more than twenty, who found the body this morning."

"I think she's the one we saw last night trying to make espresso," I interjected.

Gurn went on as if I hadn't interrupted him. "He saw her tear out of the house and run across the street screaming, so Lance caught up with her. He palmed himself off as a real estate agent just passing by, who wanted nothing more than to console her. She was scared and hysterical, so willing to talk."

"I can see being hysterical, but why scared?" I questioned this because it puzzled me.

"The girl had only been working there three weeks. She gave her notice day before yesterday, even though she got paid more money than ever before. Said it was the worst place she'd ever been in her life. Her boss made a pass at her, she was scared of the dog, and her dead mistress used to stay in her room for days at a time doing drugs and listening to Wyclef Jean. That's how come the body wasn't discovered until this morning. When the maid went in to make the bed, she found Pamela Manning stiff as a board lying face up to the ceiling, the needle and syringe still in her arm. But here's something interesting. Guess who was here yesterday afternoon for a quick visit, and left in such a hurry a fence post got knocked over?"

There was a pause, while everyone pondered this question.

"Felicity Llewellyn," Lila and I said in unison.

Chapter Twenty-two
Life Happens While You're Making Other Plans

We hotfooted it back to Felicity Llewellyn's home. Once we made sure she still hadn't returned, Gurn and I left the family to pack up and join us at the safe house *tout de suite.* That's French for move your duff; this could get ugly. However involved with Manning Mrs. Llewellyn was, a shoot-out with one's hostess was not done in Lila's circles, Mom being more or less on the conservative side.

Instead, we opted for a quick departure and a 'plans changed' missive left with a confused Delphine. We decided the Alvarez Clan should do a disappearing act for a day or two from everybody, even the Feds.

"I wonder how much the FBI knows?" I glanced over at Gurn maneuvering the car down a one-way street several blocks from our destination. "Do you think they know about Manning and Llewellyn?"

"I would say not much gets by them, Lee. But this sure got by me. I wonder where the lady in question is?"

"With Manning, I suppose. But maybe not. She still has her social obligations in New Orleans. Richard will find out with a few fast searches. If she's legitimately doing something for the Governor's Ball, we'll know soon."

"What made you and your mother suspect her of being involved in this?" He stopped at a red light and looked over at me.

"That's the best explanation for how Manning's been a step ahead of us the whole time. And Mom's been wondering why Mrs. Llewellyn invited them to stay with her. She and Mom had a passing acquaintance in Palo Alto, nothing more. Yet Mrs. Llewellyn insisted they come, especially once she heard Vicki was opening her new shop in the French Quarter."

"Makes sense, Lee. Richard said Manning was known as quite a ladies' man before and during his marriage." Gurn depressed the gas pedal and the car eased forward, only to stop several feet behind a large garbage truck. "They probably traveled in the same social circles in Palo Alto, especially before her husband died. From what Richard tells me, maybe that's why the widow Llewellyn moved here shortly after Manning disappeared."

"And she's got money up the wazoo all of a sudden, maybe from being a partner in a child porno ring. Mom became suspicious about a tie-in last night. That's why she didn't want to talk about any of this over breakfast. She thinks Mrs. Llewellyn knew about Richard's marriage to the sister of one of Manning's victims, so when Vicki was coming here to open her shop, she and Manning probably wanted to keep tabs on things.

"You're right. Maybe Felicity Llewellyn even had the library bugged."

"She certainly laid it open to us, tea and all."

"What is going on?" Gurn tensed up and looked out the windshield with about as much ill-humor as I've ever seen in him. "Oh, man, the crowds are revving up again for another football game. We'll never get through."

I looked out at the scene, having paid little attention to it before. Hundreds of people, dressed in variations of the New Orleans Saints costumes, clamored around us, hopping on and off the sidewalk and into the street. Even at the early hour, many were holding drinks in their hands, having a fine time and probably an early morning buzz.

I reached for the door handle, preparing to get out of the car. "Look, you go ahead and find a place to park. I'll get out here. It's only a half a block to the apartment and I want to get it ready before the family shows up. I've got the keys."

"It's just for a couple of nights and there are two sets of twin beds, bunk beds, and a pull-out sofa. What's to get ready?"

"I know, but it's going to be a tight squeeze and I don't even know where the extra sheets are."

He shrugged and smiled at me. "That apartment slept six before, but it was six guys. It's different with women, so whatever you think best." He crooked his neck, looking up through the windshield at the sky. "I don't like those clouds up there. It wants to rain, as my mother would say, and maybe more."

"Thank you, Mr. Weatherman."

I bounded out of the car before he could comment on my comment and headed toward the apartment building. Able to move faster by foot, I picked my way through the throngs of happy people. About four doors from the apartment, I saw the back of a black man standing on the sidewalk, the crowds walking around his stationary body. He was pivoting in a slow three-hundred-and-sixty degree turn looking for something or someone. Within a split second, I recognized his profile as one of the two men from Colbert's Motors. I squatted down behind a parked car wondering what he was doing here. Was it just a coincidence or was he looking for me?

After about thirty seconds, I peered around the fender and the gargantuous butt of an older man wearing plaid Jamaica shorts. I couldn't see my mark; I couldn't see much of anything with Mr. Butt in the way. With the crowd's ebb and flow, my mark could have been anywhere. I rose and scurried along the sidewalk, weaving in and out of citizens until I saw him walking about thirty yards ahead me approaching Bourbon Street. I followed at an easy pace.

Just as he was nearing Preservation Hall, he suddenly glanced behind him and looked directly at me. Sad to say, criminals have a sixth sense, too, not just us good guys. Once he saw me, his reaction was about as big as they get, along the lines of Little Red Riding Hood spotting the Big Bad Wolf. He started running, pushing his way through the crowds. So did I. Run, push, run, push. It's in the job description.

A cleaning crew was coming out of Preservation Hall carrying buckets, brooms, and garbage cans. Saturday night is a big party night in this town and Sunday is cleanup day. My man saw the open gate and shoved two workers aside to dash inside the courtyard of the Hall.

I jumped over one of the men still lying on the ground with a quick apology and followed my man into the small courtyard. Right away you could tell there was no back exit. I felt a momentary gloat. I didn't have to draw my gun, because I have a black belt in Karate. If we're toe to toe and you're not armed – and even sometimes if you are - look out, brother. You're mine.

I sprung at him. He surprised me by leaping away and on top of the lid of a garbage can. Young, nimble and desperate, he climbed up the side of an eight-foot, stucco wall separating the Hall from the next building. He threw himself onto the roof of the shed on the other side.

He'd knocked the garbage can on its side when he pushed off, and it took me a few precious seconds to upright the damn thing. I jumped on it, made a dive for the top of the wall, and tried to pull myself up. Desperate, yes. Young and nimble, not so much.

When I made a lunge for the top of the wall, I knocked the lid off the garbage can, and lost my left shoe to its inner contents. But I hung on and managed to pull myself up, feeling the burn in my arms. I threw my legs over the top of the shed and got to my half-shod feet.

Puddles of water from the day before gathered in pools on the uneven tar top, and were sopped up by the fabric of my new dress.

I looked down at it, wet, muddy, disheveled, and found the bonus of a small rip in the hemline. I gotta get me hazard insurance.

My man had already scrambled down the other side and was nearing the base of the tree I'd admired earlier from our bedroom window. I kicked off my other shoe for balance and jumped down from the shed in hot pursuit, but he was too far ahead of me. I saw him run across the yard, circle around, and into the open back door of one of the neighborhood businesses.

I followed, jumping over rocks and avoiding broken glass, which slowed me down. By the time I reached the door he'd gone through, I knew it was too late. He was long gone. I hobbled inside, anyway, and found myself in a small boutique shoe store. It seemed like everywhere I went in New Orleans, I ran into shoes of one sort or another.

"Good morning, lady," said a small Asian man with a very slight accent. He was amused by my appearance and the absence of shoes on my feet. Not thrown, but amused. "You've come to the right store, lady. We carry shoes."

"Did a man just come through here?" I knew the answer but wanted a moment to catch my breath.

"You mean the one who ran through here like he was being chased by *Gweilo*?"

"How's that?"

"The devil. But you are a pretty girl. You do not look like the devil. But maybe you are an unhappy girlfriend? My son once knew a girl who was so --"

"Ah, no, no." Great, a chatty guy with a lot of time on his hands. Just what I needed. "Listen, you didn't happen to see where he went, did you?"

He shook his head and gestured to the hordes passing in front of his shop window, although his store was empty, save the two of us.

"You do not wish to buy shoes?"

"No, no. I'm going to go and hopefully retrieve my own."

My phone rang. I turned my back on the shopkeeper, who shrugged and went behind the cash register. I took the call without even looking at the number, figuring it was Gurn or Mom. It wasn't.

"Ms. Alvarez? It's Mama Biggs."

Right away I could tell something bad had happened. Not because she didn't call me 'missy', but because her voice was shaky, with a hoarseness that comes from dealing with strong emotions.

"What's wrong?"

"Reed's missing. My boy's gone."

I drew in a sharp, noisy breath. Very unprofessional, but it was a gut reaction. She went on.

"Last night at supper he was talking about being a detective, just like you. I told him to stop this foolishness, practice his clarinet, get good grades. I was hard on him. It was a feeling I had, a strong feeling. What he was talking about, it would come to no good. I could see it. And I got scared. He sassed me back and I, well, I slapped him. I never, never done anything like that before. His daddy used to slap his momma sometimes; him, too, but I never…" She interrupted herself, as if talking about striking the boy made the memory even more painful. "This morning I got up and went to his room. His bed wasn't slept in. He's gone."

Mama Biggs became silent then let out a sob. I could hear her fighting for control. Me, too.

"Did you phone the police?"

"Yes, after I searched the neighborhood for him. They just called me to say they found his bike at Colbert's Motors, but not him. Nowhere." She took a deep breath and gulped out, "My visions tell me this has something to do with you. I can see it, feel it."

Maybe it did. I thought of the man I'd lost only moments before. I thought of Manning's dead wife. Then I thought of the cellar beneath the boat trailer. A body could be hidden there for weeks before anyone found it.

Did the police know about the cellar in their search for Reed? I certainly never told them.

"I'm on my way, Mama Biggs. I'll be there in less than half an hour. We'll find him. Try not to worry." *That's my job*, I thought, and hung up. I turned to the man behind the counter reading a newspaper written in ideograms, possibly Chinese.

"I need a pair of closed, walking shoes. Size nine and hurry."

"Oh, it changes now? Before you do not need. Very well. See what you like. Then we talk," he said, not looking up from his paper.

"Put the damn paper down and get me a pair of size nine shoes! Now!" I banged on the counter with my open palm. There was no time for civilities.

He dropped the paper with a start and hurried over to his larger ladies' shoes. "Such a rush. Walking shoes. Hmmm." He thought for a moment and I almost smacked him. "All we have in your size are espadrille wedgies and high heels. What about these boots? I have your size in both colors."

He grinned and pointed to two pair of cowboy boots or should I say cowgirl boots, displayed on a stack of shoeboxes. One was ginger-colored suede, the shaft wearing dozens of crimson hearts sewn up both sides. The other pair was black leather. Shiny, bright red stars in various sizes crept up the shafts, apparently without an ounce of shame. Good gawd.

"Are you kidding me?" Through the front plate glass window I noticed Gurn coast slowly by, still stuck behind the garbage truck. "Never mind. Get me the black and step on it."

He leaned down, glommed onto a box, and pulled it from the pile. "Here you are."

"Peds. I needs peds, or I'll never get them on."

He ran behind the counter, snatched up two from dozens in a jar, a pair of boot hooks, and handed the lot to me. His amusement continued to grow.

I jammed my feet into the cut-off panty hose he had the nerve to pass off as peds, and crammed my feet into the boots, pulling up on the boot hooks.

Once I got into them, they didn't feel too bad. In fact, pretty comfy. I stood, taking my wallet out of my purse and tossing the credit card on his counter.

"That will be six-hundred and fifteen dollars." He wore a great, big smile.

"What?" I leaned against the counter for support.

"Handmade, lady, and limited supply. Take them or leave them." His hand hovered over the card machine, his smile never fading.

"Oh, fer crying out loud, give them to me. I don't have time for this."

He did something with something, handed me back the card, and I ran for the door.

"Lady! Don't you want your receipt?"

"No!"

I slammed the door shut and got my bearings. About five doors up was the pizza shop and I saw our slow-moving car. I ran toward it with a clomping sound that made passersby's heads snap around. All I needed were spurs and a ten-gallon hat. I flung the car door open and dove inside, startling Gurn. He looked at my wild hair pulled free of its elastic band, the muddy dress, and outlandish boots on my feet.

"What happened? You only left ten minutes ago."

"Well, that's a long time, all things considered. Forget getting the place ready. You gave Mom your keys, right? Because we need to head over to Colbert's Motors. I'll tell you why on the way. Do your best to get out of the French Quarter ASAP."

* * *

Twenty minutes later, the car tore into the graveled yard of Colbert's Motors and Gurn jammed on the brakes. Though neither of us said it, we were scared to death about what we might find when we opened the cellar door.

We leapt out of the car, and made a run for the back.

It takes a certain knack to run in cowgirl boots, a knack I didn't have, so Gurn got to the back of the building before me. By the time I arrived, he'd thrown the trailer hitch over to the side and was lifting the mound of chains. He tossed it into the surrounding brush. The back looked undisturbed, but I knew what was directly below the boat trailer. And feared what it might hold more than I can say.

The ground was still wet and the wind had picked up again, burning my face and hands, and scattering the gravel back over the cellar door. Gurn reached down and pulled up on the metal ring with a grunt and threw the cellar door open. I stepped forward and held my breath, listening to the wind and the clinking sound of the gravel we'd failed to clear fall and bounce onto the steps below.

Here's the part with the good news and the bad news.

The good news - we didn't find the body of a small boy.

The bad news - we did find the body of a woman.

Chapter Twenty-three
Don't Tell Me This is Not Getting Dicey

She lay at the bottom of the steps, face up, the back of her head blown away. What was left of her long, over-processed red hair was splayed out in a pool of nearly dried blood, indicating that with the high humidity level, her death happened much earlier. It's odd what you think about when you see a dead body. This was my second time in less than twenty-four hours, but I sure hoped it was the last. This body-finding stuff wears you down.

Gurn and I stared at her in momentary silence. A gust of wind nearly knocked me into the cellar, what with me balancing precariously in the cumbersome boots. I reached out for Gurn's arm to steady myself. The touch of my hand brought him out of shock. He turned to me.

"Something in your face tells me this is Felicity Llewellyn."

That's when I realized he'd never met the lady before, dead or alive.

"It is."

I tore my eyes away from his, drawn to the sound of the banging of the back door against the siding of the Quonset hut in the ever-increasing wind.

"Gurn, that door was locked yesterday and trust me, she wasn't down there, either. I don't know what happened here after I left yesterday, and Reed is still missing."

Gurn nodded and crossed the gravel to the building.

He went inside, while I stood inert, trying to figure things out. The police were here earlier. They would have checked the building for signs of life. They would have found Reed, if he'd been inside. The only reason they hadn't found Felicity Llewellyn was they didn't know about the bunker.

Everything including the weather was happening at a whirlwind. A sudden gust picked up a piece of paper, and like a small tornado, swirled it around until it hit me mid-section, held fast by the blustery weather. I snatched at it and saw it was a folded business card, my business card. Reed had done that with my card yesterday before putting it in his pocket. I almost sobbed with guilt and fear.

Gurn reemerged from the Quonset hut, and came to my side.

"Nothing, but it's a mess in there. Somebody took it apart pretty good. Maybe the police. But there's no blood, nothing to indicate she'd been shot there." He looked down again at Mrs. Llewellyn lying in the cellar. "It probably happened in there. In any event, we need to call the police."

He took out his cell phone about to raise it to his ear. I reached out with my hand and covered his phone, pressing down.

"No, Gurn. Don't call the police yet."

"Why not? We have to let them know."

"Reed was here."

"I know. The police found his bike."

I showed him the folded card and started talking rapid-fire, not allowing him to interrupt, even if he'd wanted to. "Something's happened to him and I've got to find him. If you call the cops, they'll make us stay here for hours answering questions, maybe even drag us to the police station, wasting time we can't spare. I need to find Reed."

"By yourself? Are you kidding? People are getting killed right and left. I'm not letting you out of my sight."

He pulled away from me and raised the phone to his ear. I lunged for it again.

"Please, Gurn. Listen, we're running out of time. Manning's known everything we've said and done probably since the family came to New Orleans. I'm sure that's how one of his thugs knew where to look for us a few minutes ago. Manning knows we've located him and we've got what's left of the files he tried to burn."

His eyebrows furrowed and he looked at me, lowering the phone again. "Then he knows the Feds might not need his testimony for a conviction of the porno ring. He's on his own."

"Exactly. But right now I'm worried about Reed's disappearance."

"You think Manning took the kid with him?"

"I do." My voice was shaky.

"That still doesn't mean you're going anywhere near him without me. He is one dangerous man."

"I totally agree. All I'm asking is, to save time let's split up. You stay here and talk to the police. I'll go and talk to Mama Biggs. She's only about two blocks from here. Maybe she's got some information she doesn't even know she has."

I felt him waffle. I pressed my advantage.

"I need to let the family know the latest development, too. But I promise not to do anything, go anywhere, without calling you first. Please, darling. A little boy's life might be at stake."

The waffle won.

He let out a big sigh and shook his head. I could tell Gurn wasn't happy about any of this.

"You've got your gun with you?"

I nodded and tapped my shoulder bag.

"Your phone's fully charged?"

I nodded again.

"And you swear not to do anything or go anywhere without calling me first?"

"Scout's honor."

"Then get going. When I call the police, I'll try to leave you out of it. Your prints are all over that cellar, though, aren't they?"

I started to run and tossed over my shoulder, "Yes, but that's for another day."

Chapter Twenty-four
Winds are Picking Up

I got nearly a quarter of a block when my phone rang. I ripped the phone out of my bag and hoped it wasn't Gurn telling me he changed his mind and I should come back. Because I wasn't going back. I wasn't going anywhere except to search for a child who was missing because of me. I looked at the incoming number.

It was my brother.

I paused, already out of breath from fighting against the wind to get to Mama Biggs' house. It had picked up tremendously over the past half-hour. Leaves and trash were being blown every which way. I ducked behind the Plexiglas of a neighborhood bus stop. The sign announcing the designated stop vibrated and squealed, metal protesting the onslaught of the wind. I put one finger in the ear not with the phone pressed against it, trying to block out the noise.

"Richard, where are you?"

There was a slight pause. "Where are *we*? We're here at the safe house, you ninny, where you're supposed to be. That's everyone, including the Rottweiler. Tío went back and found him locked in the garage. The cats have already shown him who's boss. Where are you?"

"Following developments, Richard, and not good ones. Is Lila around? Can we do a conference call?"

Whether it was the tone in my voice or the fact I'd called Mom Lila, Richard's brotherly irritation changed to professional deference immediately.

"Yes. She's moving furniture around in the living room. She's been trying to fill in time. You know how Our Lady gets. Just a minute, I'll tell her to call you. Don't hang up."

There was a short span of waiting. Someone's umbrella, bent and misshapen, skittered along the sidewalk, passing me faster than I can run. The other line beeped. I answered then pressed conference. After I made sure all three of us were on the line, I brought Lila and Richard up to speed.

"Where are you now, Lee? I'm trying to get a fix on you through your GPS."

Richard and his GPS. Honestly.

"I'm behind a bus stop, trying to stay out of the wind. But I'm heading to Mama Biggs' house. I need to talk to her. What's going on with the weather, anyway? Does anybody know? It's like a hurricane out here."

"That's exactly what it is." Richard's voice sounded worried and exasperated. "Or promises to be. There's` a tropical storm with the potential of turning into a hurricane anytime within the next twenty-four-hours. Good God, girl, don't you listen to the radio or TV?"

"I've been a little busy, Richard."

"The stall off the coast of Florida for the past few days has started moving and fast. Depending on its trajectory and how warm the water, it could build in strength, or dissipate, or veer west toward Axapta or come straight up the Panhandle or the Louisiana coastline."

"That's a lot of 'or's."

"For New Orleans, a tropical depression probably means fifteen to twenty mile-an-hour winds with gusts up to thirty-five. If it become a category one, that means sixty-five to seventy-five mile-an-hour winds and a possible storm surge of twelve to fifteen feet. The entire area is on alert for possible evacuation."

"Thank you, Al Roker." Suddenly every man in my life was a weatherman.

I must say Lila was being very quiet about Felicity Llewellyn's death. So far, she'd been silent during the whole conversation. That usually meant when she did speak up, I wasn't going to like where it was headed. I heard her clear her throat. Danger, Will Robinson, Danger.

"Liana, this is your mother. I want you to stop what you're doing and come back immediately. There will be no arguments over this, young lady."

Yup. That's where it was headed. Lila became Mom again in a very big way. She hadn't used that tone on me since I was a teenager. Even then I hated being told what to do, especially in that 'this is the queen speaking' sort of way.

"What? What?" I extended my arm and held the phone out from behind the protective Plexiglas. It almost got blown out of my hand, but I let the wind beat at it and began to shout. "I can't hear you! Gotta go. I'll call you later!" I hung up.

Actually, I might not be able to call anyone later. Phone towers have a way of going over in strong winds.

Good. Maybe I don't have to talk to anybody until I finish this.

I went back out into the elements and fought my way to Mama Biggs'. Periodically, slashing rain came at me, feeling like pebbles thrown at my face, arms, and legs. All around me I heard groans and complaints from the world at large to the fierceness of the storm.

Back in the Bay Area, any type of rain, even the most gentle, is referred to by meteorologists as a storm. What I was experiencing in New Orleans was a storm with a capital 'S'. Like most Californians, when I see the real thing, it's a bit of a shock. And why didn't I bring a raincoat?

I shivered as I ran up the three flights of the backstairs to Mama Biggs' kitchen. She must have been on the lookout for me, because I only knocked once before she flung the door wide open. Pushed in by the wind, I smashed into her and we both struggled to close the door.

I turned to face a woman who looked smaller and older than the day before. Fear and self-recrimination has a way of doing that.

"Did you find out anything? Do you know where my boy is?" She clutched at the collar of her floral robe, fingers clenching and unclenching the flannel fabric.

"Not yet." I decided against telling her about Manning's wife and Mrs. Llewellyn. There was no point in upsetting her any more than she already was. I put my hand on her shoulder. "I need to ask you a few questions. Why don't we sit down?"

Mama Biggs wasn't listening after I'd said 'not yet'. Or didn't want to. She wiggled out of my hold and paced up and down the kitchen, talking the whole time, a lamenting duet with the wind outside.

"This is my fault. I struck my boy; I drove him away. Whatever possessed me to do that? It was like demons had hold of me. And my Reed, my poor sweet boy, has had enough trouble in his young life. A mama dying on him so young; a father leaving him after Hurricane Katrina did its worse. All he had was me."

"He still has you."

She turned back and looked at me. "I got a bad feeling, so strong, that my boy is in danger. I can see him but I can't do anything to help him." She burst into tears.

I would have joined her but time was running out. I crossed the room and took hold of her slim shoulders.

"Look at me. Look at me." I shook her until she stopped crying and looked me in the eye. "You talk about seeing things and feeling things. I want to know how real they are."

"What do you mean?"

"All this insight stuff. Is it a show you put on for your customers? Or do you have a way of seeing how things are or going to be? I was partnered with a woman in Georgia once who helped me find missing data stolen by an IT guy. She worked for the police department from time to time finding lost children, too. They said she had 'the gift'.

There wasn't much other explanation for what she did. So I'm open to this, but don't waste my time if it isn't true. Reed's life may depend on it."

I let her go and she almost dropped to the floor. I put my arm around her and guided her to one of the chairs at the table. She sat down heavily. She spoke with her head resting on her chest, and eyes closed. Her voice was so soft I could barely hear the words.

"I got the gift. My daddy had it and his mama before him. No use talking about it. Nobody believes you."

"Okay, let's say I do believe you. Yesterday when you took my hands, you said for me to stay off briny or salt water. Now should I chalk that up to showmanship or did you really, truly see something?" I sat in the chair across from her and studied her hard.

Mama Biggs wiped her face with a trembling hand. She looked up and leaned into me with such intensity, I drew back. "I saw you. I saw you on a boat. Out somewhere on the water. Waves of water. Waves of trouble. Bad." She reached out a hand and touched my face with trembling fingers. "There's more. You was shot, Missy. I didn't see you after, but you was shot." She shrank back into her chair, arm falling to her side.

"Okay. Not thrilled with that, but okay." Shaken, I took my phone out of my bag, pressed Richard's number, and put the phone to my ear. Dead, *muerto*. "Do you have a landline?" She nodded and pointed to the phone at the end of the kitchen counter. "May I use it?"

She nodded and dropped her head down to her chest once more. I picked up the phone and listened to the dial tone. It takes a lot to kick out a landline. They may be stationary, but it's one of their pluses. I dialed Richard's number, hoping his smart phone wasn't out like mine. It wasn't.

"Richard Alvarez speaking."

"Richard, it's me."

"Lee! Where are you? Who's phone is this?"

"I'm calling you on Mama Biggs' landline. My phone's out."

"The tower must have blown down where you are. I told you to get a satellite phone like I have. And get back here. Mom is frantic with worry about you."

"Tell her not to worry, I'm fine. I --"

"Easy for you to say," he interrupted, with a whisper. "You're not trapped in a room with Our Lady, who's turning into a fire-breathing dragon. Vicki had to make her some Chamomile tea."

"How is Vicki?"

"Like the rest of us, anxious about you."

"Moving on, in your research on Manning, did you ever find out if he bought another boat when he got to New Orleans?"

"Another boat? Let me see. Hold on." I heard the phone clunk on a hard surface to be picked up a few seconds later. "Yes, he's moved up in the world. The Fantasy Seventy-seven. Four staterooms, marble bathrooms, a multi-million dollar boat. It made its debut back in two thousand and nine when --"

"Let's save the ad copy for another time, shall we, Richard? Does it have a name?"

"Name, name. Wait a minute. I can enlarge a photo of it." There was a pause and I heard the clicking of a mouse. "Yes, *Laura's Folly*. I guess he named his new boat after his wife's new name."

"How romantic. Right before he killed her."

"Lee! You think her overdose wasn't an accident?"

"Leave nobody talking."

"You know, sometimes your mind scares me."

"Thank you. Where is the boat docked?"

"Docked, docked." I could feel him searching through his data. "Ah! The Orleans Harbor Marina."

"You got a slip number?"

"Yes, B248. You don't think he's gone to his boat in this weather? That could be suicide."

I looked over at Mama Biggs, leaning against the edge of the table. Other than a rigid hand moving a cup of untouched tea back and forth in front of her, she sat motionless. The expression on her face showed me her thoughts weren't anywhere in the room. I didn't want to know what she was thinking. I didn't even want to know what I was thinking.

"Give me the address, Richard."

"Address, address." As realization dawned on my brother, his words became drawn out and accusatory. "Oh no, sister mine. You're not going there in weather like this."

"Oh yes, brother mine, I am." I imitated his sing-song. "And if you don't give it to me, I can look it up in the phone book."

He let out a deep sigh. "Mom's going to have a cow when she finds out about this."

"From dragon to cow. Sounds like an improvement. Oh, and try to reach Gurn for me, would you? I promised I would keep him in the loop."

"This is keeping him in the loop?"

"Address, please."

Richard gave me the address of the marina and I hung up on a sputtering brother. I put the address in my Smartphone, which was now a glorified memo pad. How the mighty have fallen. I turned back to Mama Biggs.

"You have a car, right?"

She came back to the land of the living with one word. "Yes."

"I'm going to need to borrow it for a time."

She didn't move but said, "The keys are next to the cookie jar. It's the black SUV across the street. Do whatever you want with it, just bring back my boy to me."

"That's the plan."

I reached for the keys on a large, metal keychain. The name Barefoot Mama Biggs was etched on one side; the other side was a picture of Reed set behind Lucite.

"I'll call you as soon as I know anything."

I didn't add a stupid phrase, such as, 'try not to worry'. I've never met a person yet those words worked on.

She nodded. I didn't have anything to say after that, so I left her to her thoughts. At least I would be busy, keeping my own thoughts at bay. She had the tougher job: just sit and wait.

Chapter Twenty-five
When You're In It, You're In It

I ran down the stairs and out the front door. In the few minutes I'd spent with Mama Biggs, the temperature dropped a good ten degrees and the sky had turned pewter grey. Murky, ominous clouds raced across the sky like steel battering rams. Below, the whooshing of the wind obliterated the common, every day sounds except for the most insistent and jarring. The tinny sound of a metal trash can as it bounced across the street and crashed against the curb pierced through the steady wail. Intermittent raindrops the size of golf balls came at me sideways.

A lone man, clutching a red jacket around his frame, fought to stay upright against a wind pushing him from behind, forcing him to walk stiff legged, like he was in an old-time, silent movie. Other than him, not another living soul was on the street.

Across the street sat a huge, old and dented black SUV. It looked sturdy enough to take on any tropical storm you could throw at it. Actually, put a rudder on it and you had the Merrimack.

My own car is a turquoise '57 Chevy convertible, original paint job if you please, and was the last gift from my father before he died. It was currently lounging around in the garage beneath my Palo Alto apartment, being delicate and cute.

I would never part with it, but was glad I wasn't driving it in this weather. Even in the rare heavy rainfall of the Bay Area, it tends to leak.

I climbed into Mama Bigg's hulk of a car, grateful for its protection. I started it up – one loud sucker - and pulled out. It was like driving a city bus. How a little lady managed to drive such a big car flashed through my mind.

I headed east on St. Claude Avenue toward my ultimate destination, the Orleans Harbor Marina off the Intracoastal Waterway. The stoplights were still working, doing a green, yellow, and red cha-cha-cha against the wind. Newspapers, trash, branches of leaves, the occasional umbrella, and even someone's plaid sports coat flew by. I made my way along with the other cars still driving the streets.

Around me people were boarding up windows of businesses with heavy plywood, securing them in place with what looked like industrial staplers, Katrina still fresh in everyone's minds. Hurricane shutters were already down over windows of small homes or apartment buildings from residences lucky enough to have them. Others were hammering two by fours in 'x's across frames of windows holding glass looking too fragile and vulnerable for what was going on.

All in all, I was not happy. Even the mud baths of Calistoga looked pretty good to me at this point.

I turned onto a completely deserted Almonaster Avenue, save a passing large yellow rental truck. The driver looked wide-eyed and terrified. This was the longest two-mile drive of my life. Fifteen to twenty-five mile-an-hour winds whipped at me head-on from the Waterway connecting Lake Pontchartrain with the Mississippi River. Even flooring the car, I was only going about thirty miles an hour. What should have been a six- or seven-minute drive took me twenty harrowing minutes.

When I hung a left onto France Road, the wind struck from the right, pushing the SUV into the oncoming lane.

I weaved my way back and forth, grateful there were no other cars on the road. Not a half a mile further, with arms shaking from the fatigue of battling the steering wheel, I saw the turn-off for the marina.

The Ocean Harbor Marina lay hidden behind a high white stucco wall. Announcing the marina was a blue and white sign, currently laying at a peculiar angle and bobbing in rhythm with the wind. Two wrought iron gates were chained open against the walls at the entrance. No one was in the little gatehouse checking for vehicles coming and going.

I pulled over to the side of the road to allow a pickup truck and trailer burdened with a bulbous, but imposing deep sea fishing boat named *The Lucky Lady* pass. *The Lucky Lady* was one mother out of the water, with lots of built-on antennas slashing at the winds like dueling rapiers. Both boat and trailer looked like they might blow over any minute, taking the hapless pickup with them. But of course, they were leaving this messy business behind and I was going right smack into it. Who's sorry she's not a boat?

I drove into the half-filled parking lot, veered off to the right, and found a parking space near the choppy water. Through the steady beat of the windshield wipers, I sat for a moment observing the controlled chaos. Ahead, dozens of crafts, all sizes and varieties, were like bucking broncos in their slips, straining at their tethers.

Then I looked for signs delineating the A to F piers and their slip numbers. Reading from right to left, the slip numbers started at one-hundred and one in the A slips, two-hundred and one in the B slips, three-hundred and one in the C, and so on. It seemed complicated to me. I mean, just start at number one, folks, why don't you? But what do I know about the nautical mind. The closest I've ever come to dealing with a boat is owning a pair of deck shoes, which I wished I'd had then and there instead of clunky cowgirl boots.

With a deep sigh, I screwed my courage to the sticking post, and got out of the car.

Battling the elements and people running around like they were at a Macy's white-sale, I made my way to the wide pier separating the A from the B slips. I stood at the edge studying the scene. And it was a pip. It was all I could do to stay out of the way of frantic seafarers battening down the hatches, or whatever the hell they were doing nearest the shoreline. But at the end of the pier, where Manning's boat had to be, there wasn't a soul. Isn't that always the way?

I finally homed in on slip B248 near the end of the pier. Manning's boat was still there. When the hull wasn't being submerged by waves, I even saw the name, *Laura's Folly*, so it didn't take a genius to figure out it was his. Richard was right; Manning had certainly come up in the world. No more thirty-two foot sailboats for him. This was a seventy-plus foot long, gorgeous piece of work. Child porn paid off well, like a two story yacht with all the fixin's.

The interior lights were on. That meant someone was in there. Was it Manning? Probably. Was Reed with him? Hopefully. Would Manning be on the alert for intruders? You betcha.

That last thought prevented me from walking to the end of the pier and kicking down his cabin door with my size nine cowgirl boots. One man and two women were dead in less than forty-eight hours, all connected to this monster. Like Gurn said, Manning was one dangerous man.

But I had to move fast. Just because the boat was still there didn't mean it would stay there. Boats have a way of moving around. So did Manning.

As I stood contemplating my next move, my teeth began to chatter and my jaw was clenched so tight it hurt. Time to get out of the wind, rain, and my little girly summer dress. I ran back to the car, threw myself behind the steering wheel, and turned the motor on. Shivering and shaking, I blasted the heater, sat back, and studied the layout of the marina.

To my left, two inclined boat ramps at the water's edge had water slopping onto the sidewalk.

In the water, boats were lined up before each ramp ready to vacate the turbulent H_2O elsewhere. Protected by surf breakers, a slim sailboat was in the process of being lifted out of the water by a hydraulic system. It was memorizing watching the hydraulic lift the dripping boat into the air. A waiting truck backed up a trailer onto the inclined ramp directly beneath the hovering boat. In this weather how they were going to plop that puppy onto the trailer in one piece was a mystery to me.

However, a youngish woman with a wet, blonde ponytail looked like the ringleader. With precise hand signals similar to those bringing in a plane to a terminal gate, she guided the five men handling the hydraulics, boat, and truck. I was impressed. As soon as the sailboat was secured on the trailer and the truck pulled away, the woman moved to the next ramp and another boat being lifted out of the water by another hydraulic. Obviously, the marina had this down to a science.

Nearly everywhere else, except at the end of Pier B - dagnabbit - people were darting about on their crafts, tying ropes down, securing items, undoing sails, storing gear, seemingly unmindful of the steady rain lashing at them or the bumpy ride onboard. Sailors are a sturdy lot.

In the distance, a parade of boats was motoring out of the marina's manmade channel and into the Intracoastal Waterway. There they joined larger vessels and headed under the Danzinger Bridge. This was one busy marina and there were a lot of ways to get in and out of it.

Somewhat warmer, I turned off the car motor again, steeled myself, and got out of the car. I was immediately smacked in the face by a soggy brown paper bag. I wrestled it to the ground and made my way to the long, one-story building braced against the inside stucco walls.

The extensive building contained several clubs and services marked by signs above each door i.e., Yacht Club, Fitness Center, Gaming Room, Sporting Goods Store, Mariner's Restaurant, and so forth.

Awnings made of a white eco-friendly material were already lowered in place over plate glass windows. They not only looked strong but stylish.

Remove the storm and you had one top-of-the-line, no-expense-spared, classy marina. The closest to this I've seen is the West Palm Beach Marina, where each boat has a butler and you need a credit check to use the public bathroom.

My destination was the Sporting Goods Store. Good place to start for information and maybe a rain slicker. I was cold, wet, and sick of it. I opened its door and sneezed. I thought I could feel the low pressure from the storm outside trying to get inside, but maybe it was my imagination. Can you feel low pressure? I needed to ask one of the many Al Roker's in my life.

A middle-aged man with big ears and a woman flashing more long, white-blonde hair than I've seen outside of a beauty pageant, looked at me with worried smiles. Big Ears was finishing a sale with a customer dressed like the Gorton Fisherman, while Blondie was pulling out stacks of neatly folded wearing apparel from lower shelves and cramming them into higher ones. The customer scurried out into the atmosphere leaving the front door open. I hurried over, shut the door, and sneezed again.

"Sounds like you're coming down with a cold, young lady," the man said, this time with a genuine smile. "Why don't you help yourself to some hot coffee?"

Big Ears tilted his balding pate in the direction of a small table burdened down under a silver coffee urn, white china coffee cups, sugar bowl, creamer, and a row of sparkling spoons, all lain out on a white damask cloth. All of a sudden, his ears didn't look so bad to me. The expectation of a caffeine rush can do that.

"Thank you so much." I galumphed to the table, poured a steaming cup of coffee with the aroma of chicory in it, and gulped down half the cup before I uttered another sound. Feeling warmer and actually human again, I turned to the over-process blonde woman.

"I guess the philosophy is you should put everything up because of possible flooding, huh?"

Her smile faded. Even her hair seemed to droop. I'd only asked the question as sort of an ice breaker. I really need to stop doing that. I didn't want to be thrown out of the place before I could buy a rain slicker.

"You hope for the best but prepare for the worst. That's my motto."

Okay, so it was a motto, not a philosophy. Got it.

"The boats that are leaving." I changed the subject. "Where are they going?"

"The ones heading out to the Intracoastal Waterway?"

The man asked the question crossing the room to help the woman. I nodded and he talked as he helped her move merchandize from lower shelves to higher ones.

"The people lucky enough to be around to protect their crafts are motoring up the Mississippi trying to outrun the storm. They have to get out of here before The U.S. Army Corps of Engineers decides to close three of the barge gates, now that the storm is on the move. The Corps mentioned the possible closure on the news fifteen minutes ago."

"Is that right?"

"Once the gates go in, the boats will be trapped, unable to go anywhere. A lot of these folks are from up there, anyway. You know, Ohio and the like."

"Oh, I didn't realize that. How big a boat does it take to go on the Mighty Mississip?"

"At least eighteen feet," the woman said, taking over the conversation. "There are fierce currents out there. Matt and I know from experience, it doesn't do to be in too small a craft on that water."

She giggled and lightly punched the man in the side. He giggled back and stroked her arm. I assumed he was Matt, but really didn't want to shift the conversation to their experience on the Mighty M in a small craft. I wanted to keep it on track, although, I wasn't sure what track that was.

"What happens if you head the other way?"

He looked at me with puzzled expression. "You mean, if you went down the Mississippi?"

"Yeah."

"Well, you would be heading toward the Gulf of Mexico and into Harold."

"Who's Harold?"

Now he looked at me like I was crazy. "Harold's the name of the tropical depression coming our way. What's out there right now could turn into Hurricane Harold any minute now," he said. His voice showed his question of my sanity. Actually, he wasn't the first to do so and won't be the last. I wasn't thrown by it.

"Right, right." I walked away and began fingering a wetsuit on display, complete with goggles, flippers, and snorkel. "We don't get many hurricanes where I live," I said, half paying attention to the conversation. An idea was formulating in what was left of my brain.

"Where's that?" Out of the corner of my eyes, I saw the woman turn to the man with a raised eyebrow.

"California."

"California!" The woman's revulsion toward the state came across in the one-word reply. "You couldn't pay me to live where they have all those earthquakes. Give me a hurricane every time."

"You may get your wish," I muttered, unfolding a full black wetsuit. "How much is this?"

Now the man looked at me with dollar signs in his eyes. "What stock we have left is on sale. You're holding a fullsuit. Good for all types of water temps around here, with five-four-three insulation. Regularly $385, reduced to $295. It's a Roxie, so you know it's a real bargain." He came over and took it from my hands. "Yes, this looks like it would fit you. It's important to have the right fit."

"Could I try it on?"

He was one happy man. I think the lousy weather made for even lousier sales.

The woman, who made it clear she preferred her hurricanes to my earthquakes, seemed to glitter a bit more, too. The man turned to her.

"Faye, please bring this young lady a towel from the backroom so she can dry off."

"Of course." Faye disappeared behind a lime-green curtain only to return a second later with a thick, white fluffy towel. I eyed it with glee. With a smile, she handed it off to me. I set down my empty coffee cup and picked up the towel, blotting my face and hair with the soft cotton. I love terrycloth.

"Thank you, Faye," I said politely. "This feels really good."

"There are fitting rooms right over there." I heard the man's voice behind me. "Take your pick."

"They're all free or should I say available?" Faye's humor much improved, she pointed to three side by side slated doors in the wall, tossing her blonde locks about.

I crossed to one of the doors but turned back. "And I'll need a hood, goggles, flippers, and a waterproof pouch. You got something like that?"

"Yes, yes." They said in unison. Both almost did a jig as they scampered around looking for the items. I shut the door then opened it again, addressing the man.

"Your name is Matt, right?" He nodded eagerly. "Matt, do you think you could help me with these boots? They're a little hard to get on and off."

"My pleasure."

Leaving the door half open, I dropped my purse to the floor, and sat down on a petite club chair, upholstered in the same shade of lime as the curtains. With Faye keeping a watchful eye, Matt came inside the small room and pushed the door wide open. My suspicion Faye was his loving wife seemed to be on the nose. Speaking of noses, I felt mine clogging up, while Matt eyed my heart-encrusted boots without hiding his distaste.

"A gift from my mother," I lied. "A bit ostentatious, but what can you do?"

Somewhere in New Orleans my mother's ears were burning. And if she ever found out why, she'd probably sue me for defamation of character. Regardless, I went for broke. "Her taste is in her mouth, but you can't hurt a mother's feelings, can you?"

"Certainly not." He lifted one of my ankles, turned around with his backside to me, and straddled my leg. "Now you push with the other foot."

I placed my boot right below the small of his back. He pulled, I pushed, and after a certain amount of huffing and puffing, the boot slid off. Then we did the other one. I've never owned two-person footwear before. I mean, these are really not for someone living alone.

He left the room closing the door behind him. I stripped off my dress, threw it in a corner, and towel dried my hair and body. You have to be as dry as possible in your tug-of-war with a wetsuit.

I experienced the putting on and pulling off process when I took snorkel lessons in the Bahamas one summer. And that was in a 'shortie'. The fullsuit has long sleeves and legs to the ankles. Wonderful in colder water, but a bitch to put on if you're moist in the least.

I struggled into the suit, grunting and groaning. It fit the way they should, not too loose, which allows too much water to come inside, but not too snug, where your movements are restricted. By the time I zipped up, there was a knock on the door and I heard Faye's voice.

"How are you doing in there, dearie?"

"Just fine."

I opened the door and she stepped inside holding a matching rubber hood, goggles and mask. I took the lot, threw them on the chair, and proceeded to pull my hair back in a ponytail on top of my head with a rubber band I found at the bottom of my purse. I pulled the hood over my head and tucked the bottom into the suit. Once again, not too loose, not too tight, just right.

"What about flippers?" For what I was about to do, I needed as much help propelling around in the drink as possible. Flippers were a must.

"We don't have any women's sizes left." She shook her head with deep regret.

"Bring me what you got. Maybe we can make something work."

Faye got into the spirit of it. "Just a moment. Maybe you could wear a pair of Jelly's inside one of the men's. They would take up a lot of room."

"You mean the plastic beach sandals?"

"Yes, I think we've got hot pink and purple left. What size shoe do you wear?" She threw the question over her shoulder, as she hurried back into the store.

"Size nine," I yelled after her. I followed her out in my bare feet. I did a few small Karate moves in the suit and almost took out a mannequin sporting cruise wear I hadn't noticed. Matt dashed over to steady the tottering dummy, as if he did this sort of thing all the time. Maybe he did. Such is a merchant's life. But the suit felt good. And warm.

"We've got size nine in both colors, hot pink and purple." Faye gestured for me to come over to the corner where all the women's shoes lived. "Which color do you want?"

Like it made a difference. "I'll take the purple."

I sat down and put them on. She brought me the smallest men's flippers in the bunch and, with a few minor adjustments and the sandals, they fit okay. The Jelly's looked silly, but what can you do? Life is filled with purple Jelly's.

Matt brought me two waterproof pouches with clips and a belt to attach them to your waist. I chose the larger pouch, big enough to hold a phone and a gun or two. As I was zipping and unzipping the pouch my phone did an announcement that it was working and I had a text message. An expert at this now, I went to texting and read:

L - Where R U? Phones in and out. Am with Devereux. He wants U. Be safe. Luv G

I looked up at Faye and Matt, who were hovering nearby awaiting my next command. It's good to be queen.

"Bag up everything; I need to get going." I went into my handbag for my charge card, which was getting a lot of use these days. "Oh, one more thing, I need a rain slicker. You got one?"

Wearing a slicker over the wetsuit might make it look like I had on Capri pants from a distance. No use advertising I was about to take a dunk in the Intracoastal waters.

Matt's eager hands reached out for the card. "Yes, we do. Yellow or red? Short or long? You can't go wrong. Genuine Oilskin."

"Don't you have black?"

"We keep a couple of blacks for tourists passing through, not going on the water, but we don't recommend them. If you fall in, you want to be seen."

Not for what I'm doing. "I'm going to go with the black. Short." I spoke as I texted Gurn back.

G – At Orleans Harbor Marina. Think M here on boat. Tell D to go suck egg. Luv L

Faye handed me the slicker and I shrugged into it. "Okay. Thanks. I'm in a hurry. What do I owe you?"

Her smile faded just a little and she looked up at my head. "You're wearing all of that out? Even the hood?"

"It's pretty comfy. I can change when I get home."

I offered them a bright smile. Their hesitant, returning smiles and furtive glances to one another convinced me that Matt and Faye definitely thought I was a whack-a-doodle. It was an opinion shared, no doubt, by yesterday's barkeep. I wasn't sure I would be allowed back in the state of Louisiana in the near future.

"It comes to $964.22. A real bargain with all the sales."

"Lucky me."

After a small flurry of card and paper exchanges, they handed me two bags. One contained my wet dress and cowgirl boots. The other contained the mask, flippers, and pouch.

I went back out into the storm and wondered if with the way things were going, I could ever afford to retire. Not the way I was spending money.

Even though my feet were getting wet in the Jelly's, I noticed they gripped the slick pavement well. A bonus to being foot-bound in purple. I returned to the car warmer and dryer than I had been most of the day and climbed inside. I opened the waterproof pouch and transferred my phone into it. Then I took Lady Blue out of my handbag, the steel hard and cold in my hand.

The seriousness of what I did for a living hit me full force. If Mama Biggs was right and I was going to be shot, then by God I was taking Manning out with me. The only light at the end of the tunnel was hopefully finding and freeing Reed, a kid with his whole life before him. If he was still alive. There was that. People like Manning have no thought about innocent lives.

After loading Lady Blue, I put her inside the waterproof pouch. I thought only a split second about the Smith and Wesson before I pulled it out of the side pocket of my handbag. With a dry mouth, I loaded the gun. I checked to make sure the safety was on then practiced again and again how to release it in an instant and fire. Funny, I didn't feel in the least bit like Rambo.

Chapter Twenty-six
Wet Chaos

In Pier C nearly half the boats were gone or pulling out. Looking over to the backside of *Laura's Folly*, I noticed the wide swim platform. I'd chartered a boat with one of those in the Bahamas. They make it easy to get in and out of the water, thought they can be slippery. I eyeballed the distance I'd have to swim to get from one pier to another, hoping I didn't have to get out of the way of any escaping boats. Strategically placed in various locations on each pier were swim ladders going from the deck into the water. I went to the ladder at the end of Pier C, sat down next to it, and looked around.

No one was paying attention to me that I could tell, so I lay down, rolled over the side, and onto the ladder. Pulling off my slicker, I stuffed it between pilings, and put on my flippers. I reached behind into the pouch and pulled out my phone and went to texting. I tapped in both my brother's and Gurn's phone numbers.

G&R – About to take boat ride. Don't know where. More later. L

After I returned the phone to the pouch, I lowered myself into the rushing waters, always keeping an eye on *Laura's Folly*.

To my surprise, I saw the young black man I chased earlier bound out of the pilothouse. He took the stairs two at a time, and hopped onto the lower deck of *Laura's Folly*. I pressed myself against the ladder, in case he looked my way.

He was in one big hurry, but lost some time when his hat and scarf blew out of his hands and onto the boat deck. He chased after and retrieved them then jumped from the boat onto the pier and took off for parts unknown, lithe and sure-footed. But I knew from experience, this was one fast and wiry dude.

A second later, Manning came out of the pilothouse and on to the upper deck. He also came down the stairs to the lower deck, but not as fast. Age will tell.

He began to cast off docking lines with the expertise of a man who had spent his life around boats. Then he moved to the front of the boat. Duh, he was leaving! I don't know why it took me so long to catch onto that. Once he pulled out, I'd never catch up with him.

Slipping into the water up to my neck, I began the forty or so yard swim to Pier B. Despite the wetsuit, I was shivering, a combination of anticipation, anger, and fear. No, not so much fear. I was too mad to be afraid. I hated this man for all I was worth. The anger helped me plow through the water like Johnny Weissmuller in an old Tarzan movie. Fortunately, no other boat got in my way, because the mood I was in, I would have smacked it to the other side of the marina.

Aided by the flippers, I got to the boat's stern in no time, even with the madness of the water. I grabbed onto the rails at either side of the center of the swim platform and hoisted myself up and in the nick of time. Just then the boat jerked and came to life. Fluttering like a kite caught in the wind, the Laura's Folly took off with a speed I didn't think possible. It backed out of the slip, made a left and haul-assed down the alley between the piers and out of the marina.

Clinging on for dear life, I removed my flippers and dropped them into the water. I wrapped one arm and a leg around the two center rails. It was a bouncy, perilous ride hanging on the back. Not so much because of the waves or wind, but swim platforms are not designed to be used when a boat is under way. If I hadn't had the rails to hang on to, I would have never been able to stay aboard.

But Houston, we had another problem. Once out in the Intracoastal Waterway there were other boats. Around one hundred yards behind us, a tugboat began tooting his horn. Maybe he wanted to let someone on the boat know a straggler was attached to Folly's butt. But whatever, I waved brightly and hoped he would stop tooting. Also I hoped that way up on the upper deck, where the pilothouse was, Manning wouldn't notice and come down before I was ready for him.

We outdistanced the tugboat in nothing flat, but I waved again, like I was out for a jolly ride. The surface of the Intracoastal seemed smoother, maybe because of the wake, or maybe it was the speed of the boat cutting through the water. In any event, I managed to get up the three steps at the top of the swim platform leading to the lower deck. Mercifully, that area was covered in some kind of slip proof carpeting. On the left side of the narrow back deck was a long white box with the words Emergency Supplies stenciled along the top. Rows of lashed down diesel fuel cans ran along the railing out to the bow. Or was it the aft? I can never keep that straight.

The emergency supply box was big enough to crawl behind and far enough away from the railing for me to lay flat. I didn't wonder about the diesel fuel. Manning was on the run. He needed all the fuel he could get.

Unfortunately, the railing was solid except for a couple of inches above the deck. I had no way of seeing where we were. I felt rather than saw us turn left into the Mississippi. Once heading south on the river, we picked up momentum big time. No longer with other boats to hinder him, Manning put the pedal to the metal. Air and water rushed by at a speed I wouldn't have believed such a big boat could do. For a short time there was the sameness of the up and down rhythm of the boat slapping into the oncoming waves. Gradually the crests and valleys became more pronounced. We were heading out into the Gulf and a showdown with Harold.

Hanging onto the rail, I rose to my feet and assessed the situation.

Being a stowaway was one thing, but I couldn't spend what was left of my life hiding behind emergency supplies. I had to know if Reed, or if anyone else besides Manning was aboard. I crept across the deck to the cabin wall with a line of portals in it. Raising up to one side of the last portal, I pressed my face to the last portal, and stared with a mixture of horror and relief.

In a small stateroom, Reed sat on a berth next to an end table. Even through the thick-glassed, rain streaked porthole, I could see his breathing was rapid and shallow, eyes half-closed in a tear stained face. A small bruise had formed on his right cheek and the sleeve of his t-shirt had a rip in it. The kid looked absolutely scared to death, but exhausted and resigned to his fate. Every now and then he tugged at something with his left arm. I looked down. His left wrist was manacled to a post.

That's when I understood the phrase about something making your blood boil. I could feel rage race through my veins and arteries like hot lava. Time to stop this Manning son of a bitch.

The sound of movement above and hurried footsteps going somewhere caused me to freeze. The overhead sounds thudded more away from me than near. A few seconds later, Manning opened the door to the stateroom. My right hand was holding onto an overhead rail for stability, but I pulled back and leaned against the wall. I was afraid to move, so I unzipped the pouch with my free left hand and pulled out one of the guns. I glanced at it. Lady Blue. Good enough for me.

I heard the muttering of a voice and the sounds of movement again. I took the chance and leaned in to look into the stateroom again. Manning's back was to me, but Reed was facing the window. He saw me and his eyes opened wide with astonishment. Before he could say or do anything I put my finger to my lips in a shushing gesture, banging my chin with the gun. He looked at me, nodded, and glanced away. Manning, meanwhile, was concentrating on unlocking the shackles, his back still to me.

Let's be clear about this. If it weren't for the uncertainty of the porthole glass being bulletproof, I would have shot Manning in the back then and there. Save nobility for the movies. I wanted to rescue the kid and get off a boat heading into a hurricane. However, it was within the realm of possibility the windows were bulletproof and I didn't want the shot to ricochet back at me.

So hugging the wall, I crept around to the sliding door of the lower passageway. My hope was to enter quietly, but I got over that notion real quick. First, the door wouldn't budge. Probably locked from the inside. Second, even if I got in, I would only be in the passageway. What was I going to do, knock on the stateroom door and wait for Manning to say come in?

Just as I was going over this in my mind, the door to the stateroom burst open. I pulled back and Manning came out, dragging Reed behind him and hauling him to the inside stairs – or whatever the hell it's called on a boat – and up to the top deck and pilothouse. I turned to the outside stairs and snuck up as quietly as possible until I got about half way. Thank God for the Jelly's. Not only were they noiseless, they gripped the slick surfaces like nobody's business. I'm going to buy stock in these things.

I glanced out over what I could see of the horizon. No land in sight, just ugly, mean water. The waves were becoming more frequent and intense now that we were in the Gulf of Mexico. The boat dipped and crested on larger waves, the wind and rain bit at me from every angle. There was a sudden lurch. I lost my balance, banging my knee against one of the metal steps, and made a grab for the guardrail.

I heard the door of the pilothouse slam open. Manning's voice bellowed out over the wind and water, in a taunting, singsong tone.

"All right, Ms. Alvarez. Come out, come out wherever you are. I know you're here. I was radioed by the captain of the tugboat that someone was on my platform. I can't think of anybody else who would want to stow away on a boat heading into a hurricane."

Between the storm and the hood, I couldn't make out every single word, but heard enough to cause me to freeze in place. I released the safety on Lady Blue, still in my left hand. There was a moment of silence. I reached back and touched the Smith and Wesson inside the pouch with my right. I wasn't sure what I was going to do, but I had two guns. I had two chances to get this right. I heard Manning's booming voice again, this time over every other sound.

"I'm going to count to three, Ms Alvarez, and then I'm going to shoot the boy."

I heard Reed let out a cry and struggle briefly.

"Now I'd hoped to have him along during the journey for some amusement on those long, boring nights, but I *am* willing to kill him now if necessary." He paused. "One," he stretched out the word. "Two…"

I stood and hurled myself up to the top of steps, extending my left arm full out, gun in hand, bracing myself against a wall. The barrel aimed at his forehead, I took a wide stance on the deck in my purple plastic Jelly's. I was as ready as I would ever be.

Manning looked at me with amusement and surprise. "Why, very good, Ms. Alvarez."

He turned his gun away from Reed's head and pointed it toward me. Reed squealed and tried to pull away. Manning had him in a vise-like grip and didn't even bother to look down at the struggling boy.

We stood there, no more than eight feet from one another, guns aimed at one another's forehead, trying to keep our footing in the rolling and pitching boat. But there was no way either of us could miss from this distance. My only solace was that if I went, I would be taking Manning out with me.

"I wasn't sure if you would come prepared," he shouted. "I would have hated to shoot an unarmed woman."

"You didn't seem to have any trouble shooting Felicity Llewellyn," I shouted back over the fury of the storm. My left hand held my Detective Special, but my right hand touched the pouch behind me.

I saw Manning lose his cool for the first time.

"That bitch! I'm glad she's dead. That stupid bitch. Deliberately gave Pammy an overdose. She killed my little girl. And bragged about it. I was only screwing her as part of the deal. Llewellyn had big, rich contacts. She made a lot of money from what we were doing, too. That bitch thought if my wife was out of the picture, I would take her away with me. As if."

———————————————————

He let out a sardonic laugh that forced the rushing winds to recede in my ears, it was that ominous. Then his lower lip quivered.

"My wife called me as Llewellyn was shooting her up. By the time I got home, the bitch was gone and Pammy was dead. Pammy meant everything to me. I loved that little girl."

He looked away for a split second, fighting for control of himself. I made a slight move forward, but he straightened up. This time he returned the gun to Reed's head.

"Drop the gun, Ms. Alvarez, or I'll kill the boy. I swear. Right here and now." I hesitated. "Do it!" He screamed, tapping the side of Reed's head with the gun.

Reed let out a small cry lost in the storm. Horror written all over his face, he stood stock still, just staring at me.

I lowered the gun, my mind racing. I released it from my hand. The top aft deck had an only two thin guard lines protecting me from the elements and water, fathoms deep.

The boat lurched. A big wave had hit across the right side. Water washed across the forward deck. I fought to stay steady. I felt the cold, wet currents wrap around my ankles almost like a living thing, pulling and pushing at me.

The sluicing water was powerful enough to take Lady Blue, slide it across the deck, and drop it into the water.

I didn't hear or see it happen, but I knew it did. My eyes never left Manning.

I was like a golfer I once knew who credited her success on the green to never losing sight of where the ball had to ultimately wind up. Practice your swing, she'd say, learn to do everything right, but when the time comes, forget it all and focus only on the hole in one. Manning was my hole in one.

The SOB gave another sardonic laugh and swung his gun around on me again. If I could get mine out of the pouch before he shot me dead, maybe I could save Reed and me. Or maybe I couldn't. At least, I had to try.

But you got to hand it to kids. They are one inventive, resilient lot. Instead of struggling to pull free, Reed took advantage of another lurch, and shoved hard against Manning, throwing him off balance.

That was the split second I needed. I made a grab for the Smith and Wesson. Never taking my eyes off the center of his forehead, I whipped my arm around, locked my elbow, and fired exactly at the same instant he did.

It was a Zen moment for me. I didn't feel the bucking of the boat, the wind, the rain, or the bullet piercing my left arm. All I was aware of was the small, dark red circle suddenly appearing in the middle of Manning's forehead, the look of surprise on his face.

As fast as all that went, what followed seemed to happen in slow motion. The impact from the bullet threw Manning's head back making his body arch, almost like he was an acrobat going into a back bend. The boat did the rest. Once again, a large wave struck the right side, putting the boat at a dangerous slant. On dead feet, Manning stumbled backward. Still with a vise-like grip on Reed's small, thin arm, Manning hit the railing and started going over, pulling the child with him.

I was also thrown against the railing, my left arm not working to help me hang on to it. I dropped the gun, which slid into the drink just like Lady Blue had. My right hand now free, I made a lunge for Reed.

Chapter Twenty-seven
Being a Hero Is Not All It's Cracked Up To Be

Just in time, I got a hold on Reed's t-shirt, then grabbed him by the neck. Throwing myself down on the deck and against the railing, I yanked Reed down with me, trying to counter the weight of a dead man pulling in the other direction.

Manning's body tottered on the thin rail. For a moment, I thought all three of us might go overboard. I managed to wrench Reed free, and the man fell into the swirling, never-ending waters of the Gulf.

The boat rocked and shuddered. Reed and I clung to each other, struggling with the terror of it all. Finally Reed looked up at me, features distorted with fear and shock. I couldn't tell where the rain began on his face or the tears ended.

"He was going to shoot me! And he tried to take me over the side with him. He was going to kill me!"

The timbre of Reed's voice replicated the howling of the wind, growing in intensity with each word. I saw his small body shake in waves and realized it was probably him I felt shuddering, as well as the boat.

"Reed," I shouted over the wind. "It's all right now. We're all right now." I wanted to wrap both arms around him but couldn't seem to move my left one. It felt numb except for the burning hot spot below my shoulder and a weakness all over.

Meanwhile the boat battled the waves, while salt-laced wind and water burned our faces. Foam gathered around us and in the corners of the upper deck.

"We're going to die; we're going to die," he cried out, his voice ending in a wail.

"Not if I can help it. But I can't work my arm, so you're going to have to help me do this."

Hyperventilating, he noticed my arm for the first time. "You're shot! You're bleeding! He shot you! Oh, sweet Jesus!" Wailing, he burst into tears.

I grabbed Reed's shoulder with my good arm and shook him then gave him a hug.

"Stop it, Reed. Stop it, please. I need your help right now. This is no time to panic. Stop!"

"I'm scared." He swallowed hard. His whine almost got buried inside his shaking body and the sound of the wind.

"Too bad," I yelled in his face. "We don't have time for it. This eff-ing boat is heading right for a hurricane. Maybe we're already in it. We need to get inside the pilothouse."

It was taking a lot of effort to try to calm the boy. And all I really wanted to do was lie down. On a bed. In a dry room. With my cat and a martini. I also felt a little nauseated. Maybe it was the constant motion of the boat. Maybe it was being shot for the first time in my life; there was that.

If the kid was going to be a liability instead of a helpmate, we were in serious trouble. Well, *more* serious trouble. And I was fresh out of ideas.

"Reed. I'm scared, too. And I'm wounded. You have to help me save us. We need to do this together."

I looked at him and he looked at me. Reed hesitated then nodded. I could see a boy entering manhood.

"Now help me up." I bent my left arm at the elbow and held it close to my body. It didn't make it feel any better, but I felt more protected. It was hard trying to balance my body like that. Dizzy, I leaned against the railing and couldn't quite stand.

"Come on." He stood straight up but was thrown against the railing by a shift in the boat. That didn't deter him. He reached down and starting pulling on my good arm. "Come on, Lee. We need to take care of that arm."

When the kid took charge, he didn't mess around. I was fine with it, though, and struggled to get up, fighting weakness as much as the elements. Reed wrapped his arm around my waist and together we labored to get inside the pilothouse. Once we closed the port side door, the noise of the storm was softened but that didn't make it any better.

I looked out at the unobstructed view through the panoramic windows into a world of green-grey nastiness. We were being battered from all sides by an astounding power. I'd never seen anything like it before. And I've never felt so small and helpless.

Compared to the outside catastrophe, the cabin looked calm and serene, windshield wipers beating a steady rhythm on the windows. In front of two high-backed, brown leather chairs bolted into the floor, four huge monitors sat mounted atop the control console. Each monitor showed the churning waters we were plowing through from the front, back, and at either side. The view wasn't good in any of them.

Directly in front of one of the pilot chairs was an old-fashioned pirate's wheel. Out of place in the era of high-tech bells and whistles, it looked like one more thing on a megalomaniac's wish list.

Reed and I struggled against the pitching of the boat and made our way to the console. Dripping blood, I leaned against the captain's chair. I studied the dozens of dials and paraphernalia, colored lights blinking malevolently at me. I was horrified. It was like being on the bridge of the Enterprise in a Star Trek movie, but scarier, because there wasn't one Starfleet officer in sight.

"Help me off with this." I indicated the hood of the wetsuit. "It's giving me a headache."

I unzipped the wetsuit a few inches, bent over, and tugged at the hood. Reed grabbed both ends of it and ripped it off my head. I tore the rubber band out of my hair. Dry, but in masses of curls, it sprung free like a jack-in-the-box.

"Ah, so much better."

I shook my head, causing dizziness to strike again.

After opening and closing my eyes, I looked down at the console, determined not to let it overwhelm me. After all, I am a professional. Right.

"Reed, I'm thinking that Manning put the boat on automatic pilot before he left this cabin and it's probably still on it."

"Yes, ma'am. I saw him punch something over here before he dragged me out on the deck."

"Good. Moving right along, I'm hoping you know something about electronics, 'cause I sure don't."

"I have an IPad, but it's at home."

"Any resemblance?"

"No ma'am."

"Okay, let's can the 'yes ma'am, no ma'am' stuff. Just call me Lee. Think you can find the radio in all this mess?"

"Is that it up there, Lee? Looks like there's two of them."

Reed pointed to two rectangular boxes screwed overhead in a shelf below the ceiling, one above each chair. The radio over the pirate's wheel was on, a yellow screen flashing the number sixteen. Now that I concentrated on it, I heard the murmur of static and some kind of squawking. A microphone on a coiled wire was hooked to one side.

I snatched at the mic, just as I noticed a tall wall of water coming right at us. The boat was bow down, going into the valley of a smaller swell. The oncoming wave was twice the height of the boat, traveling like a son of a bitch, and looked about as solid as a brick wall.

"Hang on!"

Those two words were all I managed to get out before wave and boat collided head on. I was thrown into the captain's chair. Reed was tossed to the floor. The entire boat shook like a six-point-oh earthquake, and a cacophony of creaking wood surrounded us, the boat protesting the assault. Although the furniture was bolted down, pillows, charts, pencils, a baseball cap, anything not secured, flew around the room.

There was the deafening sound of water breaking overhead and smashing against the windows. The lights sputtered for an instant and then darkness enveloped us. We were inside the wave.

The boat shot out almost at a forty-five degree angle but leveled off, crashing down onto the ocean's surface with a loud splat, like a boulder being thrown into somebody's pool. The lights flickered back on and a motor kicked in beneath us, thudding and pounding. A new panel light showed up, flashing the words 'Bilge Pump Activation' in bright red. Okay, this just might be the time to panic.

"Reed! Reed!" I swiveled the chair around and saw him lying near the port side door. The impact had caused him to slide across the room. "Are you okay?"

"I'm okay." To my relief, his voice sounded stronger than I thought it would.

He struggled to sit up and shook his body like a small dog. Reed used the wet bar at the back bulkhead of the pilothouse to pull himself to his feet.

"You better come and sit in the other chair. It might be safer."

My voice gave out on the last few words. I was feeling strangely weak and otherworldly. I looked down at the blood dripping to the floor and decided to ignore it. I depressed the button on the side of the microphone that was clutched in my good hand.

"Mayday, Mayday, Mayday. Or whatever you say at a time like this. Help! Help. We need help."

"Oh, sweet Jesus." Reed's face drained of color, as he pointed to the never-ending spastic ocean in front of us. "There's another one coming."

His voice no longer carried terror or fear, but something akin to awe. I swiveled around following the direction of his stiff, frozen hand.

We both stared out. The rain and wind was hitting from every side now, and under us the gulf swelled and peaked, in ever-undulating mountains of grey-green and frothy white.

Everything seemed even more ominous, darker, and bigger. I concentrated on the moving ridge coming at us.

"Not so big, not so big. But hang on, anyway."

We both grabbed at the helm to brace ourselves. The bow disappeared for a moment inside the swell, but resurfaced just as fast. The wave was only half the size of the preceding one, maybe twenty feet or so. Was I becoming blasé? The radio came to life above my head. We both looked at it.

"This is the United States Coast Guard, Houma, Louisiana. How may we assist you? Over." The voice was male, sounding young, professional, and unemotional.

"The Coast Guard!" I almost kissed the microphone. "Help!"

"Please state the nature of your emergency. Over," he said. He sounded like a waiter at Denny's taking a breakfast order.

"The 'nature of my emergency'? How about I've been shot, I'm with a child who was kidnapped, we're in the middle of a hurricane, and the only person who knew how to drive this tub fell overboard several miles back. You do the math."

"Understood, Ma'am."

Out of the corner of my eye, I saw Reed stand and return to the bar near aft back. "Where are you going?"

"Lee, you're bleeding all over the floor." The kid, feet spread out for balance, waddled to the back bar, while he shouted over his shoulder. "We have to stop it. I think there's an emergency kit under the bar. I thought I saw him take something from there yesterday."

"Ma'am, what is the name of your vessel and your location? Over." The unseen voice floated out into the pilothouse.

I turned back to the radio still feeling a little woozy. The fury of the storm, static, and how I felt blocked out some his words to me.

"Say again."

"State the name of your vessel and the location. Over."

"The name? Ah…*Laura's Folly*. Location? Somewhere in the Gulf of Mexico. We want off!"

"I understand the name of your vessel is *Laura's Folly*. Are you taking on water? Is the engine operational?"

"I wouldn't know any of that. I've been too busy being shot. I need medical attention right away. Get. Us. Off. This. Tub."

"*Laura's Folly*, are you saying you need to abandon ship? Over." Said like, do you want fries with that?

"One of us is not listening."

"I repeat, *Laura's Folly*, are you abandoning ship? Over."

"Yes," I bellowed. "We took a vote. We are abandoning ship."

Reed returned with a good-sized emergency kit. He set it on the helm and opened it up, digging through the contents in between fighting to stay on his feet.

Another swell, maybe not as high as the last one but clear as glass came at us. For just a split second, I thought I saw the body of Manning suspended in it, arms and legs akimbo, but his eyes looking directly at me, red bullet hole prominent between them. I let out a small scream, the hand clutching the mic pointing at the oncoming wave.

"Do you see him?" My voice came out strangled, not sounding like mine at all. "He's right there."

"Who?" Reed looked out the windshield.

Manning was gone in a flash.

"You must have. He…he was there."

There's nobody out there. And I was looking right where you pointed."

The swell hit. It took us up into the stratosphere, and held us there for a second. We fell back onto the ocean with a thud. Reed clutched onto the armrest of my chair then proceeded to take out gauze and wrap it around my arm. I looked up at his face. He'd seen nothing. Maybe I hadn't either.

I broke out into a cold sweat, heart racing. With all that was going on, I hadn't had time to think about the fact I'd just killed a man, but maybe my subconscious knew it only too well. The radio voice came alive again.

"Please give us the coordinates of the vessel and number of persons aboard. Over."

I fought the pain in my arm and in my mind. I got control, finally.

"Two. Two persons. A boy and myself. And you need to save us or we're over. Over."

"Understood. Please state coordinates of *Laura's Folly*. Over."

"Ahhhh…" I looked at the flashing dials on the console. "Where the hell would I find those?"

I heard loud static and thought the radio had gone kaflooie. Then there was silence. Just as I was about to panic, I heard the voice again.

"*Laura's Folly*, this is the United States Coast Guard, Houma, Louisiana. *Laura's Folly*, do you copy?"

"Yes, yes," I said.

"We are receiving a message from the United States Navy Aviation Rescue Swimmers. We will patch them through. Over."

Who or what was United States Navy Aviation Rescue Swimmers? A few more squawkings. Then I heard a distorted voice slightly familiar to me, but detached and formal.

"*Laura's Folly*, do you read me? This is Commander Gurn Hanson of the United States Naval Reserves aboard the *HSM Nine Nine*. Over."

"Gurn, this is Lee." My voice cracked in the middle of saying his name. "Where are you?"

"I'm on a helicopter, babe. The AIRR is coming to get you."

"I don't know what AIRR is and I don't care. Just come get us."

"We're on our way. What's this I hear that you've been shot? Are you all right?" His voice changed, love and worry shading his tone, as sure as if he was standing beside me. Only he wasn't. Time to put on my big girl panties.

"It's just a flesh wound."

It was almost a casual statement, like it happened to me all the time. I didn't mention that I was bleeding all over everything and had bouts of dizziness. Or that I'd killed Manning, sent him to Davy Jones' Locker, but moments ago King Neptune tossed him back at me. Or maybe he didn't. Time for all that later.

"It didn't hit near any major veins or arteries. Reed is fixing me up. Over."

Gurn let out the breath he'd probably been holding inside since he'd heard. His voice returned to being more official.

"Good, good. *Laura's Folly*, we are commencing an air rescue mission and should rendezvous with you within twenty, twenty-five minutes. Over."

"You are? But I don't know where we are." I wailed then caught myself. "Listen up, *HSM Pinafore*, how will you find us?"

"We are locked onto coordinates from both the GPS in your phone and the FBI tracking device aboard. We know where you are within forty feet. Over." More squawking and a faint exchange of voices. "Is the auto-pilot on?"

"You mean, who's steering this thing? Well, it sure isn't me. All I know is we're crashing into waves at about a hundred miles an hour."

"Not possible. Top speed for that boat is fifty-five miles an hour, roughly forty-seven knots."

"Well, it feels like a hundred miles an hour."

"Copy that." I could feel his smile. "Is the boat hitting the waves bow first?"

"Most of the time, yes."

"Are the bilge pumps working?"

"One of these gadgets says they are. Should I believe it?"

"No reason not to; that's their job. You would be alerted to a malfunction. Do you have on life-jackets?"

"Life jackets?" I looked at Reed and we both shook our heads. "No, should we do that? Do you think we're going down?" The panic caused my voice to raise a few decimals. Even Reed began to hyperventilate.

"Life jackets should be worn at all times, Lee, no matter what the conditions. As for *Laura's Folly*, she's a seaworthy craft and can take on weather like this, barring the unknown."

"I hate the unknown."

"This is only a category one hurricane and if you weren't injured, you could probably ride it out."

"Well then, thank God I'm shot. I don't want to ride it out. Whoa!" The last word was in response to going up on a crest and slamming back into the ocean. "This is one crazy ride. Get us out of here!"

"Copy that. I will contact you again in a few minutes. Stand by. Over."

"Where would I go? Hey! Don't leave us." Silence. I turned to Reed. "Okay, you heard the man. We need to find some life jackets. They're the orange, bulky things."

"I saw some under the bar." Reed stood and walked to the back with much more control of his body than I would have had. He returned less than a minute later. He was already slipping his over his head. It was big, but he adjusted it with a few tugs of the ties.

He thrust another inflatable preserver at me. I set down the mic and took it with my good hand. Reed studied me.

"Don't worry. I'll help you into it."

The moment I attempted to straighten my left arm, I saw stars. I tried not to cry out, but Reed must have seen the pain written on my face.

"I'm sorry, Lee, but we have to do this. Nice and easy," he said in a very grown up voice, as he took my left wrist and gently put it through the armhole. I felt sweat dripping down my face and let out a sob masked in a shudder. He wrapped the vest around me and hooked the front of the jacket over my chest. I managed a smile. He returned it.

"Okay," I said. "All nice and legal now." We slapped another large wave head on and I was thrown against the back of the chair. "Next step, how do we tell where we are?"

"Maybe this?" Reed sat in the other chair and pointed to a glowing blue square box to the left.

I stretched forward. Inside the box was a flat drawing of the northern hemisphere laid out behind a white grid. A small blue light was blinking in the Gulf of Mexico. That was probably us.

"Reed, is that showing what I think it's showing?"

"It also shows the longitude and latitude down here." He pointed to a double row of digital numbers, changing in small increments by the second. "We learned about longitude and latitude a couple of weeks ago in school."

I looked at him with astonishment and pride. The radio sprang back to life, complete with static.

"*Laura's Folly*, this is the Navy Aviation Rescue Swimmers. Do you copy? Over."

"Gurn? I mean, Commander Hanson, this is *Laura's Folly*. Over." Maybe I was getting the hang of this. No, I wasn't. Another wave hit us slightly portside and we rocked and rolled for a time. I felt nauseated but fought it down.

"*Laura's Folly*, I need to verify your coordinates. Can you locate the marine chronometer and read me the longitude and latitude? Over."

"Yes, we think we have it." I read from the glowing blue box. "Top row of numbers are twenty-eight point eighty-four, seventy-eight, sixty-two. Next row. Minus eighty-nine point forty-seven, fifty, ninety-eight."

"Roger that. We are confirmed. Next, do you see the autopilot? It should be a black box, looking like a small computer monitor. The word pilot should be written somewhere on it."

"I see it," shouted Reed. He pointed to the autopilot, which if it had been a snake, would have bit me. And considering the day I'd been having, it would have bit me hard.

"We see it," I said, trying to imitate Reed's enthusiasm and sense of adventure. He was starting to have a grand time. I was glad, but on the other hand, we were in the middle of a frigging hurricane in the middle of the frigging ocean. I mean, frigging good gawd.

"Are there any numbers in that box? Over."

"Yes, it's got a bunch of numbers in it," I said.

"Those are your **predefined reference course**. Read me the numbers one at a time."

"Top row, minus, three, three, period, zero, four three, zero, seven, two, five, nine, zero, zero, zero, zero, zero. Bottom row, minus, seven, one, period, six, two, five, two, eight, four, one, seven, zero, zero, zero, zero, zero. What's with all these zeros, anyway?"

"It's somewhere in the Pacific, off the coast of Chile. Your final destination has been set into the auto-pilot and the boat is adjusting to the seas and weather as you go along."

"That's good, right? We don't have to worry about anything except getting rescued. Then *Laura's Folly* can go wherever it wants."

"Not exactly. I need you to change the auto-pilot coordinates so the boat goes directly into the eye of the hurricane."

"Say what?" If you can reel from a sitting position, I did it. "Repeat that, please." I stuttered.

"You're only one nautical mile from the eye now, but you're running parallel to it."

Gurn's voice took on the tone as if he were talking to a child. I was more of a babbling idiot. He went on.

"*Laura's Folly* needs to change course for you to be picked up in the eye of the hurricane. There will be no rain or wind in the eye. It will be a safer rescue all around, especially with your injury."

"I don't like the sound of this," I interjected.

"You will have to take it off of autopilot before you put in the new coordinates. Also, when you come into the eye, you will have to decrease your speed. We don't want you to stall but we do need you to decrease your speed. That will keep you in the eye for the longest amount of time possible. I'll tell you what to do, but don't touch anything else on the console. Do you copy?"

"Holy shit."

"I repeat, do you copy?"

Reed leaned in and spoke into the mic. "We copy."

"Copy, copy," I added.

"Good. Here are the new coordinates. Do you have pen and paper?"

"Yes," Reed said, reaching up and pulling down a pencil from a clip. He ripped a small sheet of paper from a holder beside it.

Gurn said the coordinates twice, while Reed wrote them down. I read them back to Gurn and once it was decided we had the same numbers, the time came for us to disengage the autopilot.

"Before we do that, let's throttle back. Reed, do you see two side-by-side levers? They should be right near the wheel."

"Yes, sir."

I looked over at a kid who was a little scared but having the time of his life. He came to the other side of me, reaching both hands out over the gears.

"You'd better share this chair with me, Reed. Keep you from falling over," I said, scrunching to the left of the seat. Reed is a skinny kid, so he managed to get his bum in beside mine.

"Let me know when you're ready." Gurn's voice was loud but comforting at the same time.

"I think we're ready," I said.

"Ready, sir," Reed said.

"Good. Reed, I want you to pull both levers at the same time - and keep them even – and stop in the center. Then read me your speed. It should decrease as you pull back."

Reed wrapped his small hands around the throttle levers and pulled them about half way toward him. I felt the boat slow down, just as we got slammed with a wave.

"Yes, sir. We're at twelve knots, sir."

"Just a minute." A rustling sound came over the mic then static and voices in the background. We waited for a full thirty-seconds before Gurn's voice came back on air, pressing and filled with alarm. "*HSM Nine Nine….Laura's Folly*, do….copy?"

"Yes, yes." I panicked then shouted. "But I'm losing every other word."

We heard static going in and out along with a soft screeching sound.

"*Laura's Folly, Laura's Folly*, do you read….? I'm trying another frequency." Static almost covered his voice, but I could still hear the urgency in it. "Can you read me?"

"We do, but there's a lot of static. What's going on?"

"Lee, Richard just contacted me. They've deciphered most of the documents and…" The rest was lost to static. A few words came through. "found….not just….but the email list shows…."

"What? Say again. I didn't understand what you said. The email list?"

Static. "I said…" More static. "….name is there."

"Who? Who's name? I didn't get it. Over."

"I expect that would be my name, Miss Alvarez, they found on the email list." Delphine Robochaux's rich, contralto voice filled the air, less jazzy now and far more lethal. "We were careful about keeping my name off the documents, but Manning did email me from time to time."

Chapter Twenty-eight
Changing Players

I rose and wheeled around to face Felicity Llewellyn's housekeeper standing at the top of the stairs coming into the pilothouse from below deck. Her trim, athletic figure was wearing a one-piece, navy blue bathing suit. Hair and body dripping, she aimed her rather impressive gun at me. I kept my right thumb on the mic's talk button. Whatever happened, I wanted the boys in the helicopter to hear every word. I looked at her and tried to do a curled lip similar to Elvis Presley's smirk.

"I had a feeling you were too good to be true, all that To The Manor Born stuff."

She bowed her head, with a little smile. "I try to be a valuable and conscientious servant."

"How did you get onboard?"

"Who's voice is that?" Gurn's tone held command, but he was clearly thrown. "It sounds like Delphine."

"Yes, it is. I'm wondering how she got here." I raised an eyebrow in Delphine's direction.

"As you can see, you're not the only one who can swim out to a boat, Ms. Alvarez. I got on forward. There's a handy little ladder there. I've been following you most of the day, my pet. I knew I could count on you to lead me to Manning. I'd lost him in all the ruckus or rather, he deliberately lost me. Fortunately, I always have my bathing suit in the back of my car, so when I watched you buy the wetsuit at the marina, I knew what you were up to.

Manning was trying to make a run for it, leave me holding the bag. He shouldn't have done that. It made me angry."

"Delphine Robochaux, your resistance is futile." Gurn's voice was firm and unemotional. "We have evidence of your participation in a --"

"Shut him up," Delphine demanded.

I raised the mic to my mouth. "She insists you shut up, Gurn. And as she's pointing a gun at Reed and me, I'd appreciate you doing what she says." I turned back to Delphine. "If you've been on the boat the whole time, what took you so long to show yourself?"

"There was nothing for me to do but come out now. I usually have a backup plan, but regarding you and the boy, it took me awhile to come up with something. Should I kill you? Or leave you alive as my hostages? As long as the boat was on autopilot, heading for Chili, I stayed in the shadows. But now your rescue has ruined everything."

"Working for Felicity Llewellyn was your cover. You were Manning's silent partner."

It wasn't a question on my part, but a statement. She shook her head slowly, a grin crossing her face. I felt Reed shudder, as he leaned into me. My new nemesis went on.

"Not his partner, his boss. I'm the second in command of the entire operations. Manning worked for me, took orders from me. Although it was his idea to plant the voodoo doll in your brother's car."

"Nice touch."

"We thought so." She laughed heartily.

"You're going to be laughing out of the other side of your face when you find out you've been blown," I said. "Manning was turning State's evidence before a Grand Jury day after tomorrow. Then he decided to screw the both of you and make a run for it."

Delphine thought for a moment, eyebrows furrowed. "Ah! We knew there was a leak somewhere."

"I liked you better when you were a housekeeper."

She threw her head back and let out another laugh, this time straight out of a bad horror movie.

"Those days are over, thanks to Manning and Llewellyn. I have a fortune waiting in a place where the law can never touch me, once I get there. Felicity Llewellyn," She repeated the name with a scoff. "It was a pleasure to be rid of her."

"So it was you who killed her. Manning did look a little surprised when I told him about her being dead." I mused for a moment. "I thought her death a little cold-blooded, even for a lowlife like him. His were crimes of passion. Yours, more thought out."

"Thank you. I pride myself on planning things well, as a rule. Yesterday I told her he'd phoned and needed to see her right away at Colbert's Motors. I didn't want to kill her at her home. It tied in too closely to me. The bunker seemed ideal. When I met her there instead of him, she was shocked. The idiot actually thought she and Manning were in a legitimate business together, making all that money through second mortgages. Not that she really cared, as long as she got laid. But her lust for him had gotten out of hand."

"I can see that. She should have never given Manning's wife an overdose thinking she might have him all to herself. Attracts too much attention," I said.

"Exactly, so I took care of her. I didn't think her body would be found for several weeks, but your finding her like that changed my plans for a leisurely departure for places unknown."

"The best laid plans of mice and men."

"Yes, I'm in the position of having to improvise now. I followed you here to take care of Manning. I didn't see you shoot him, but I saw him fall overboard from the deck below. Thank you for getting rid of him for me. Of course, there's the next order of business. That would be getting from here to my island. And that's where you two are going to help me."

I raised my eyebrows in surprise.

"Fat chance," I said. "I'm only going to help you into a jail cell."

"Cocky like all the rest of the Alvarez. But you aren't unintelligent, I'll give you that. I've learned a lot about your family by listening in on your conversations. Of course, Lila stopped revealing anything day before yesterday. I think your bitch of a mother suspected the house was bugged."

"Hey! Don't you be calling my mother a bitch." *That's my job.*

"Delphine, what makes you think you can get away with this?" Gurn's strong voice sliced through the air like a knife. I had almost forgotten about him, but I'd kept my thumb on the button, so he heard every word. He went on with great authority. "We're listening to every word you say. If you give yourself up now, we can work out some sort of deal. You can turn state's evidence. I'm authorized to offer you the same deal given Manning. Or --"

"Shut up, Mr. Hanson. Here's what's actually going to happen. You are going to back the chopper off and let me take this boat to Chile or I'm going to kill this woman and boy right here, right now. You understand me, Mr. Hanson?"

There was a moment of silence, where just the sounds of the wind, rain and water could be heard. I guess Gurn was weighing his options, which were damned few. He finally spoke.

"Very well. We'll do it, as long as you promise not to hurt anyone. Then what?"

Not to be outdone, I put in my two cents. "How do we know you won't kill us once this boat gets to Chile? You already said that was your plan." I put a protective arm around Reed. "That's saying we manage to make it through the other side of this hurricane."

"This is only a category one hurricane." Delphine shouted her words to me with another laugh. "I've been through two of them and on a smaller boat than this. As for killing you, that was the original plan, but it's changed. You're worth more to me alive. You'll have to trust me on that."

Something in her eyes told me I could trust her about as far as I could throw *Laura's Folly*.

"If she kills us, she wouldn't have any hostages to use to get away," Reed, who up to now had been silent, said looking at me.

Delphine nodded toward him appreciatively. "Smart boy." Louder she said, addressing the microphone in my hand, "Mr. Hanson, we're going to keep the coordinates of the original settings off the coast of Chile. We three aboard are going to go there on this boat. Once there, I'll be met by friends of mine with a waiting seaplane. I'll fly to my small island, where the United States has no extradition rights whatsoever."

"You own an island?" I was stunned.

"The kind of money I make can buy you a lot of real estate in this economically challenged world of ours, Ms. Alvarez. As I said, once I get to my island, Commander, my friends will give you the lady and the boy back, unharmed. How's that?"

"Well, that's good enough for me." I leaned back and rested the wrist of the hand holding the mic against the throttles. "Oh, my arm," I said aloud, feigning weakness. Not much of a feign, really. I leaned into Reed who was hovering by my side. "Hold on to something," I whispered. He was surprised, but gave me an imperceptible nod.

I let go of the mic and pushed the throttles forward to the max with one quick thrust. I could barely grab the lip of the station with my good hand, and brace my left leg against the seat of the chair, before the boat leapt ahead like a jackrabbit being chased by a hungry fox. Reed held on, but was jerked to the full extension of his arms.

The frontward momentum threw Delphine backwards. Arms flailing in the air, she instinctively searched for balance and stability. Her body slammed against the starboard door, knocking the wind out of her. The gun went off somewhere in the ceiling with a shocking report.

Before she could regain herself, I ran to her then pivoted around. Aiming the heel of my little purple jelly shoe at her knee, I kicked as hard as I could. There was a sickening crunch, cartilage doing something bad.

In a protective gesture, Delphine bent over toward her knee, just enough for me to reach up and twist the gun out of her grasp with my good hand. I clipped her one behind the ear with the butt of it. Hard. She went down like a rock.

Shaking, I leaned against the sidebar breathing hard, having expended more energy than I had to give. I held on for dear life, as the boat raced to God-knows-where at what felt like the speed of light. Maybe Antarctica?

"Reed! Reed, throttle back to under a hundred miles an hour, would you?"

I looked over at the boy still frozen in place. At my words he turned around and grabbed the throttles, the noise in the pilot room taking a decided nosedive as the speed of the craft lessened. Only then could I hear Gurn's voice yelling over the radio.

"What's going on? Report back! Report back. Over."

I wobbled toward the front of the pilothouse and fell into the pilot's chair. "I need to sit down. I really do. Reed, grab that rope over there. Think you can tie her hands and feet, while I watch?"

"I won two prizes for naval knots in Boy Scouts. I'm on this like white on rice."

I had to laugh. He ran over to the wall, retrieved a coiled rope, and managed to roll the unconscious woman over on her stomach. Then he tied her hands and feet together faster than I've seen a cowboy tie a doggy at a rodeo, impeded very little by the storm. If I'd had a sign with the number ten written on it, I would have held it up.

"*Laura's Folly*! Do you copy? Answer me." Gurn's voice sounded frantic.

I grabbed the mic, depressed the talk button, and spoke into it. "Sorry for the delay in responding, *R.P.M. Lusitania*, or whatever. We've captured Delphine Robochaux and we're trussing her up like a Thanksgiving turkey. You can come get her along with us. Nobody's hurt except her. She may be walking with a cane for a few months."

"Good, good," Gurn said, expelling air into his microphone. He quickly went on, "Lee, how are you doing? Over."

"I'd like to get out of these wet clothes and into a dry martini. Ow!" The boat rolled from side to side and my bad arm struck the back of the leather chair. My jaw hurt from being clenched so tightly, but not as much as my arm. Nothing had ever hurt as much as my arm.

"I'm glad to see your sense of humor is intact." Gurn's tone changed back to official. "Let's take care of this autopilot problem now. Are you ready? Over."

"Yeah, ready. Let's do it."

"Depress the autopilot by holding it in to the count of three. That will shut if off. Tell me when you've done that."

I did and the light changed from blue to green around the autopilot.

"It's off."

"Reed, you still there, son?"

Reed came back to the console and leaned over the mic. "Yes, sir."

"What is your speed?"

"It's between ten and twelve knots, sir."

"Good. Put your hands on the wheel and keep it steady until we can put the autopilot back on. Think you can do that? Over."

"Yes, sir." Reed grabbed the wheel like he had done it all his life.

"Okay, I don't want to scare either of you, but we need to get this done as soon as possible and put it back onto autopilot. Lee, there should be an icon for a keyboard somewhere beneath the screen."

"Yes, there is."

"Press that and tell me if a small keyboard comes up on the computer screen."

"Yes."

"Good. One line should say the word longitude and below it, latitude."

"Yes, both lines are there."

"Start putting the numbers in. Just be sure to put in the plusses, minuses, and periods exactly where they should be. Say everything out loud to me as you put them in. Over."

We got hit portside by a powerful wave and it took me two tries to get the numbers in correctly. I was having bouts of uncontrollable shaking coming at me faster and faster, while Reed fought to control the wheel. But finally, we managed to boot up the autopilot again.

"Mission accomplished." I slid back in the chair, exhausted. "We're getting hit from the portside now as well as the front. Is that bad?" I pulled at Reed's arm and he sat beside me.

"The boat has slightly altered direction, but you'll be coming into the waves at an angle, so there shouldn't be a problem."

"Glad to hear it. So are we done?"

"Not quite," said Gurn, his authoritative voice filled with regret. "Reed, my man, you still there?"

"Yes, sir."

"You should be in the eye of the hurricane in less than ten minutes. It will be calm. At that time, you are to pull back the throttles to five knots, no more, no less. That will keep you in the eye for as long a time as possible and prevent stalling. The helicopter should arrive approximately five minutes later and we will execute the rescue at that time. Do you copy?"

"Yes, sir."

"Good. As soon as you are locked into five knots, go out to the foredeck and await our arrival. Understood?"

"Understood," Reed and I said in unison.

"Reed." Gurn's voice hesitated. "Reed, take care of Ms. Alvarez."

"I will, sir."

"Then over and out."

"You don't look so good, Lee." Reed said after a moment, looking into my face. "And I have to take care of you."

"Don't worry about it. You're doing a fine job," I said through chattering teeth. "I'm just a little cold."

"I'll warm you up."

He wrapped a thin arm around me and leaned into my chest. I gave him a hug.

"Mama Biggs sent me, you know. She loves you and she's sorry she slapped you."

He looked up at me with a faint smile and nodded.

"I shouldn't have run away like that. I wanted to show her I could be a detective, so I rode my bike to old Colbert's place to look for clues. When I got there, that man was coming out of the front of the building. He grabbed me and said 'You'll do' or something like that."

"Did either of you go around to the back, where the boat trailer was?"

"No, he grabbed me in front. I tried to fight him off, but he put me in his car and brought me to this boat."

"Did he...hurt you, Reed?'

Reed shook his head. "He hit me once, but then he locked me up in the room below. I didn't see him again until you came."

I never felt such relief in my life. We rode toward the eye of the hurricane holding onto one another.

Chapter Twenty-nine
You Gotta Be A Trouper

Silence engulfed me and brought me out of a coma-like sleep. Were my ears plugged up? One moment a cacophony of sounds, vibrations, and wild nature assaults you, takes over your life, and then suddenly, nothing. No rain, no wind. Even the waters, while still choppy, were much calmer.

"Reed! Look out there!"

He, too, was looking around him, eyes wide in disbelief. "Man, this is weird. I've never been in the eye of a hurricane before. What's that yellow glow?"

"I think it's sunshine."

We heard movement behind us and both turned to see the housekeeper struggling against her bonds.

"She don't need to bother, you know," Reed whispered to me. "She'll never be free. I know what I'm doing."

"I'll bet you do," I whispered back. "But let's hope she doesn't untie those ropes, Reed," I said loud enough for Delphine to hear. "Because I'll have to shoot her if she does."

"Now surely, Miss Alvarez, you and I can come to some mutually beneficial terms." Delphine's dulcet tones never sounded more charming or seductive, although I could hear a wince of pain due to her swollen knee. "We can work together, you and I. I can pay you a lot of money if you'll only --"

"Not going to happen, sweetie," I interrupted her. "I've seen what you do to your co-workers."

She persisted. "That doesn't have to be the way it goes. I'm sure you and I --"

"Reed," I interrupted her again, while looking at the boy. "Are you wearing any socks?"

"Socks? Yes ma'am." Reed looked at me, puzzled.

"Good. I want you to take one off so I can stuff it in her mouth for some peace and quiet."

"I been wearing them for two days," he said in a dead serious tone of voice.

"You hear that, Delphine?" I looked behind him at the woman lying on the floor. "You've been warned, so shut up." She did.

The mic was still clasped in my good hand and I raised it to my mouth, depressing the key. "Hello, HMS....ah....oh, who cares? Are you there? We're finally in the eye." My words were drawn out, almost lazy. I'd tried to speak faster, but I couldn't seem to.

"We'll be there, *Laura's Folly*, in less than five minutes."

In the distance, I heard the beat-beat of chopper blades. Gurn went on.

"Throttle back to five knots then proceed to the foredeck. Repeat, proceed to the foredeck. Do you copy?"

"Yes, sir," said Reed, taking the mic from me. He pulled back on the throttles. "We're at five knots, sir."

"We see you. The *HSM Nine Nine* is almost upon you. Over and out." Gurn said.

"Let's go, kiddo." I tried to lift myself out of the chair, but was having difficulty standing.

"What about me?" Delphine's voice will filled with fear. "You're not going to leave me here, are you?"

"You? Not hardly," I said. "I'm sure there's a big reward for you out there. And someone has to put this child through music school. It may as well be you."

"Come on," Reed said, tugging at me. "Stop talking. We need to get outside. Here, let me help you up."

He grabbed onto my right arm and pulled.

I struggled out of the soft leather and stood, more unsteady than choppy waves would cause.

I leaned on the kid against my will, but he was stronger than I expected. And I was weaker. Overhead, I heard the sound of a chopper closing in, invading the relative calm. Once we got outside, we both looked up from the deck, and the blast of wind from the blades almost knocked me over. I stumbled and Reed propped me up against outside wall of the pilothouse. I slid down and sat, legs outstretched, head resting on my chest, while he ran to the end of the deck, waving his arms at the chopper. The helicopter lowered itself slowly until it was almost upon us.

I don't remember much after that; I think I passed out. I was roused by the sound of Gurn's voice, bellowing in my ear.

"You got to wake up now, honey. Come on." He shook me a little as he pulled me to my feet. I hardly recognized him. He wore a black wetsuit, with a helmet and goggles covering his head. If it weren't for his voice, I would never have known it was him.

"Reed, where's Reed?"

"He's already onboard. So is our villainess, trussed up just like you said. Reed does a mean knot. Come on, darling, try to stand. Help me out here." He raised me up to a standing position.

"How did you manage to get here? Did you hire the helicopter?"

"Better than that. I have friends in high places. I pulled in the last of my markers from some buddies from the Persian Gulf. And then some." He wrapped a strong arm around my waist. I leaned into him.

"And then some?"

"Let's just say in exchange for their services, I've agreed to name my next cat Rodriguez, Miller, Kowalski, and Littman, or Romikowli for short. But you're worth it." He half lifted, half carried me to a shallow but long metal basket with straps.

"I guess it's a good thing Baba is only a year old."

"Yeah, I'm going to have to take real good care of her."

He laid me down, strapped me in, waved and yelled. I reached up and stroked his cheek. The roar of the helicopter drowned out any more words, but his lopsided smile reassured me all would be okay. The basket rose into the sky. Gurn climbed the rope ladder at the same pace as I did. I felt two people grab the basket and lift me out into the helicopter.

Shortly after, a man took my pulse and temperature. Reed, my little hero, hugged me before he was shifted aside by someone else, this time a woman. She cut away the rubber sleeve of my wetsuit and swabbed at my wounded arm with something that burned like crazy, thank you so much.

Then I saw the face of a man looking vaguely familiar. Fear stabbed through me like a knife. It was the same man who burned the files, the one I chased, and saw leaving Laura's Folly. One of Manning's henchmen! Did the men aboard the *HMS Piddley-Squat* know about him? I pulled back and began to thrash about, trying to free myself. When I found it was useless, I pointed a weak finger at him.

"You, you."

"It's all right Lee," said Gurn, coming out of nowhere. "This is Special Agent Jeremiah Grovner. He's one of the good guys."

"Yes, ma'am. You can call me Jerry."

"But I chased you earlier. Over a wall." By now, my voice was hoarse.

"What?" He couldn't hear me over the drone of the blades, and turned to Gurn standing next to him. I noticed small microphones over each one's mouth.

"She says she chased you over a wall," Gurn said to him.

"Oh! Yes, ma'am. Sorry about that. I wasn't quite sure who you were and couldn't let you catch me. I was undercover. But you gave me a helluva run." He grinned down at me.

"But what were you doing at the marina?" I was confused.

"What?" He tapped his helmet at his ear and shook his head, indicating he couldn't hear me.

"She says she saw you at the marina," Gurn repeated.

Given the constant din, I wished I'd known sign language. Jerry leaned over me and shouted.

"Yes, ma'am. Manning thought I was there to get last minute instructions, but I attached a tracer to the hull of the boat when he wasn't looking. That's when I saw the boy inside the boat. I was going for reinforcements when Manning took off, you with him. I would have tried to save you from going with him, Ms. Alvarez, told you who I was, if I had only seen you."

"Now you tell me."

"What?" He looked from me to Gurn.

"She said…never mind." Gurn shook his head, gave me a quick kiss, and stepped back. He turned to Reed, hovering nearby, and shouted to him. "Come on, son, we need to sit down, and prepare for what's ahead."

They moved away. I heard a deafening roar as the copter lifted into the air, its blades beating an even stronger rhythm.

"What's ahead?" I didn't like the sound of those words. "What does that mean, 'prepare for what's ahead'?"

The two paramedics on either side of me began throwing straps across my body, pulling them tight, and securing them. Even my head was put into a vise-like contraption and I couldn't move it. I had read about the dungeon of the Tower of London, and this seemed to me this was step one of the kingly torture. I guess I struggled, because one of the paramedics put a hand on mine in a reassuring manner, before shouting in my face.

"It's all right, ma'am. We just need to tie you in for the ride ahead."

"Ride ahead?" I whimpered, so I'm not sure he heard my words.

"It'll be a little bumpy, but you'll be fine. Your vitals are good, so you just relax, okay?" He patted my strapped in hand.

"Bumpy?"

"It's nothing to worry about." He smiled into my vise-gripped face. "We have to take a little trip again through the hurricane to get back to New Orleans."

"What? You mean we're going back into the eff-ing hurricane I worked so hard to get out of? Oh, no. Let me off this chopper. Noooooooo!"

Chapter Thirty
Celebrations Are in Order

"Just how many cocktails do I get for a quarter?"

"The ordinary person gets up to three drinks during lunch for twenty-five cents each. You, however, get none." Gurn smiled at me, grey-green eyes sparkling.

"I knew that." I flipped the long fringes of the white embroidered shawl I was wearing in his direction. "Just fanaticizing."

I'd draped the shawl over the left shoulder of the turquoise and lime green silk outfit Mom had given me. The heavier silk of the shawl and the pure white complimented the three-piece turquoise pantsuit, also silk, and hid my slinged arm from sight. I liked that.

Five days after the ordeal of *La Boot*, I was raring to go. I felt marvelous, glad to be alive – which had been questionable there for awhile – and loving the Big Easy. True, I had my left arm in a sling and still hadn't had a Sazerac Cocktail or any other cocktail for that matter. I was half way through taking mega antibiotics. Booze was off the table during the duration, but one must adjust. I can adjust really well, especially when I'm given a gorgeous vintage silk shawl to cover my boo-boo. Gurn is so thoughtful. His mother trained him well.

After being patched up during an overnight stay at the hospital, I was released and told to take it easy. I saw the silver lining at the end of that particular soggy cloud right away.

The family and Gurn spent the next several days knocking themselves out decorating, unpacking, sorting, hiring staff, distributing flyers, and doing a myriad of last minute things getting Vicki's hat shop ready for the grand opening. But under doctor's orders I couldn't participate. Aw, gee.

We no longer had to stay in the safe house, and returned to our luxury digs at the **Mariage Frères Chateau**. I spent the first day lounging by the pool in the company of two leashed but affectionate cats. I had bonbons; they had liver treats. I may have been the one who was shot, but their story was they had suffered, too.

On days two and three, I took rides on the sightseeing buses back in operation after the hurricane. Tour busses are the first to know when a street opens up for business. Fortunately, Harold had done a minimum of damage and most major streets were open within twenty-four hours.

Putting aside that a knowledgeable guide fills your head with local history, facts, and figures, it's a great way to see the Big Easy, while sitting on your duff with your finger in your ear. In that regard, I tried to be very compliant with doctor's orders.

Day four found me sitting on a stool in a corner of The Obsessive Chapeau on opening day. I got to watch the controlled chaos of Vicki's booming business from a catbird seat, once again, with my finger in my ear. There's something to be said for this walking wounded stuff.

The big hit was Vicki's Panama hat line. Made in the classic fedora style, and woven especially for her shop **in the small town of Pilé in Ecuador. The town is considered to make the best** Panama hats **in the world.** They sure cost enough.

Vicki's twist was that hers were woven in pastel colors instead of white. The ice-cream colors dubbed pistachio cream, lemon sun, strawberry swirl, grape froth, and orange crush were softer than soft hues of their namesakes.

The women's hats had wider brims and higher crowns, but every hat was finished off with a black suede band.

At three hundred a pop, I marveled at just how many hats could fly out the door in a single day. Ka-ching, ka-ching.

On the fifth day, Gurn followed me down the hall of the Commodore's Palace to the lectern, behind which stood the host, a good-looking lad in his mid-twenties. I couldn't help but notice the streaks of man-made sun running throughout his thick brunette locks, made even more notable by one of those every strand in place haircuts. Here was not a Supercuts kind of guy.

It reminded me I was long overdue for a conditioning and trim, currently forced to wear my frizz ball in a topknot, this time to hide the split ends. Salt air, seawater, and being shot can be murder on a hair-do.

The host found our name in the computer before him, and handed us off to a young lady dressed in the society matron's ubiquitous uniform i.e. basic black dress, pearls, hose and three-inch black heels. We followed her bouncing ponytail – the only indication she was barely out of her teens - through a large and airy old-fashioned dining room.

Tables were already half-filled with diners, ladies decked out in their finery, and gentlemen in their well-fitted suits. It was like watching a re-run of Mad Men on TV. Or given Lila Hamilton Alvarez's dress code, our own offices at Discretionary Inquiries back home. I felt a sudden rush of homesickness for Palo Alto and everything California. It was time to go home.

I'd read that the Commodore's Palace had once been a private home. Hard to believe. It's almost the size of a palace, although the feel is less formal. Smothered in old-world southern charm, it seems to be an ode to an era gone by.

Ponytail paused for a moment, and stood to one side, letting a large group of well-dressed, older men pass by. We followed her lead. While we waited, a thought occurred to me. I took the opportunity to pull Gurn aside and ask a question on the QT.

"Gurn, you never told me and I keep forgetting to ask, did you ever find out whose gun it was Tugger found under the floorboards?"

He looked around, drew me into a tight corner, keeping his voice low. "Believe it or not, the only person it could have been was Dennis Manning."

"What?"

"Yes, when the Feds were negotiating with him a few months back, they brought him to the safe house for a couple of days until they hammered out a deal. They took him to a firing range once, where they say he used a Smith and Wesson. Why he would stash it under the floorboards is anybody's guess - maybe his idea of protection - but he was an odd man."

I felt the color drain from my face. "You mean, I killed him with his own gun?"

"You had no choice."

"No."

"You did what you had to do."

"Yes."

I thought for a moment. "I would do it again if I had to, but it's hard to live with."

"We all do things that are hard to live with." Gurn gave me a quick hug. "I'm sorry the gun your father gave you went down in the briny deep, but I'm glad you didn't go along with it." He smiled and kissed me on the nose.

"Me, too." I grinned up at him. "You always know how to make me feel better."

"I'll get you a better gun."

"Thanks, but no thanks. I don't want somebody I love to give me anything like that again. It's not good to get sentimental over a weapon the way I did with Lady Blue."

"Just tools of the trade from now on?"

We both laughed.

Ponytail cleared her throat from a short distance away, not wanting to interrupt but indicating the passageway was clear and we should continue our journey.

We followed her through French doors and into a private dining room.

It was a lovely room, light and airy, swathed in sunlight, with a mantled fireplace at one end. Instead of flames, lit candles filled the air with the faint scent of vanilla. The outside wall gave a spectacular view of the gardens through floor-to-ceiling windows.

Below the chandelier, a beautifully decorated round table was set for formal dining. Silverware and porcelain china sparkled at each place setting and a low flower arrangement of lavender and pink flowers – Vicki's business theme colors - was centered on the white damask cloth.

Reading from left to right was the family, Mom, Tío, Richard, and Vicki. Added to the lineup were Reed and Mama Biggs. Mom told me later that after the ordeal of Reed's kidnapping, she'd invited the Biggs to join us, hoping to create happier memories of the Alvarez Family for them. The group was laughing and chatting, half-hidden behind balloons and ribbons.

"Hi, everyone," I said pushing aside a set of pink balloons only to have them snap back and smack me in the face.

Given the plethora of balloons and ribbons, it was little wonder no one saw us enter until I spoke. Surprised, the table turned in our direction and began to applaud. I wasn't sure what was going on. Hadn't I just seen the family the night before?

Then they began to sing, "For She's a Jolly Good Fellow," with Reed leaping up and playing along on his clarinet. After the song, everyone broke into applause again, while I stood there, embarrassed and speechless.

Gurn sat down at one of the two empty chairs, grabbed my right hand, and pulled me into the remaining chair. To my left sat my mother, who beamed at me with rarely given pride.

Dressed in a beige linen sleeveless dress, she managed to make what I purport to be the most boring color in the world work. She always does. Blonde hair sleeked back, she wore her usual pearl button earrings.

Near the top of the collarless dress was a small gold and pearl broach in the design of a fleur-de-lys. Other than her diamond engagement and wedding rings and a gold watch, she wore no other adornments. Mom is from the 'less is more' school of thought, while I am from the 'pile it on, what the hey, you only live once' school of thought.

Two servers came in with opened bottles of champagne and began to fill the fluted glasses in front of nearly everyone. Tío pulled a chilling bottle of sparkling cider from a silver bucket on the table and poured some into the glasses in front of Vicki, Reed, and me.

After the bubbly and apple juice were dispensed, a smiling Vicki stood, looking sensational in that Vogue, yet kooky way of hers. And this is with the addition of her pregnancy bump.

Standing atop her usual platform heels to make up for being only five foot one, she wore a long bias cut sleeveless dress of sewn together earth-tone squares of tie-dyed fabric. Vicki finished the look off with a hand-hammered copper necklace dangling half-way down to her waist, and one of her own beaded berets in soft bronze and orange colors set to one side of her curly, auburn hair. My darling sister-in-law has what the French call *je ne sais quoi*, which roughly translated means, I haven't a clue why that should work but it does.

Vicki lifted her glass of sparkling cider and looked at me.

"'Lee, this toast is to you. A toast to the best --"

She suddenly stopped talking. While the initial words came out strong, she seemed near the point of tears. I wondered why. Yes, we'd found her sister's rapist, but there appeared to be more.

Vicki wiped her face, took a deep breath, and started over again. "A toast to the best sister-in-law a girl could have. It's not many people who would risk their lives for someone else. Lee, I think you know how grateful I am for all you've done for me." She fought for composure. "And for Robin."

Her eyes filled with tears, as did mine. She paused before going on.

"Forgive me, but I have some wonderful, wonderful news about my sister."

Vicki reached down for Richard's hand while she spoke. He held on to hers and looked up adoringly. She swallowed hard and went on.

"As most of you know, for the past nine years, Robin has been unable to speak more than a word or two, if that. Months would go by, sometimes as much as a year, and she wouldn't say anything, just stare out the window. But this morning she spoke a full sentence. Shortly after that, she said even more. The nurses said she had an actual conversation with the doctor. It's like a miracle."

The family's reaction was huge. Gasps of astonishment went around the table, then another round of applause. Reed and Mama Biggs, not knowing much of the history, nonetheless smiled at everyone's joy. Vicki took a deep breath and continued.

"They can't predict how much she will recover, but for the first time, they are hopeful, very hopeful. I don't know if it has anything to do with Dennis Manning truly being dead now, but ever since he did die for real, she seems to have turned around. I'm sure you're thinking this can't be right; it's only a coincidence, but still..."

She broke off and looked down at the table, trying again to recover her emotions. Richard stood and enveloped her in his arms, crooning words I couldn't hear. They held one another fast, rocking back and forth. At that moment, there was no one else in the world but the two of them. It was a beautiful thing to see.

"'There are more things in heaven and earth, Horatio, than are dreamt of in your philosophy'," Mom mumbled, looking out into space. When she realized she'd spoken out loud, and that we were staring at her, she said in explanation, "Hamlet."

"Oh, I read that," Reed said. "Shakespeare, right? One bad-assed dude."

"Reed!"

Mama Biggs' reprimand of him was so strong on the one word, the entire table burst out laughing. Vicki and Richard joined in the laughter and sat down, their private moment finished. After the laughter peaked, Gurn spoke up. The grin I love so much nearly broke his face.

"Well, that's one way of putting it. Shakespeare was one bad-assed dude, for sure."

"But out of deference to the man," Mom said, in her best lady-like manner, "it would be more appropriate to say he was a genius. We can save the expression 'bad-assed dude' for someone like Bruno Mars."

"You know who he is, Mrs. Alvarez?" Reed stared at Mom in admiration. "You are one cool lady."

"Now that, young man, is entirely appropriate." Mom pointed a finger at him with a smile on her face. "But let's continue our toast to my lovely and determined daughter, Liana Margaret Alvarez. To Liana."

Mom lifted her glass in my direction. Everyone followed suit with murmurs and exclamations of 'to Lee' or 'to Liana' with the exception of Reed.

"Who's this Liana Margaret?" No one answered.

I smiled and swallowed down the apple juice. In no way is apple juice a replacement for a good glass of champagne. Just sayin'.

"Speech, speech," yelled out Richard.

"*Si*," Tío, said, applauding again. Everyone took up clapping. Embarrassed, I stood and cleared my throat.

"Well, gosh. Thanks a lot. I have no idea what I should say, other than that's the last time I get on a boat, if I have anything to say about it."

Everyone laughed and I warmed to the subject. I do have the touch of the orator about me, especially with a trapped audience.

"This time I was rescued by Gurn." I turned and looked at him. "Thank you, sweetie."

"My pleasure," he said in a serious tone.

"But before that and not so long ago, I was knocked out and taken aboard a boat off the coast of Princeton-By-The-Sea. That go-round I was rescued by my mother – thank you, Mom - who lost a favorite pair of stilettos in the process. She still mourns the loss of those shoes."

"Liana, I do not *mourn* their loss," Mom said, correcting me. "Although I have *yet* to be able to replace them."

She gave everyone a look that said she was making one of her rare jokes. We all laughed. Rustling occurred and I suspected I was losing my audience, but pressed on, anyway.

"Suffice it to say, water and I don't seem to get along. We may have a short history, but it's a damp one. So it's the terra firma for me from now on. On dry land I seem to be able to take care of myself and I like being self-sufficient. Yes, yes. I know what you're thinking: no man is an island. Or woman, either. Ha ha."

I laughed. No one else did. I looked around at faces that had no idea what I was talking about. I sort of lost track of it, myself. I cleared my throat.

"But please let me say, I only did what had to be done. I'm no hero. As the great poet, Henry Wadsworth Longfellow once said --"

"Yes, yes. *Thank* you, Liana." Mom stood, interrupting me. "You're still recuperating, dear, and we don't want you to use up *all* your strength. Why don't you sit *down*?"

And taking the hint, I did. Mom smiled and became the ever gracious lady once more.

"The Alvarez family welcomes Leticia Biggs and her grand-nephew, Jasper, to help celebrate this occasion. I believe Leticia also has something she would like to say."

Mom took her chair again, gesturing to Mama Biggs. I might have known Mom would find out Barefoot Mama Biggs and Reed's given names and blurt them out to the masses. She has a knack for that sort of thing.

Mama Biggs stood up, dressed for the occasion in a floor-length yellow and green dashiki embroidered in golden threads. It was exquisite.

She was even wearing shoes on her feet, gold open-toed sandals in honor of the occasion.

"Thank you Lila, honey."

Mom blanched but smiled. I don't think my mother has ever been called 'honey' in her life, and certainly not when she was in the room. But it might have been payback time for Barefoot Mama Leticia Biggs. That would have been my call.

"I want to thank all of you for inviting Reed and me here today to help celebrate with your family." She turned and addressed me. "If it wasn't for you, Lee, my boy wouldn't be with me. You saved my boy."

She wiped a tear from her eye and brought up from under the table a beautifully wrapped box in a vibrant dashiki cloth in hues of purple and blue. A silken blue bow topped off the wrapping. She reached across the table, and handed it to me.

"This is for you."

I took the box from her, and pulled at the luscious ribbon, thinking I would never part with it, maybe using it only on holidays as a collar for Tugger. The lid to the box came off easily, as it had been wrapped separately from the bottom. Beneath the soft, white tissue paper was the gorgeous Voodoo doll, complete with stand, from Marie Laveau's collection.

"Mama Biggs! I thought you had a buyer for the doll. Why, this is a priceless heirloom."

"Not as priceless as my boy, Missy." She sat down and wrapped an arm around a grinning Reed. "And you close your pretty mouth now, except to say thank you, and take the gift like you should."

I held the doll up, displaying it before the assembled. Ohs and Ahs filled the room.

"Thank you. I'll treasure this forever, Mama Biggs."

"You just keep those two cats of yours from eating it, that's all." The tone of her voice changed and became similar to the one she used to make sure Reed was practicing his music and not goofing off behind the palm trees. "I heard about them. Your own mama says they are as spoiled as they come."

"They're not spoiled, Mama Biggs," I said with a big smile on my face. "They're not spoiled, Mom," I said as an aside to my mother.

"Yes, they are," Mom said. "I found them on the kitchen table when we arrived at the safe house and they chased the dog into a closet."

I leaned down and whispered, "That means nothing, Mom, nothing." I straightened up and added in a louder voice, "Don't you worry, Mama Biggs, I'll put this beautiful reminder of New Orleans on a top shelf they can't reach."

"There is no shelf they can't reach," said Gurn, with a laugh.

"You're not helping, sport," I said.

"I think it would be much safer in the family home, Liana," Mom said, "enclosed behind the glass doors of the dining room breakfront. I said as much to Mama Biggs earlier today when she showed me the remarkable piece of American heritage she insisted on giving you."

"Oh, you did, did you? So that's where this chit-chat is going. Well, fat chance. You just want to have it at your place. And it's not American heritage, for your information. It comes from the Caribbean. Ha ha. And the doll stays with me."

I could have saved my breath. This is probably one of the reasons I am not a great orator or even a mediocre one. Nobody seems to listen to me for longer than ten seconds at a clip. Any further protestations I might have had were drowned out by Vicki's off-the-charts cooing in appreciation of the doll.

"Oh, Lee! That is the more gorgeous thing I've seen in years. And the clothes! They're so authentic. May I look at it more closely?" She reached over Richard and took it from my hands.

"Well, sure," I said, "but I want to make it clear that this doll is not going...."

No one was paying attention to my feeble power play, so I shut up. Vicki examined the doll thoroughly then gave it to Richard.

The doll got passed around to everyone at the table, with conversations, exclamations, and compliments bouncing off the rafters.

I was losing the battle to have it in my own apartment instead of the family digs, with each minute that ticked by. Sure enough, at Mom's turn to hold and admire the doll, she slipped it into its box and set it by her side. My doll had been commandeered. The end.

I decided to be philosophical about it. Tugger doesn't really eat stuff he shouldn't and neither does Baba. Both are very culinary in their tastes. But they have been known to bat things around the apartment, especially things of interest. I've learned to keep my collection of handbags behind closed doors ever since I found my Judith Leiber **Minaudier** clutch in their litter pan. I don't care to think about why they put it there.

While everyone was laughing and chatting, Reed got up, and came by my side, blushing. He was smartly dressed in a grey three-piece suit, the vest even holding a pocket watch. A perfectly tied, blue paisley bowtie completed the picture, showing a portent of the handsome man he would someday become.

After the doctors talked with and examined him, they determined nothing happened other than what Reed had told me. Another few weeks of therapy and talking it out, they said, and he probably wouldn't even need a nightlight in his room anymore.

Mama Biggs was another story. There's no nightlight for the cuts and bruises on a parent or guardian's heart. She said she'd stop walking him to and from school when he was about twenty-five. Sounded about right to me.

He stood at my side and I could tell Reed wanted to say something to me privately. I turned away from the table and gave him my full attention. Reed was hesitant at first, and then his words spilled out like water over a dam.

"I really am grateful you came after me and all. But I have to say, and I hope you don't mind me saying this, what you do for a living is dangerous. At first I thought it was exciting, and I wanted to be a detective just like you. But I don't think so now, when I look back on it. Why, we could have been killed."

"Yes, we could have. This is why you have to stick to your clarinet lessons, study hard, and get a college degree, so you don't have to do what I do."

"But you went to college. You graduated from Stanford."

"Yes, but there were extenuating…don't pay any attention to what I…what I'm saying is….ah….don't you want to eat your soup while it's hot?" I pointed to the steaming soup tureens being set in the middle of the table. "Looks yummy."

"Yes, ma'am, I do. And thanks again for saving my life, Lee."

"Anytime. Don't mention it."

"Okay." He scampered away.

The first course, wild snapping turtle soup, was being ladled into individual soup bowls with great showmanship by a very efficient older man who seemed to have done this sort of ladling out thing for much of his life. At that point, very little else was said and we concentrated on feasting.

Following the turtle soup, huge plates of the Commander's Salad were placed before us with flourish. Hearts of romaine, slivers of Parmesan, house-made bacon, French bread croutons, grated *Gruyère*, smothered in a creamy black pepper dressing. Undaunted, we moved on to the main course, Chicory Coffee Lacquered Quail with Fire roasted chili and *cochon de lait boudin* over smoky bacon wilted greens with Tabasco pepper jelly & sticky coffee syrup. Had I saved enough room for dessert? You betcha.

But before the dessert showed up, a waiter entered, came silently to my side, and thrust a folded note into my right hand. With a nod, he glided out of the room before I was hardly able to acknowledge him, let alone give him a reply. I read the hand-printed note with no signature.

Dear Ms. Alvarez, I would like to see you about the Rottweiler in your care. I'm sorry to disrupt you party, but I'm waiting out in the hallway.

Having watched this brief exchange, Gurn gave me a questioning look. I shook my head, kissed him on the cheek, and rose.

"Forgive me, I'll be right back, everyone. I need to see a man about a dog."

"Liana," Mom said, in her best chiding voice. "You needn't be *quite* so explicit as to why you are leaving the table. In particular --"

"No, really, Mom," I interrupted. "I have to literally see a man about a dog. Someone is here to claim Manning's Rottweiler. Tío, do you want to come with me?" I looked down at my uncle, whose expression of surprise matched my mother's.

"*Si, si.*" Tío stood up and dropped his napkin to the seat of the chair. He continued talking as he came by my side. "I will not turn over the animal to just anyone. They will have to prove to me they have the right to have the dog returned to them. Leaving the *pobre* animal in a garage during a hurricane is not being a responsible pet owner."

Drawing himself up to his full six feet tall, he took me by my good arm and we left together. I leaned into him.

"True, true, Tío, but were you planning on bringing Rocco back to Palo Alto with you?"

"*Es posible*. He is a good dog. I will not abandon him."

"And no one wants you to. But what say we see what this is all about?"

Chapter Thirty-one
Some Things Come out In The End

We stepped into the hallway, where I found Detective Devereux waiting for us. Dressed in a dark blue suit and wearing a red tie, I'd never seen him look so well kempt. And he seemed nervous. This surprised me. Something was up. I noticed at his side he held a faded but thick parcel. There was a moment of silence. I was the first to break it.

"Is this your note? Why didn't you sign it?" I waved the small paper in the air.

He gave me a hesitant grin. "Didn't I? An oversight. Or maybe I didn't because I wasn't sure you would come once you knew it was me."

"So the dog is just a ruse?"

He gave me a shrug before he said, "No. I'm here about the dog. But there is another thing that can't wait. Not any longer."

He hesitated again, this time on the word 'another'. What the hey? I forged ahead. After all, dessert was waiting.

"Okay, you've piqued my curiosity. But Rocco is in the protective custody of my uncle not me. He's the one you need to speak with about the dog." I turned to Tío.

"*Si*, I do not understand why someone is coming forward now to claim him, *señor*."

Tío stood tall and unyielding.

I suspected an unworthy claimant would have to pry to dog's leash from his unconscious hands.

"Actually, nobody's come forward for the dog, except me. Otherwise, he would go to the pound. I had a Rottweiler when I was a kid. They're a great dog, gentle and kind. My kids - my boy, Donald, in particular - want a dog and I thought we could save this one. But of course, if you are going to put in a claim for the dog, that's another thing."

"Your son wants a pet? He is how old?" Tío started the grilling process.

"Donald is eleven going on thirty. He plans to be a vet when he's older; a big animal vet, horses, cows, you know. Right now he's got six rabbits, a squirrel he's nursing back to health, two parakeets and a cat. But he wants a dog. But look, Mr. Alvarez, if you plan on taking the dog with you to California, I won't fight you on it."

"Your Donald, he sounds like a good boy."

"He is. He loves every four-footed creature on earth. Takes after his mother like that. She's the same way. Last year we had a baby goat for a while. The mother refused to nurse him so my wife and Donald bottle-fed him every four hours for a month. Our backyard looks like a barnyard most of the time. But like I say --"

"You give me your address, Detective. I will bring Rocco by later this afternoon. If he likes Donald and Donald likes him then the dog you may have."

They both beamed at one another.

"That's great." Devereux reached inside his breast pocket and pulled out a card with his free hand. "Here's my home number and address. We'll be there the rest of the day."

Tío took the card and extended his hand. Both men shook on it. I stared at Devereux, waiting.

"Time for this other thing, Detective?"

"Yes, but I need to speak to you alone." Devereux looked from Tío to me. "Please."

"Sure," I said. "It's all right, Tío. I'll be there in a minute."

With a small look of concern crossing his face, my uncle walked down the hallway toward the dining room. I turned back to the detective.

"What's up? And what's with the good will and manners all of a sudden? You have yourself cloned or something?"

"Look, you've got a right to be on your guard a little --"

"A little?"

"But can we drop the tough act for just a minute? I'm here to set something right."

"Should I alert the press?"

His lips tightened a bit. Whether it was my unyielding attitude or something else, I couldn't tell. Nonetheless, he looked at me with what passed for sincerity. I decided to do as he asked.

"Okay. Tough act tabled for a minute. What's on your mind?"

"First of all, there aren't going to be any charges brought against your sister-in-law. I thought you'd like to know. Not by the FBI or New Orleans Police Department."

"That means the nonsense about Vicki killing Bernie Gold has officially come to a close?"

He nodded. "I found out today there was a partial print of Manning's on the wrench that killed Gold."

"So the Powers That Be knew all along it had been Manning."

"The FBI knew. We were never given that information. They were just putting pressure on your family, hoping you would back off. Give them some time to find him themselves."

"It didn't work. What about my role in all this? You think I might be arrested somewhere down the line?"

Devereux shrugged, but took a step back. I took one back as well. The void between us increased.

"No body, no gun, Miss Alvarez. Very hard to prove you shot somebody. Especially, as the boy only heard one shot and saw Manning shoot you. He never saw or heard you fire. All Reed can remember was the man fell over the railing and tried to pull him overboard.

You saved the child, even with a bullet in your arm. You're a heroine, even though some might say there are holes in your story big enough to drive a truck through."

"Are you driving a truck, Detective Devereux?"

He shook his head. "Not me. I'm a sedan man, myself."

He smiled at me. I smiled back. Some sort of truce happened, or maybe we lowered the sabers midway.

"Here's something I thought was interesting." His eyes narrowed in on me, even though his smile stayed in place. "*Laura's Folly* washed ashore near Destin, Florida, day before yesterday. It was in pretty bad shape, but the Coast Guard says the boat is still worth a couple of mil, even in its current condition. It's going up for auction in a week or two."

"No kidding."

"No kidding. The rest of Manning's estate has been confiscated by the government, but according to my sources, the boat has some kind of deal connected to it. I understand Discretionary Inquiries was instrumental in its undertaking. All I know is the proceeds from the sale of the boat goes to the Manning children. Care to enlighten me as to how you pulled that one off?"

"Let's just say we were in possession of certain information that could be turned over to the FBI if they made a few concessions regarding the boat and Manning's kids."

Devereux burst out laughing. "I see D.I. still has a moving line where the law is concerned."

"We like to think of it as discretionary."

He shrugged again, his face gaining a more solemn look. "A nationwide child pornography ring has been closed down, with all guilty parties being held accountable. That's a rare accomplishment. Fortunately, Delphine Robochaux has been cooperating --"

"Sung with the lungs of a canary, eh?"

"In an effort to lessen her caged time, she couldn't sing names fast enough."

We gazed at each other in mutual understanding.

Here was the real reason for a truce; the bad guys were going down. Devereux went on.

"She even handed over Rodrigo Santiago, the number one man, and all his bank accounts."

"Glad to hear it. All's well that ends well."

"Yes."

"Well, good."

I fidgeted. So did he. I cleared my throat. So did he. I was puzzled. We'd said just about everything that needed to be said and yet he was still hanging around. What's up with that?

"Then that about wraps things up?"

"Yes. No. Not really. There is one more thing…" Devereux brought the package he'd been holding at his side up and grasped it with both hands, almost as if it was a peace offering.

"You were right, Miss Alvarez. When I lost my brother I was loaded with guilt. Did I somehow cause my own brother's death? So I blamed your father for everything. It was the only way I could live with myself, I suppose. But I was wrong to blame anybody, other than the shooters. My wife's been telling me that for years, and I finally decided to listen to her."

"I think I like your wife."

"You're a lot like her in some ways, stubborn, opinionated, and not afraid to say what's on your mind."

"Now I know I like her."

"Anyway, this is for you." He pushed the paper wrapped parcel to me.

I took it from him with my good hand. It was heavier than it looked and felt like whatever was inside had been wrapped in something cushiony, like bubble wrap or a towel.

"What is it?"

"After my brother's death, all the weapons were confiscated from the crime scene. That included your father's gun. There it is. The chamber's empty. The bullets were removed by forensics." He nodded toward the package.

"But that was years ago. After Dad was cleared, why wasn't it returned to him?"

"They could never find it. It wasn't the department; it was me. I kept moving it around in the evidence room, misplacing it. Once we even sent him back the wrong weapon, mismarked. I did that, too. Roberto returned it and asked again for his own gun back. I knew he wanted it. I knew it was special to him. Something about your mother having given it to him."

I started to speak but he held up his hand and went on.

"I'm not proud of what I did, but it's done. You return the gun to your mother, with my apologies. If you or your mother want to file a complaint with the department then so be it. I've already told my boss, and I've been given a reprimand. If your family wants to add to it, try to have me suspended or demoted, I've got it coming."

I felt a burst of anger at Devereux for being so petty, so mean-spirited. Keeping something that should have been rightfully returned to my father, just to screw with his head, made me see red. Then my emotions did a flip-flop. Maybe I was tired of a war I didn't have anything to do with, a war that seemed out of place and unworthy of us all.

"I don't think we need to carry this any further, but I'll check with Mom. She'll probably feel the same way I do. Let's try to make the past the past; move forward."

He studied me for a moment. "You have a touch of the Pollyanna in you, you know that?"

"Ah, the old Devereux resurfaces. And by the way, up yours."

The detective threw his head back and gave out a hoot of laughter before he said, "Old habits die hard." Then he sobered and looked at me. "Tell your uncle I'll be waiting for him at the house this afternoon. That dog will never have a better home. That much I can promise you."

He strode away without a backward glance even though my eyes were boring into his back.

Devereux got half way down the hallway and just when I thought we would never speak to each other again in of our lifetimes, he turned around to me. A smile streaked across his face but was gone in an instant.

"You're a good investigator, Miss Alvarez. I'll say that for you. Just like your father. I don't think he was totally blameless in what happened, just like I think you asked for what you got on the high seas. But you're a person who needs to right a wrong. I can appreciate that."

He turned around and left, striding tall and purposeful down the hallway.

Wow. He'd used the same phrase Mama Biggs did, about me needing to right a wrong. I guess I'm more transparent than I think. I looked down at what was in my hand and fought the urge to unwrap the gun and take a gander at it.

But I knew Mom was the one who should see it for the first time in nearly two decades. I covered the package with my beautiful shawl, feeling sad and unsettled, but with some kind of ending in sight.

Chapter Thirty-two
Honor Comes Home

The door from the dining room swung open and Mom entered the hallway.

"Liana, there you are. Dessert is on the table. We've been *waiting* for you. The festivities are *awaiting* you. It's not good to keep our guests *waiting*."

"Mom, I'm glad you're here." I clutched at the package, unmoved by her urgency, even though the word 'waiting' had been used three times. "Just the person I wanted to see."

"Oh?"

Her Dresden blue eyes focused in on me. She knew something important was going down. I told her briefly of Devereux's confession, explanation, and, of course, what he had given me to give to her.

"According to Devereux, this is the gun you gave to Dad years ago."

I removed my shawl to reveal the package. Before I gave it to her, I swept a loving hand over the top of the outside paper, thin, dry, and stained by years of its own waiting.

There was no response from my mother, other than a deep intake of breath. I passed it over to her like it was the Holy Grail. She took it in the same manner and wordless, unwrapped the thin outer shell of paper, revealing a batting material used before bubble-wrap became so popular.

Inside a glittering, steel gun lay, looking much the same as it probably had twenty years before.

Moments went by and I said nothing, giving her time. She stared at the gun, before running the shaky tips of her fingers over a section of its handle.

"The words are still there, just as I had them inscribed."

Her voice was emotionless and all the more powerful because of it. I held my breath and was quiet, letting her go on at her own pace. I saw her slip back in time, focusing on things long gone.

"I was so happy when your father left the police department. Before that every day when he went to his job, I was afraid he might never come home again. When he started Discretionary Investigations, doing more benign work, I was thrilled. Nobody, I thought, would ever be in danger dealing with computer software and hardware, intellectual property, and so forth. We could be almost normal. Our children would grow up and go off to live their own lives. He and I would grow old together. Then he had the aneurism. He was dead before he hit the ground. All that worry about him being shot and meanwhile, a ticking time bomb inside of him…."

Her voice trailed off. She came back to the present, seeing me, as if for the first time.

"You are so like him, you know. Your energy, verve, way of looking at things; the light I see in your eyes, I saw in his eyes. That's why I'm short with you sometimes. It's not fair, but it's the truth. I never forgave him for leaving us like that. So sometimes, I take it out on you."

A solitary tear ran down her cheek.

"It's all right, Mom. I never take it personally."

Which was a bald-faced lie, but then we Alvarez women seem to make those kinds of lying statements all the time. I don't think she even heard me; she was so lost within herself.

"I gave him this gun the day we opened the doors of Discretionary Inquires. I wanted it be the beginning of a new era for us." She caressed it again. "At the bottom of the grip I had the words, 'Honor Above All' inscribed. See? Because that's how he lived his life. Honor came before everything."

"I know."

"I miss him so much."

"I know."

"I will never love another man the way I loved Roberto Alvarez."

"I know, Mom."

I'm not sure when the child becomes the parent or the parent the child, but at that moment I knew it happened. I reached out to a still grieving, lonely woman and enclosed her in a hug, even with my one game arm. Her suffering was my suffering, and was even paramount to anything I could feel or ever had felt. She and I clung to each other for a moment, eternity, not long, forever. Real time is not a part of this sort of thing.

Lila Hamilton Alvarez was the first to break free. She dabbed under each eye with a delicate fingertip, careful not to spoil her makeup or stain her finger. When she finished, she thrust Dad's gun at me.

"I want you to have it, Liana."

Stunned, I pushed it back to her. "No, Mom. The one Dad gave me is gone, but I want you to keep the one you gave him. Besides, you love it."

"I don't 'love' it, Liana. It's just a weapon. And I *insist* you take it, even thought you managed to lose two perfectly good weapons in a single day."

The last part of her sentence was a throwaway, but I heard it quite clearly. She tried to force the gun on me again. I took a step back, still not taking it from her. And I was pissed.

"Wait a minute. I didn't 'lose' them. I know right where those guns are. The bottom of the Gulf."

Mom grabbed my hand, pulling me toward her.

"This is not a *criticism* of you, my dear, merely an *observation*." Mom spoke in a strong, critical tone. "What I'm saying is to have lost *two* revolvers in one day might show a certain amount of recklessness."

"Recklessness?"

"Or *lack* of concentration."

"Lack of concentration?"

"Possibly? You should *think* about it, Liana."

"Hmmm." I faltered. "How about if I say…" I paused, not sure of the right words to end this discussion. "How about if I say I will give it some thought?"

"In that case, I don't think we need continue this conversation."

"Thank you, Jesus."

"Please do not use the Lord's name in vain, Liana."

"I use it as a prayer of thanks."

"Regardless. Now, I want you to have your father's gun. I know he would have *wanted* you to have it. With the *proviso*, of course, you will try to be more *careful* in the future, dear."

"Excuse me," said a male voice from a distance, after a slight cough.

"You know, Mom," I said, ignoring the male and his stupid cough, "You can be so tough. You weren't there. You have no idea --"

The cough sounded again, a little louder this time and with more authority. "Ladies, I don't mean to interrupt but --"

"What do you want?" We asked in unison, turning in the direction of the cough.

I looked over to see Gurn standing nearby, suppressing laughter.

"Ladies, things are winding up inside, the soufflé is getting cold, and Vicki needs to leave soon and get back to the shop. How about you settle this, whatever it is, later and we get back in there?"

"Devereux returned Dad's gun and Mom wants me to have it. It's the one she gave him twenty years ago, but I'm not taking it." I pushed it back toward her, hard. "And that's final, Mom."

"Liana, you are being *petulant*." She pushed it even harder toward me.

"Ladies, ladies. May I see the gun in question?"

Gurn's smile never ceased, but our conversation earlier clicked in the back of my mind. I shrugged, relaxed, and backed off, seemingly giving in.

Mom handed the gun to Gurn as she arched an eyebrow at me. She, too, backed off and crossed her arms. I could see a little toe-tapping done on her part out of the corner of my eye. She thought he was going to weigh in on her side. Gurn took the Detective Special and examined it from every side, deep in thought.

"Honor Above All," he read. "I'm sure this means a lot to you, Lila. A Detective Special was a nice weapon twenty, thirty years ago, but firearms have improved so much, I don't think this is quite up to the task nowadays." He smiled at her, pearly whites glinting in the sun streaming in from the windows behind me. Gurn went on. "And you want Liana to have the very best and latest, don't you? So I've got a suggestion. Why don't you frame Roberto's gun and put it on a wall in your office or your desk for everyone to see? The gun that started it all."

"That could work," I put in, as my mother would say, with verve.

"I don't know." Mom was hesitant; surprised she was losing the battle.

"Possibly? You should think about it." I used the same tone she'd used on me. I was ignored.

Gurn went on as if I hadn't spoken. "Another suggestion would be to put the motto, Honor Above All, over the doors of D.I. -- ah, Discretionary Inquiries."

My man continued his award winning yet sincere smile. The corners of Mom's mouth turned upward. I could feel her waiver. Gurn went on to seal the deal.

"I'd do business with a company that promoted a quality like that, ma'am."

Wow! He'd ma'am-ed Lila Hamilton Alvarez. She loves that sort of thing. My mother cast him one of her own award winning smiles. I felt like I was at the Oscars.

"You know, Gurn, you should consider selling real estate. You're quite good." Still smiling, Mom looked him squarely in the eyes.

"Thank you, ma'am, but no. I'm content with being a Certified Public Accountant."

Mom scoffed Big Time. "Certified Public Accountant, indeed. I believe there's more to you than meets the eye."

It was the first time anyone besides me had challenged Gurn on his professed career of pushing around numbers. I stepped back and let the champs dance around the ring, so to speak. This was getting good.

"I'm afraid not, ma'am. What you see is what you get. It's true I have a few interests on the side --"

"Ahah!" Mom and I interrupted in unison, me more of a back up than the lead singer.

"—Such as NROTC and supporting my D.C. affiliations, which I am not at liberty to discuss. But other than that, I am your plain, ordinary CPA."

Mom and I studied him in silence. His face wore the mask of sincerity. There would be getting no more out of him on the subject, dagnabbit. Finally, Mom spoke up.

"You're going to marry my daughter, aren't you?"

"Yes, ma'am, if she'll have me."

Okay, the conversation had taken an unexpected turn. I decided not to faint as I was wearing my new silk three-piece pantsuit. Otherwise, look out floor. I did try to force speech from a mouth that felt like it was filled with the sands of the Sahara. Or the sands of Death Valley; I was homesick for California. I think I gurgled, not unlike the sound of a stopped up sink finally being freed of a clump of hair by a plumber. Meanwhile, Mom continued, center stage.

"You won't treat her like her first husband."

"No, ma'am."

"If you do, you will have to answer to me for it. I didn't interfere between she and Nick, but I feel now I should have."

Wait just a ding-dong minute. I'm being talked about like I'm not in the room. What's up with that? I decided to try speech again, let them know who was who around here.

"Hey!'

Okay, it's not Shakespeare, but it should alert someone I'm still among the living.

"She was a different person then," Gurn said, ignoring me and returning Mom's cool, appraising stare. "And married to a different man."

"Hey!"

Nothing like talking to a wall. Two walls, in fact. I took a deep breath to throw out another yell, but Gurn started talking again.

"I think Liana Margaret Alvarez is the most remarkable woman I've ever been privileged to know. She's intelligent, beautiful, loving, funny, original, and very much her own person. I would never try to control her in any way; I only want to cherish the woman she is."

Okay, so maybe I'll just be quiet and let the man talk.

"I will honor and love her forever, ma'am, but that's only, as I said before, if she'll have me," he said.

Mom reached out, touching Gurn on the shoulder with slim fingers for a flash of a moment. "Of course, she'll have you."

Watch it, Mom. I'm the one who should be saying that. Potential bride and all that.

"Hey!" I finally yelled for the third time, only to have it continue to fall on deaf ears.

My mother went on. "But you are marrying the entire Alvarez Family, dear boy. Remember that."

"Yes, ma'am. It gave me pause, but I still want to do it."

Mom wasn't sure she'd heard right. At best, she didn't quite know what to make of his remark, so she remained silent and smiling.

I giggled. Life with a man who could throw my mother like that had a definite upside. Mom looked from Gurn to me. It was refreshing, someone conceding I was standing within earshot.

"In that case, I will return to my Creole Bread Pudding Soufflé and leave you both to discuss your future."

"And take the gun with you, Mom." It was my parting shot and I delivered it for all I was worth.

Without acknowledging I'd spoken, Mom did an about face and went back into the dining room. I watched her leave then turned to Gurn, pulling myself up to my full five foot eight inches. With an arched eyebrow not unlike my mother's and a stern look upon my face, I challenged him.

"Well?" And I meant it to sting.

"Well." Gurn echoed back the word with a smile. "You have to admit, my talking about marriage got her off the subject of making you carry your father's weapon."

I felt my jaw drop and I must have shrunk down to four foot ten.

"You mean, you didn't mean…"

"What do you think, Liana Margaret Hamilton?" He gave me his lopsided grin, green-gray eyes sparkling, as he walked toward me.

"Aw, stop using my middle name. What a way to spoil a mood. All it does is make me want to do is smack you."

"Then I'll never use it again. I promise." He drew closer and pulled me into his arms. "Let's renew that mood, Lee, my darling Lee, love of my life, Lee."

I wasn't paying attention, but continued along my vein of thought, even though he was smothering my neck with kisses. It's hard to concentrate when a man does that, but I did my best.

"Besides, who are you to talk, Mr. Gurn Hanson?" I broke free of his embrace. "Where'd you come up with a name like Gurn, anyway? I never heard of it before you."

"If you'd listened to Steve Martin, you would have."

"Steve Martin, the comic?"

"The very same. My father was a big fan. Steve Martin created a character called Gern Blanston, so my father named me after him. Only dad spelled it wrong. Instead of an 'e', he used a 'u'." Gurn let out a guffaw. "That's my dad."

"I like your dad."

My voice was soft. Gurn's voice took on the same timbre as mine.

"I know. He likes you. So does my mom. And you know how I feel. You mean everything to me. I can't imagine my life without you. And I'm hoping you feel the same way."

"So I guess it's time we…talk."

Then we kissed, and the room temperature soared.

~~

Books by Heather Haven

The Alvarez Family Murder Mysteries
Murder is a Family Business, Book 1
A Wedding to Die For, Book 2
Death Runs in the Family, Book 3
DEAD...If Only, Book 4
The CEO Came DOA, Book 5
The Culinary Art of Murder, Book 6

The Lee Alvarez Mystery Novelettes
Honeymoons Can Be Murder, Book 1
Marriage Can Be Murder, Book 2 (October 2017)

The Persephone Cole Vintage Mysteries
The Dagger Before Me, Book 1
Iced Diamonds, Book 2
The Chocolate Kiss-Off, Book 3

Noir Mystery Stand Alone
Death of a Clown

Collection of Short Stories
Corliss and Other Award-Winning Stories

Multi-Author Boxed Sets
Sleuthing Women: 10 First-in-Series Mysteries
Sleuthing Women II: 10 Mystery Novellas

About Heather Haven

After studying drama at the University of Miami in Miami, Florida, Heather went to Manhattan to pursue a career. There she wrote short stories, novels, comedy acts, television treatments, ad copy, commercials, and two one-act plays, produced at several places, such as Playwrights Horizon. Once she even ghostwrote a book on how to run an employment agency. She was unemployed at the time.

One of her first paying jobs was writing a love story for a book published by Bantam called *Moments of Love*. She had a deadline of one week but promptly came down with the flu. Heather wrote "The Sands of Time" with a raging temperature, and delivered some pretty hot stuff because of it. Her stint at New York City's No Soap Radio - where she wrote comedic ad copy – help develop her long-time love affair with comedy.

She has won five awards so far for the humorous Alvarez Family Murder Mysteries. The Persephone Cole Vintage Mysteries and *Corliss and Other Award Winning Stories* have garnered several, as well.

However, her proudest achievement is winning the Independent Publisher Book Awards (IPPY) 2014 Silver Medal for her stand-alone noir mystery, **Death of a Clown**. As the real-life daughter of Ringling Brothers and Barnum and Bailey circus folk, she was inspired by stories told throughout her childhood by her mother, a trapeze artist and performer. The book cover even has a picture of her mother sitting atop an elephant from that time. Her father trained the elephants. Heather brings the daily existence of the Big Top to life during World War II, embellished by her own murderous imagination.

Connect with Heather at the following sites:

Website: **www:heatherhavenstories.com**
Heather's Blog:
http://heatherhavenstories.com/blog/
https://www.facebook.com/HeatherHavenStories
https://www.twitter.com/Twitter@HeatherHaven

Sign up for Heather's newsletter at:
http://heatherhavenstories.com/subscribe-via-email/

Email: **heather@heatherhavenstories.com**.

She'd love to hear from you. Thanks so much!

The Wives of Bath Press

The Wife of Bath was a woman of a certain age, with opinions, who's on a journey. Heather Haven and Baird Nuckolls are modern day Wives of Bath.
www.thewivesofbath.com